THE REPLACEMENTS

Also by David Putnam

The Bruno Johnson Novels

The Disposables

THE REPLACEMENTS

A Novel

David Putnam

Oceanview Publishing

Longboat Key, Florida

ISBN: 978-1-60809-137-9

Published in the United States of America by Oceanview Publishing
Longboat Key, Florida

www.oceanviewpub.com
10 9 8 7 6 5 4 3 2

PRINTED IN THE UNITED STATES OF AMERICA

Dedicated to the greatly missed and irreplaceable
Kyle Benjamin Allen.

1990-2014

THE REPLACEMENTS

CHAPTER ONE

The day the house bled started out sunny and warm. I was a rookie street cop in South Central Los Angeles. I worked uniform patrol for the sheriff's department, a job that could impact the community in so many positive ways. I ferreted out the predators, either put them in jail or prodded them until they moved on to another neighborhood. I liked working with the kids the most. I tried to find them before they were corrupted by the cancerous part of the street. There were the lost causes, but most kids wanted to better themselves and were hungry for guidance.

The absolute worst part of the job was bearing witness to the lowest ebb of humanity. I never could understand the motivation, the reasoning, the excuses for harming children. Because there weren't any. Not in this world or any other.

The day of the horrible bleeding house incident started out great. A Blood by the name of Little Ghost had been dodging me for weeks. Anytime I was able to feed my handcuffs with a predator gave me a warm feeling. He'd set up shop slinging rock cocaine two blocks from a middle school, and I hadn't been able to nab him. That day I put on a gray raincoat over my uniform and snuck up on him through a back alley, caught him right in the middle of a hand-to-hand deal.

So I was having a good day until the call to "keep the peace" came my way. I pulled up to a house in East Compton. White Street, west of Atlantic. A house like any other on the street, light blue with dark blue trim, maybe maintained a little better with a mowed lawn and a trimmed hedge. A man in slacks and a long-sleeve blue dress shirt stood out front wringing his hands, his expression one of genuine concern. I pulled up and parked half in the driveway, half in the street, and got out. "How can I help you, sir?"

"My name's Micah Mabry, and I'm worried about my kids, Jonas, Betsy, and Sally. Jonas is five, Betsy's seven, and Sally, she's…she's eight. Yes…yes, she's eight last October. I knocked and knocked and they won't answer the door. Please, you have to help me. Please."

"Okay, Mr. Mabry, slow down and start from the beginning."

"Right, right, sure. My wife Bella and I are separated. We're getting a divorce."

"I'm sorry."

He waved off the apology. "It's okay, it's a long story. But two nights ago she was supposed to meet me at McDonald's. I was supposed to get my three kids for the weekend."

Dispatch hadn't told me this was a hostage exchange—the term used for child custody conflicts. The adults never acted like adults, and the losers were always the children caught between parents they loved, with their petty conflicts and wounded egos. The parents' bitter emotions were the worst to deal with in these incidents. People became irrational. Child custody calls tore at my gut. I couldn't stand to see children cry and I always had to suppress the urge to do something about it.

Mabry continued, "She never showed up. I've tried to call her for the last two days, so I came over here. Listen, I'm going to tell you up front, she has a restraining order against me, and I'm not supposed to be here."

No wonder she wasn't answering the door. I couldn't allow him to stay if he was telling the truth about the TRO, the temporary restraining order. I said, "Do you have the court custody papers signed by the judge?"

"Yeah, yeah, sure." He pulled them from his back pocket. I checked; they were complete and in order. He was right, it was his turn to have the kids. "Okay," I said, "Here's the deal. All I'm allowed to do in this case is take a report and submit it to the DA as a violation of a court order, a PC 166.4—"

"You can't make her give me my kids?"

"No, you have to have your attorney pull her back into family court."

"Come on, that can take forever."

"I know, I'm sorry." I sat in the front seat and filled in the report form while he stood in the open door of the patrol unit staring down. I knew he was staring at me, and I couldn't look up at him. He pulled out his wallet. "Deputy Johnson, you have kids?"

I was raising my daughter on my own and found it damn difficult to juggle her upbringing with an ever-shifting patrol schedule. I knew how hard it was to raise children and disliked him a little for throwing the kid card.

He held out his wallet, the plastic sleeves cloudy from overuse. The kids were cute. What child wasn't? I wrote the case number down on a business card, got out, and stood in the open door. I handed it to him. Micah Mabry stared at the card as if it were a disappearing lifeline.

I said, "Ah, hell. You knocked?"

"Yes, yes. I've been here for an hour. I've knocked again and again the entire time. I know they're in there. Please, Deputy?"

Son of a bitch. I reached in and picked up the mic. "Two-fifty-five-Adam, start another unit to back. I'm going to force entry."

I'd hardly unkeyed the mic when Sergeant Foreman came up on the air. "Negative, Two-fifty-five-Adam. Stand by, I'm responding."

Once Foreman arrived, no way would he do anything other than what the book said.

I tossed the mic onto the seat. The window configuration of the house, outlined in dark blue paint against the light blue of the house, made the windows look like the eyes of a monster.

I walked with purpose to the front door. I'd made up my mind and didn't want to think about the consequences. I knocked loud enough for the neighbors to hear. No answer. "What's your wife's name?"

"Bella. Her name's Bella, but this won't do any good. I've tried."

I believed him and was beginning to have a bad feeling about the entire situation. I yelled, "Bella, this is Deputy Johnson with the Los Angeles County Sheriff's Department. I need you to open the door. Come to the door and talk to me. Now." Something was wrong about the whole setup. Anxiety rose up in me, and I could no longer follow proper protocol.

I looked down just as water, a little at first, then more, seeped under the door and out onto the porch.

I stepped back and booted the door.

CHAPTER TWO

The door burst inward. The inside knob embedded in the drywall and kept the door from ricocheting back. Water flowed in a wave from the house out onto the stoop. Little rivulets of blood floated on top of the water coming toward me. I drew my service pistol. "Stay here."

"Just try and make me."

"Then stay behind me." I would have had to beat him down to keep him from following.

I stepped in. The water was three to four inches deep. A peculiar odor rolled out across the water—humidity mixed with a tangy iron residue—along with a heavy dose of sorrow.

Two steps to the left was the open entrance to the kitchen. The two sink drains were clogged with towels, the faucet on full blast. It had to have been that way for hours and hours.

Behind me, Micah Mabry wailed, "My God. Oh my God."

Focus. I had to focus. I already knew and feared what I was going to find. Three more sloshing steps and the short hall gave way to the spartanly furnished living room. On the couch lay an inert person, a woman. Micah Mabry pushed around me, sobbing, wailing. The woman wore a thin, transparent nightie, soaked down to her waist with blood. Locked in her hand, resting on the floor at the base of the couch, was a .22 pistol. She'd shot herself in the chest.

Micah Mabry stood there frozen, shoulders slumped, his chin on his chest as he wept. He whispered, "Why, Bella?"

With wooden feet, I sloshed back to the main hall heading for the bedrooms, a deep pain in the pit of my stomach. I didn't want to go. No way did I want to do this.

The blood path on the water had not mixed and was a small stream atop a river of water. My black boots swished it together to a consistent pink. I moved past an open bathroom door. The bathtub and sink ran over, their drains clogged and faucets running full out. Why had she clogged the drains and turned on the water? What could have possessed the woman?

The gun, heavy in my hand.

My socks soaked, sloshing in my boots.

In the first bedroom I found two dead, both shot in the head.

Young children. The young girls: Betsy and Sally. The older one, Sally, her golden hair in a fan on the pillow, her one whole eye locked open, staring at the ceiling.

These children had depended on their parents to keep them safe. My face turned wet with tears.

With each child I felt for a pulse, their skin waxy and stiff. And terribly cold.

Oh, so terribly cold. I turned and went to the last bedroom. One more. The same as the others. The youngest, the boy Jonas, five years old. Yet he was different than the others. Bella had not shot him in the head. He had blood on his chest, close to his heart.

One of my senses pulled me out of my trance. What was it? Focus.

Jonas' skin had been warm and pliable. I turned back, fumbled at his neck, probing for a pulse.

Thready.

Thready, but still there. He clung to life. Five miles to the hospital. It would take longer to wait on the paramedics. I scooped Jonas up and ran. Water splashed up on the walls.

As I passed the first bedroom an image flashed in my adrenaline-fueled flight. Micah Mabry on his knees at the bed keening, a child in his arms.

Out front, Jonas in my arms, I only slowed to gently ease us into the front seat of the patrol car. I slammed the door and jammed the gearshift into reverse, smoking the back tires as I held the delicate child in my other arm. In drive, going forward, I brought my knee up to hold the wheel in place while I grabbed the mic and keyed it. "Two-fifty-five-Adam. I have a one-eight-seven with four down. I am responding code three to St. Francis. Advise St. Francis I'm rolling in hot with a critical child."

The dispatcher replied. "Two-fifty-five-Adam, ten-four, I'm making the notification now."

"Two-fifty-Sam." Sergeant Foreman came up on the frequency. "Negative, Two-fifty-five-Adam, pull over and stand by for paramedics."

I came out on Atlantic and dropped the mic, grabbed the wheel just in time to avoid hitting a Ford Taurus.

Back to the knee driving. "Two-fifty-five-Adam, I have heavy traffic on Atlantic northbound. Are there any Lynwood units available to block intersections?"

"Two-fifty-three-boy, Bruno, I got Alondra, twenty seconds out."

"Two-fifty-one-Adam, I've got Compton, I'm there now."

The station watch commander, the lieutenant, came up on the frequency. "Negative. Lynwood units do not block the intersections. Two-fifty-five-Adam, pull over and stand by for paramedics."

I shot past Alondra, the intersection blocked by Two-fifty-three-boy, also disobeying direct orders. Deputy Ortiz stood outside his patrol car, arms raised, stopping traffic. I keyed the mic. "Is there anyone for Rosecrans?"

"Negative. Negative." Lieutenant's tone said there was going to be hell to pay. "All Lynwood units stand down."

"Two-fifty-Tom-one, I got your back, Bruno, I'm shutting down Rosecrans now."

I shot past Compton and Rosecrans making excellent time. I only had Century Boulevard left, the largest, most dangerous intersection—and there was nobody left.

The boy in my arm, held lightly against my chest, let out a little gurgle.

A bad sign.

"Come on, kid, hold on. We're almost there."

We came up fast on Century. The entire intersection was shut down with two fire trucks. Fire fighters stood in the street waving me on. I took the corner with five big blocks left.

I pulled into the back of St. Francis. Three nurses and two doctors waited for me with a gurney. They yanked open my door and took the child, ran with him on the gurney. They disappeared into the hospital. I couldn't move. I shook all over. Blood soaked my uniform shirt. Feet cold and numb in wet boots, I sat there a long time before I was able to put it in gear and head back to my crime scene, one I'd had no right to leave in the first place.

CHAPTER THREE

Twenty years after the house that bled, I was tending the cabana bar at La Margarite in San José, Costa Rica. The usual suspects were in attendance, and I mean just that—four regulars who started around noon and stayed for hours, day after day. All four expats from the US. All four had fled under dark or morally corrupt circumstances. Like me, all four were criminals.

I'd brought my patchwork family to San José to dodge the law in the US.

The US could extradite those who sat at my bar, but instead, they worked under the theory that Costa Rica could deal with the nefarious and disreputable hiding out in their country. Only a few had been extradited since the treaty in 1992. Why bring them back for an expensive trial and incarceration?

Everyone who was not a local in the small village just outside San José had something to hide. I, too, had fled under unfavorable circumstances. I needed to know with whom I associated as a matter of self-preservation.

The first three of my regulars had been no challenge at all, not with my prior law enforcement experience. When time allowed I worked on the fourth. The last holdout, Jake Donaldson, was a hard nut to crack.

With the first three, I'd employed an elementary interrogation technique. When I had one of them alone, before the others arrived, and after he'd had a few drinks, I'd admit to my own culpability in a major criminal enterprise. Not the real ones, of course. Looking them in the eyes, trying for compassion, and then, when the time was right, I'd reach over and lay my hand on their arm. It was the touch that did it. They opened up every time, like little children standing in front of their mothers with their slingshots clutched in their fists behind their backs.

Mike Olivares and John Booth were both tax evaders owing $1.5 and $2 million, respectively, to Uncle Sam. With interest and penalties, that number would easily triple. Neither had to worry too much about the US government coming south to scoop them up. Not for taxes. Not for that paltry amount.

Ansel Tomkins, the most cunning of the three, had been a certified public accountant who'd managed a big movie star's finances. An embezzler, he'd robbed the fat piggy bank and left the movie mogul with nary an IOU. I'd read about it in the *LA Times,* a paper they usually left lying around the bar. These men missed their abandoned lives and avidly pored over every inch of every column. Or maybe they just wanted to see if they had made the news again, craving an additional spotlight in their fifteen seconds of fame.

I hoped they hadn't seen my ugly mug on the front page nine months ago. All of *that* mess had calmed down now. The bullet wound in my ass had healed. The scar tugged and pulled if I stretched to reach the Patrón Silver bottle high on the top shelf. Though it was likely the men had seen my picture and read the story, they never put it together. Lucky for me. Once given the information, the Feds would gladly sneak down on a black bag operation and snag me up in an illegal extradition. They were beyond mad that I had slipped through their fingers on the lam. The main reason why I wore shirts that covered my BMF tattoo, an identifier from another lifetime. I'd also changed my name from Bruno Johnson to Bob Johnson. Johnson was like Smith, there were tens of thousands of us. I always wore an old Cincinnati Reds ball cap and dark sunglasses. Not a great disguise, but enough that I didn't think anyone so far south would identify me.

The hotel insisted that the television suspended from the

ceiling remain on. When I turned to take some glasses out of the warm soapy water, Barbara Wicks, in a Montclair Police Department blue uniform, appeared on a CNN news item. For a long moment I stood there stunned, watching, unable to move.

Her husband had been the one who'd shot me the first time three years ago, and again nine months ago. But that was a long, sad story, one I was trying hard to forget.

The four gold stars on her collars indicating chief status caught my eye. Nine months ago when I had left, Barbara had been a lieutenant. Good for her. She had worked hard, first as a patrol officer, then as the department's first female homicide detective. She had excelled as an investigator and quickly moved up to watch commander. And now chief.

Way back, Barbara and Robby had been good friends of mine. I missed them both. The camera came in tight on her face. I stared at the screen. "At seven thirty yesterday morning, eight-year-old Sandy Williams was taken from her home on Buena Vista Street in the City of Montclair. The suspect jimmied the back door to get in, as the parents were home preparing to go to work. Montclair Police Department is working every possible lead, and we are using every available resource. This is a crime of unimaginable horror, not only for the Williamses, but for any family with children. The citizens in our city have to be able to feel safe in their own homes."

"Hey, Bobby J," Ansel said, "turn that crap off. We don't want to hear it. It'll ruin our buzz."

I kept my eyes on the screen, eager to hear the rest, and I tried to keep the anger out of my tone, "Ruin your buzz? How do you think that child, Sandy Williams, is feeling right now?"

I'd taken—rescued, really, eight children—though some might describe the rescuing as kidnapping—and brought them to Costa Rica. Had this suspect taken Sandy Williams like I had taken my children? Taken her from an abusive home, where she'd been doomed to a life of pain and agony? Taken her with no other intent than to trundle her down to Costa Rica, where it would be safe for one and all? No chance, there were no statistics for what I'd done with my kids. No one had ever rescued children like I had done. Mine had been a one-time shot.

This kidnapping was the worst kind, the suspect's motivation too difficult to ponder. I knew the odds were not in Sandy's favor. This kidnapping, like most others, was not going to end well.

My attention returned to Barbara Wicks on the screen. "We now have compelling evidence that the East LA kidnapping of Elena Cortez two weeks ago is related. We have put together a joint task force with Los Angeles County Sheriff's Department and with the FBI as advisors. If anyone has any information about either of these children, please contact us at the number listed on your screen." She looked into the camera. I couldn't help thinking she was looking right at me, right through me. She paused, then: "Now I'll take questions."

***

So this was a serial kidnapping. Some animal was on the loose. My first instinct was to return to the States and manhunt him. Of course, I had to resist. I wanted to listen to the rest of the broadcast, but couldn't. The thought of what those kids were going through cut too deep. I lowered the volume with the automatic control and tried to distract myself by washing the rest of the glasses and filling drink orders for Becca, the server working the pool area. Lots of tropical drinks with little umbrellas and ice-cold Mexican beers.

Images of the children continued to pop up unbidden. I needed a stronger distraction. What I really needed was to go for a long run. That would clear my head, straighten things out. But I couldn't leave the bar. All I had left was to talk to the regulars. A mild distraction was better than nothing.

Ansel, if that was his real name, held up his empty highball. "Hey, Bobby J, how about doin' this again?" I filled his glass with Jack and Coke and made the seventh tick on the paper I used to keep track of 'who' drank 'what' and 'how many.' I set down the drink in front of him. He took the glass and leaned over the bar for a private word, his breath sweet with whiskey and mulled cherries. The other guys were talking amongst themselves and weren't paying attention to us. "Hey, Bob," Ansel half-whispered, "you been working ol' Jake? You get a story outta him yet?"

I shook my head, "No luck."

"Man, that's driving me nuts not knowin'. You know what I'm sayin'? I'm thinking real estate fraud. He skedaddled with all the proceeds from some big land grab. He looks like some crotchety old realtor, don't he? Whatta ya think?"

Ansel didn't have a lot of imagination. I'd fed the guys the story that I had fled the States on the heels of a major real estate fraud. I said, "Let me try something else."

Three of my customers at the cabana bar—Ansel Tomkins, Mike Olivares, and John Booth—had had an overwhelming desire to tell their stories. Their consciences demanded it. With the help of Jack Daniel's and the need to wallow in self-pity, they'd all opened up.

All except Jake Donaldson.

Jake's insistence to hold on to his dirty little secret had always piqued my curiosity. I decided to take a different tack with Jake today. This time I'd conduct my interrogation with his drinking pals sitting right next to him. I'd try for a little peer pressure.

Jake was older than all of us. His head balding with wispy white hair, his skin tanned nut brown from the intense sun. He possessed that old man kind of strength with little body fat to hide the sinew and muscle that rippled when he moved. He'd been hiding out down here the longest.

I stepped over from Ansel, the Jack bottle in hand, and re-filled Jake's glass, intent on further softening him up before getting started with the softball questions. He'd been hitting the Jack harder than normal. After each glass I poured him, he'd slump a little lower over the bar. I'd ask him where he grew up, how many sisters and brothers did he have—that kind of thing—that, if answered, revealed little by little a history of the man. I stood there not marking down the ticks for each drink, trying not to be too

obvious. The other three pretended not to be watching or listening, and whispered to each other as Jake's inebriation continued
in earnest. Finally, I said, "Jake, old buddy, what'd you do in the
States before you came down here? What were you into, huh,
buddy?" He didn't answer right away. His cheek touched the
smooth bamboo bar as he began to speak, his words aimed down
the length of the bar, not directed at anyone in particular, jum-
bled and incoherent.

I said, "Jake, old buddy, sit up, look at me. Come on, man, sit
up. What did you just say?" I thought he'd said I was his best friend.

Jake's head rose and swayed as if too heavy to hold, his eyes
bleary, unfocused. I repeated the question, "What'd you just say?"

His jerky head turned, looked down the bar at his three fellow compatriots all intent to know his secret. Jake, his voice a low
croak, said, "He was my best friend."

"Who's that, Jake," I asked. "Who was your best friend?" The
four of us held our breaths waiting, watching his eyes. With a "best
friend" used in the past tense, maybe I didn't want to know this.

He raised his head, face flushed red. Tears brimmed and
rolled down, leaving glistening trails.

This was bad, too much emotion. Now I didn't want to hear
this man's tortured secret. I'd been toying with these men for my
own security and some entertainment, but this one wasn't going
to have a happy ending.

"Jake, wait, don't."

With his mouth in a straight line, he brought a drunken
hand up and waved me off. "Freddy. That's who. My best friend,
that's who. You black bastard. I know what you're doing. I know
you've been talking to these assholes about me. So you want to
know the rest of the ugly truth? I'll tell yeh, you black bastard."
He swayed on his stool. Waved his hand in a wider arc. "I'm not
like these other pussies here, these spineless little chickenshits
with their petty white-collar crime bullshit."

In the six months I'd known him, Jake had never opened up
like this, never used such strong words. I realized, in part, this

came with his new South American persona that included an accurate portrayal of a harmless nerd, a geek. But now he was shedding that skin, revealing the real man. I had awakened a sleeping ogre. I was getting old and rusty and had not seen the signs. Here was a street-smart crook, and I had pushed his buttons. I wasn't afraid of him; I was forty-five to his sixty-five, and I outweighed him by thirty pounds. And I was sober.

Though another major consideration, Jake had on a light linen jacket that could easily conceal a weapon. I remembered what Robby Wicks, Barbara's husband, used to always say, that God created men, and Samuel Colt made them equal. Robby had died by those words. My next thought was, what would Marie and the kids do if this wrinkled, bag-of-bones of a man threw down on me, shot me dead?

In the last nine months since I'd been in Costa Rica, I had allowed my instincts to wane. I would never again disregard my street sense and let it fade away like that.

I straightened up and pulled my shoulders back. I did what I used to do while working the streets on the Violent Crimes Team for the Los Angeles County Sheriff when confronting a rabid predator: I returned his stare the same as you would with a vicious dog.

"If you're going to tell us, old man, get to it. We're not getting any younger."

CHAPTER FOUR

Jake's mouth dropped open and his eyes probed mine, trying to figure me out. His tongue whipped out, lizard like, and wet his dry lips. "All right, you black bastard, I'll tell you." His head jerked to the right to see his pals, "And if any of you cocksuckers rat me out, it'll be the last thing you ever do. You can bet your ass on that. You hear? You hear me? You sorry sack of pussies."

No one answered. They were all too scared. Jake had never talked to them this way. He'd always been quiet, calm, told quaint anecdotes of urban living. Ansel Tomkins, the CPA to the movie star he'd ripped off, one of Jake's three pals sitting at the bar on his left, looked away, brought a shaky hand up and scratched his cheek to bleed off a little tension.

In a bizarre mood shift, Jake seemed to decompress and took the situation down a notch. While we all watched a little stunned, Jake slowly spun his stool around until he faced the bright blue ocean capped with white, blown up by the afternoon breeze. When he talked again, he used the same harsh words, but his tone had lost the hard edge, gradually melting back into the Jake we knew, the quiet, mild-mannered old man everyone liked to drink with.

"Those Mexican assholes, they were the ones did it. I did it, sure I did. But it was those chili-eatin' Mexican assholes was the cause. They were makin' cheese in the bathtub next door. I know it sounds damn silly to start off a horrible story like this with bathtub cheese, but that was the way it all began.

"The smell...damn, you boys should've taken a whiff of that rotten smell, you'd a done the same. The whole damn neighborhood reeked like Mexican dirty socks, a million of 'em. Sure, I called the code enforcement boys. They came and raided the house. *But it was only cheese, after all.* That's what the code enforcement supervisor told me when he went ahead and walked across my yard, right up to my door. Burned me to those chili-eaters, sure as God made little green apples. The code enforcement boys took all their cheese and issued them a summons to go to court. A summons, for cripes sakes, and nothin' more.

"That's when it really started. Sure, right then." Jake hesitated, his eyes lost on the blue horizon. The boys at the bar exchanged glances. Ansel seemed to recover from his fear and shrugged at the others.

Jake swallowed hard, in profile, his tan and prominent Adam's apple rose and fell against the bright blue, cloudless sky. "Them assholes decided to put in a fence to wall me out from their front yard. 'Okay by me, bring it on.' That's what I yelled when they started diggin' the ditch for the foundation. Sure, I said it just like that, 'bring it on, you assholes.'"

He hesitated again. And we waited. I had a feeling I knew how this story would end. I was glad I no longer worked the streets of South Central Los Angeles, so I wouldn't have to deal with domestic disturbances in person ever again. Including the news I'd just heard. Though compelling, Jake's story still could not entirely push out the kidnapping and the image of Barbara Wicks on the television.

Jake continued on. "Couple a days later, my best friend Freddy came over. We sat on the porch and had us a few beers. That's when Freddy said it. He was the one that lit the fuse. He said, 'Jake, look at that, would yeh?'"

"'What's that, Freddy?' I ask."

"'They come right over on your side a the property line. Look, look.'"

"I got up, walked out to the street and checked that little

line-marker doughnut thing in the sidewalk. Sure as shit, Freddy
was right. Those shit-assed brown bastards had crossed the line.
Well, we got into an argument, me and Freddy and two of them
Mexes. We started pushin' and shovin'. That's when the cops
showed up. They broke it up. But the assholes threatened me right
in front of those cops, said for me not to go to sleep or they'd
burn down my house.

"Me and Freddy, we went into my house and, when it got
dark, we put guns by all the windows and doors and we watched.
We were ready for 'em, you can bet. We were ready, sure we were."
Jake's voice trailed off again.

"Long about midnight—I was godawful tired by then, and
I admit a little irritable waiting for them chili-eaters to attack—
Freddy—my best friend Freddy, he said, 'Think I heard a noise
out back.' Freddy, he was covering the back door, I had the front.
I said, 'Well, dammit, man, you got the back, go on out and check
on it.' I didn't think nothin' of it, thought it might be ghosts in
old Freddy's head."

Jake's voice broke as tears came in earnest now. "Them Mexes came right then. Knocked on my front door. I'd been ready all
night, tense and tight as a wound spring. I yanked open that front
door and said, 'Okay, you sons of bitches.'

"I shot the .44 Magnum. The noise and flash...it...it stunned
me. I wasn't ready for it." Jake swallowed hard. "Freddy, my best
friend, stood on the porch in front of me holding his chest. His
eyes...his eyes pleaded with me to take it back, to take back what I
had just done. He wanted to live, and I had stolen his life.

"You see, Freddy, he'd gone out back and the door closed,
locked him out. And he'd come around the front.

"I cried like a baby."

John Booth muttered low, "Jesus H—"

"Before he fell off the porch, dead, I yelled, 'How come you
didn't say it was you, Freddy? How come you didn't say?'"

Ansel reached over to put his hand on Jake's arm.

Jake jerked away. "It was his fault really, I guess."

Oh, God, what a terrible story, and I had been responsible for him telling it. The poor man.

Jake slid off his stool and ambled a few steps down the beach before he turned back and pointed a finger at me, his eyes squinting from the sun. He lifted his thumb, his hand now resembling a pistol. For a long second he held it, pointing in a threatening manner right at me. He turned and continued down the beach.

Ansel tossed back the rest of his drink, set the glass down hard on the bar, "Hey, Bobby J, do that again, but make it a double and hold the ice. That was something, wasn't it, boys? That sure was something to tell your grandkids about."

I did as he asked, while the other two sat solemn, brooding over the loss of their drinking buddy and his revelation. One thing I learned working the streets was all about human nature. Jake would never come back, not now, not after we all knew. Ansel took another drink, then said, "I never thought old Jake was down here on a murder beef. No sir, never would've guessed that one in a million years."

Ansel talked while I refilled Olivares' and Booth's drinks. His words melted into the fading day as I, too, remembered a similar, life-changing incident. Long ago, I'd bumped up against evil on the other side of a similar door in a house that bled. A day didn't go by I wasn't reminded that not all humans believed in keeping children safe and out of harm's way.

That's when my world jerked back into focus. I stood at the cabana bar looking out at the blue water. That's when I saw Barbara Wicks, the woman who'd just been on the television, the chief of police for Montclair, and Robby's widow, walking across the beach toward the cabana bar, her black heels kicking up sand.

What in the hell was she doing in Costa Rica?

CHAPTER FIVE

Why was she approaching from the beach and not from within the hotel? Could there be thirty or forty Feds along with the Costa Rican police hidden in and around the personal cabanas and tourist sunbathers? Was Barbara's approach a diversion so they could sneak up and take down a BMF, a Brutal Mother Fucker, wanted in the States on multiple felonies? I didn't turn and look. If they were there, it wouldn't matter anyway.

Barbara was a beautiful woman with brown hair going gray. Her face wore the haggard lines brought on by stress and sleep deprivation, and, to be fair, probably a little grief. Her now-deceased husband, Robby, had been the leader of the Violent Crimes Team, of which I'd been a member. We'd called ourselves the BMFs, Brutal Mother Fuckers. We'd had many a barbeque and beer in their backyard.

Robby's death had been the direct result of my actions. When he'd shot me in the ass—the second time he'd shot me in two-and-a-half years—he was trying to take me down. He was after Wally Kim, the kidnapped son of a South Korean diplomat who had a million-dollar reward on him for his safe return. Deputy John Mack of the Los Angeles County Sheriff's Department had then shot and killed Robby with a 12-gauge Ithaca Deerslayer shotgun.

I fought the urge to turn back to the television to see if Barbara's image was still there, hoping to make this nothing more than an apparition of guilt, retribution for what I'd just done to Jake. The news broadcast had been taped, and the flight to Costa Rica only took six hours—an obvious explanation.

She smiled. "How's it hangin', Bruno?"

"Get you something to drink, Chief? Something pink with a little umbrella?" I played the cool fugitive, suppressing every instinct to leap over the bar and run for my life. No matter how hard I tried, I couldn't come up with a logical reason for her standing there other than to take me down. Just because she'd been in the process of divorcing Robby didn't mean she hadn't loved him. Taking me in could be a matter of principle. Unlike me, some people still lived by principles. That wasn't necessarily true; I did have principles, just a different set.

I thought Costa Rica was far enough away so I hadn't worked at changing my appearance. A disguise would not have fooled Barbara Wicks. Robby hadn't married her because she was a fool, not by a damn sight.

She looked at the three compadres all watching her every move. "You boys need to find someplace else to drink. Bruno and I need to talk." She didn't know I was living under an alias. Didn't know or didn't care.

Her business professional dark slacks and a peach blouse displayed no law enforcement insignia. Her assertive, no-nonsense demeanor was all she needed. The boys got up mumbling that they had something to do or someplace they were supposed to be, and walked away. Ansel stopped and said, "Hey, Bruno, see you later?" He'd used my real name instead of Bob and winked. He was the smartest of the three and sensed the same dreaded outcome, a conversation that might end with my arrest.

"Sure, come on back later and the first one's on me." Meantime, my hands had been working all on their own mixing a Cosmo, her favorite drink. I set it in front of her. I wanted to blurt out, to ask her—no, to beg her—to tell me why she was there. I had to know if my life, as I knew it, was over. She slid up onto the stool, took the drink, and sipped. "What an absolutely beautiful view. This is a hell of a place to work, Bruno. You did good."

My mind clicked in on the obvious reason for her appearance. Wally Kim. What a dumbass for not thinking of it outright. She was there for Wally Kim. I had promised John Mack I would give Wally back. I just hadn't gotten around to it. Of the eight children I had saved from abusive homes, Wally Kim had a good father, one I hadn't known existed when I'd liberated Wally. Through the South Korean embassy, I'd set up a meeting to give Wally back. The meeting was scheduled for tomorrow. The embassy called early in the morning after Marie had gone to work, and I hadn't told her yet. I could have called her at work, but she was going to be upset. I wanted to tell her in person, hold her in my arms and whisper it in her ear, be there to comfort her.

All the kids we took were doing great, flourishing in their new healthy environment, one that none of them had ever had. I regretted that we had not had the time to prepare Wally or the other children emotionally for Wally's departure.

That was how Barbara had found me. Somebody from the embassy must have called her, told her where I was hiding out. Maybe that was why she was sitting at the bar sipping a Cosmo. Maybe the cops had already raided our bungalow, seized all eight children, which included my grandson Alonzo. Marie, the love of my life, and my father may now be in custody, pending extradition.

All because of me.

My heart sank. Of course, this was the only logical conclusion. We'd had a good run. Why had we thought we could get away with it in the first place?

Barbara set her drink on the bar and looked back down the beach. "That guy who just walked away, the dried-up old fart who looked like an old kicked-around walnut, that was Melvin Milky, you know. He made me as a cop."

I took up a white towel and wiped down the bar. "Don't know who you're talking about. Didn't see him."

She nodded as if she believed me. She pulled out a slim cell, from where I couldn't guess, and texted while she talked. "I am absolutely sure that was old Melvin." She finished her text and took up her drink. Had she just made up the name Melvin Milky for Jake Donaldson, and was using it as an excuse to text her back-up to swarm in?

"Okay," I said, "come on, tell me. I can't stand it anymore. Why are you here?"

She sipped her drink, her expression unreadable.

"Barbara?"

She smiled, set the glass down. "I think you know why." She nodded behind me.

My stomach dropped the same as if I'd been in a high-speed elevator falling a hundred floors. The police were waiting out there, I knew it, could feel it. She must've been nodding toward her backup. I thought of Marie and the kids and Dad.

I got mad. "I didn't think you, of all people, would come this far to stab me in the back like this."

She chuckled. "Bruno, what the hell are you talking about?"

I didn't like being the fool. I spun around. No storm-trooper cops were creeping up. A few tan and lobster-red tourists milled about the pool, drinking and talking. The place was quiet. I looked up at the television. The station was replaying the inter-view with Montclair Chief of Police Barbara Wicks, on a continu-ous loop like the press does with sensational incidents.

I spun back to face her, pointed up, over my shoulder. "The kidnapped kids? Those kids? Barbara, I don't have *those* kids. You've made a long trip for nothing."

Her smile fled, shifted to stone-cold. "Now what are *you* talk-ing about?"

"What are *you* talking about?"

She leaned over the bar, reached out, placed her hand on my arm, and said, "I need you to come back and chase down the guy who's taken these two little girls."

CHAPTER SIX

Barbara *didn't* know about my kids. She didn't know about Wally Kim. Could it be that her sole purpose in traveling all those thousands of miles down to Costa Rica was to ask me to…no, no way in hell. That didn't compute, not at all.

"I can't step a foot back in the States. You know that."

She took a sip and stared at me, said, "You know I wouldn't ask you if it wasn't important."

"Why me? And don't try that old saw that it's because I'm the best at this kind of thing. I won't buy—"

She waved her hand, "No, that would be ridiculous and you know it."

"Oh, thanks for that, Barbara."

She laughed, "You know what I mean."

I waited until her laughter died. "Tell me." I didn't want to know, not really. This had to be some link back to my old life, and it wouldn't be good. None of my old life had been good. That wasn't true, I had met Marie in my past life, and she was the best thing that ever happened to me, bar none.

Barbara again lost her smile, "You're my only chance, and you know me, I wouldn't be here, hat in hand, asking, if there was any other way. I wouldn't ask you to hang yourself out like that."

This time I was the one who couldn't speak, and only nodded.

Her cell buzzed on the bar. She left it, not caring if I saw it, displaying a little trust. I couldn't read the text upside down and didn't want to. She said, "It's about your boy Milky." She nodded over her shoulder in the direction Jake Donaldson had walked off. She pushed another button and a photo came up on her cell screen. I didn't need to turn it right side up to recognize Jake. She picked up her phone, moved it closer for me to see. "That him? That the guy who just walked off?"

"Nope, close, but it's not the same guy." Of course it was, but I wasn't going to rat.

She looked surprised, "Maybe you're not the right guy for this job. Maybe I'm wrong. The Bruno Johnson I used to know has changed."

"What are you talking about?"

"Used to be, no matter what, with you, a crook was a crook was a crook. Robby said you were a bulldog when it came to 'fighting the tyrannical oppression of the underprivileged.'"

The name "Robby" coming from her lips caused me to cringe. With it came a stab of grief and sorrow. At one time, Robby had been a good friend. "Maybe," I said, "but that was then, this is now. Times change. You change with them, or get eaten up." My own words came out cold, desolate. But I was alive, and Robby was the one taking the cold dirt nap.

"All right, all right," she said. "Let me tell you a story and, if you still feel the same, I'll let you tell me whether or not I should drop the hammer on your friend Milky."

"That's okay, this hypothetical Milky, he told me all about it, and it sounds like what happened might've been a terrible accident."

I didn't really think that. By his own words, Jake, aka Milky, had swung his front door open with the intent to fire, with the intent to kill. That was murder no matter who stood there, friend or foe. But were there extenuating circumstances that mitigated his actions? Years ago, in my book, before I went to prison for gunning down my son-in-law, there had been no such thing. You did the crime, you went down for it, hard or easy, your choice.

Barbara began, "Milky used to live in Fresno. He killed a black guy on the sidewalk out in front of his house. It started with a stupid argument that turned to racial slurs. Milky pulled this huge hogleg from his waistband and, without provocation, shot him dead because he was black."

Any empathy I might have had for Jake was gone. Barbara had no reason to make up this story. Jake had now morphed into the kind of animal I had chased while on the Violent Crimes Team.

Barbara continued, "According to the report, Milky had the gun under his jacket, out on the sidewalk. He shouldn't have had the gun out there in the first place, which proves intent. Milky claimed that the victim came at him with a knife. Milky fled the scene and, by the time the deputies arrived, there was no knife. There were no witnesses. The Sheriff's Department handled the incident and could not get the DA to file. And here's a little bit of ugly irony for you. The sheriff screwed up and released the gun back to Milky. Maybe they had to, but I wouldn't have. Milky left Fresno because it got a little too hot. Too many people wanted a piece of him. When he happened to settle in our little town of Montclair, I was working homicide and caught the case. He blew this guy right off his own porch. Point blank, right in the heart. He thought it was his Hispanic neighbor. Again, no witnesses. Again, no other motive than prejudice. He ran like most all of those cracker assholes do. And, until right now, we had no idea where he'd landed. We issued a warrant and we've been looking for him ever since.

"Oh, and the slug, went right through Fredrick Landsberg, the victim. We dug it out of a kid's playhouse across the street. It matched. Milky used the same gun, the .44 Mag that he used to kill that sixteen-year-old kid in Fresno."

A sixteen-year-old? To make matters worse, Jake had gunned down a sixteen-year-old kid!

Barbara cocked her head a little like she always did when trying to decipher a problem, trying to decide to say something further. "Be careful. I saw Milky when he left, what he did with his hand." She mimicked Jake Donaldson and made a gun with her index finger, her thumb as a hammer.

I asked, "Wasn't this Fredrick Landsberg his best friend?"

She scoffed. "Landsberg's wife told me that her husband met Milky that same day at a filling station, and Milky paid him forty bucks to help him protect his property against the influx of, 'the Mechican scourge.' And she said it just like that too."

I was stunned. How had I totally misread Jake? I didn't know what to say. "Don't worry about him. He'll lay low for a while and then take off. He'll go to Panama or Cuba." I didn't say the words with enough conviction to convince even myself.

She continued, "We never recovered that gun. The psych profile report believes that he's probably devolved mentally, and in some sort of freaky way, worships that gun. Bruno, he looked right at me tonight. He knows me from Montclair. I was the patrol sergeant working overtime the day of the shooting. I'd been the one to respond out to his house earlier that same day to mediate a neighborhood disturbance. And, get this, it was over some bathtub cheese. So watch yourself, the way this went down, me walking up, he might think you ratted him out."

"Perfect."

She said, "I'll notify the FBI and tell them he's down here, but there's not much they can do if he's wanted for murder. Costa Rica won't approve the extradition if there's a possibility of the death penalty."

I said, "Forget Milky, answer a simple question about this other thing, about these two kidnapped kids. Why me?"

She took another sip as she probed my eyes. This close examination made me uncomfortable. She finally smiled and reached with her hand to touch me again. I stepped back.

"Okay," she said, "for several reasons." She raised a finger to tick them off. "One. I know it's trite, but it's true, you are the best at what you do. Robby said you were the best he'd ever seen at tracking down assholes. And with that man's ego, you have to know how difficult it was for him to say."

I wished she wouldn't keep saying his name.

"Two. Because I know who's involved."

"If that's the case, put a team together and follow the suspect. Pick him up in the morning and put him to bed every night. He'll trip himself up."

"We can't find him, and you know how important time is in a kidnapping."

"Listen, I know you have people who are good at turning over rocks. The news reports said you have a joint task force with Los Angeles County Sheriff's Department. Get John Mack. He's good." I'd said John's name to see if she'd react. He was the only one who knew where Marie, my dad, and the kids had landed in Costa Rica. While I spoke, I started having a bad feeling about where she was leading me.

She was good, didn't even twitch. John Mack had been the one to tell her where I lived. Had to be. But I had trusted him with my life or I wouldn't have told him. He had to have a good reason for telling her.

John Mack had the skills; he would have no problem tracking down this suspect, but he still had a job and a career to consider, where I didn't. If John found the suspect and the suspect didn't want to talk, John wouldn't put the guy's nuts in a vise like I would and twist until he gave up the kids' location.

"You want someone off the grid to come in and black bag this guy, that's it, isn't it?"

She didn't answer, just stared.

"No?" I shook my head and looked into her eyes, trying to glean the answer she found so difficult to utter. "It's something else, isn't it? It's because of who it is, right?"

She nodded.

"Who is it? Tell me."

"He left a note, Bruno, said he'd only deal with you. He wrote your name in the note, Deputy Bruno Johnson. I have the note. Only my department knows."

"Me? Why me?"

She didn't answer. She didn't answer because I'd asked the wrong question.

I said, "Who?"

"Bruno, it's Jonas Mabry. Not the father, Micah—the kid. Jonas."

My head swam and my knees went weak. I grabbed the bar for support.

CHAPTER SEVEN

In an instant, I was transported back to that day the house bled and relived the incident, complete with all the regrets. The water. The blood. The two dead girls. The race to the hospital with Jonas Mabry.

I snapped out of the memory and returned to reality. My current life was still running full tilt. I was in Costa Rica tending bar in a cabana on the beach with Barbara Wicks sitting all alone, her Cosmo glass empty. She must've recognized my need to zone out, to relive that horrible event, and didn't shake me out of it. Why would she? The memory only served to further her cause.

Sweat beaded on my forehead and rolled down into my eyes. My voice croaked. "Micah Mabry, the old man?" I swiped at the salt burning my eyes.

"No, Bruno, you heard me. I said *Jonas Mabry.*"

I had heard, but my mind, for protective reasons, had blocked it out. His name in this context made me sick to my stomach, reminded me of failure, one strongly attached to a heavy dose of guilt.

Jonas was the small child I'd held in my arms as I rolled code three to St. Francis. He'd survived, only to be shoved into the foster care system. His father had had a nervous breakdown over grief and guilt. The last I'd heard, the father, Micah Mabry, had not responded to treatment. I couldn't blame him. Under the same circumstances, I'm not sure I would have been any different.

"Why me? What does he want with me?"

"He said in the note that he wants to pay you back for what you did. Are you going to go, Bruno?"

"Pay me back? That doesn't make any sense, not when he kidnaps kids to get my attention."

"Bruno?" I had waited too long to give Barbara Wicks my answer. She said, "If for nothing else, you do owe me."

She didn't need to throw that one out there. I had all but decided to go. How could I not go, given the circumstances? I had saved Jonas Mabry, only for him to be ruined by the social welfare system. I had known better. Why had I not adopted him myself? The opportunity had been ripe for adoption. I went to see him in the hospital, housed in intensive care for three weeks, not expected to live. After they moved him to a regular room, his father still had not come to see him. I brought him books and read to him. He didn't say a word for several weeks. I couldn't imagine what it must have been like to see your own mother standing over you with a gun. The hospital discharged him, and social services placed him in a good home. I saw to that, vetted the folks myself. He didn't want to go with them; he wanted to stay with me. Then I was transferred to the Violent Crimes Team and my schedule turned hectic, all but impossible. The job became my life and we lost touch. Regrets. Twenty years ago I was a different person, still too selfish and self-centered. I wanted my career and didn't want to be burdened with a second child. I was already caring for a young daughter.

Jonas would be twenty-six now.

I asked, "What did the note say?"

She took out a crumpled-up piece of paper that had been in her pocket the entire flight down. She smoothed the note on the bar. I didn't want to look, words a magic carpet to the past, someplace I didn't want to ever revisit. But I had only moments ago. The letter printed in all capitals, crooked, written with a shaky hand: *"TWO DOWN, ONE TO GO. I'LL ONLY SPEAK TO DEPUTY BRUNO JOHNSON. GET HIM. DEPUTY BRUNO JOHNSON OWES ME A GREAT DEBT THAT NEEDS TO BE SETTLED."*

I couldn't believe this note came from the child I knew. Now he's a psychotic. "So there's going to be a third?"

"Yes."

"And you think I'll have some emotional connection with Jonas, and will be able to get through to him, and get him to tell me where he's stashed the kids, is that it?"

"Yes." But she looked away.

"And?"

She didn't answer, which meant, worst case, I'd run Jonas down, ask him nicely and, if that didn't work, ask him the hard way. I *did* have an emotional link to Jonas and, under normal circumstances, I would not be able to interrogate him in the manner she thought I could. But if he had taken two small girls—just the thought made my blood turn hot with anger. Of course I would go. How could I not?

I would have to explain my departure to Marie. I'd met Marie the night almost three years ago when Robby Wicks took me into custody for the killing of my son-in-law, who'd abused my grandson to death. I did two years and got out on parole. That's when Marie and I started our relationship full of romance and love and caring and respect. Now I had to tell her I had to go back. No way did I want to hurt her like this.

I looked Barbara in the eyes and nodded. She didn't smile, but reached out and laid her hand on my arm. "Thank you."

Her gratitude touched something in me. A form of forgiveness I'd craved so badly for what had happened to Robby. I leaned over the bar and hugged her. She hugged back. Tears burned my eyes. We stayed that way a long time. "We're still good?" she asked.

"Yeah, we're good."

My mind immediately went back to Marie. How would I break this to her?

"Is that note a copy? Can I have it?"

Barbara handed it over. I folded it and put it in my pocket.

"How am I going to cross back into the States?"

"I'm going to leave that up to you, for obvious reasons. When you get up there, you're going to be on your own. If you get caught by the police, I won't be able to help you. I'd love to stay and catch up, and I promise we will when this is all over." She slid off the barstool. "I have a turn-around flight back. The mayor doesn't know I'm gone, and he'd flip if he did. I shouldn't have left town, let alone the country, not with this major investigation going on."

"I understand." I didn't have the focus to chat anyway. Marie didn't deserve this. She'd thought once we made the dangerous journey out of the States with our precious cargo, we would never have to worry again.

"It's going to take me a few days to get back, maybe even a week. I'm going to have to walk across the border."

She lost her smile. "I need you on this now, like, right now. You read the note, another kid is going to be taken, and those girls are in the hands of a psychopath."

Why me? Why three kids? What debt could I owe him? What was Jonas thinking? That was the real problem. Jonas had slipped over the tenuous edge of sanity and into his own psychotic world.

A kernel of an idea popped into my head. "If I get lucky, I'll be there tomorrow night."

CHAPTER EIGHT

Marie volunteered at the local clinic three days a week, partly for altruistic reasons, and partly to keep her hand and mind in the medical field. She didn't want to lose her edge. By now, the kids' physical wounds had healed. The emotional ones went deeper and were more difficult to overcome. Volunteering as a physician's assistant still allowed her plenty of time with the children.

I gave the hotel an excuse and the inside bartender relieved me. As usual, I moved through the streets in a circuitous route, doubling back over and over again, but now I was on high alert. Jake Donaldson wasn't just a pissed-off old drunk. The timing for me to leave town couldn't be worse. At least no one knew where I lived; I'd made sure to keep it that way.

Except for the main roads, the people on the streets were similar in size and clothing and movement. Anyone from north of the border would be easy to spot. I stopped at a café, ordered a coffee I didn't want, and watched the street's ebb and flow. This also gave me a chance to think, to make sure my decision remained sound.

Fifteen minutes later I turned down an alley free from debris and graffiti, something difficult to get used to. I climbed an old jacaranda tree like I always did and peeked over the thick, eight-foot-high wall surrounding the huge house we rented. For $500 a month, the house came with a groundsman, a housekeeper, and three meals a day. With the help of John Mack, we'd brought $250,000 with us, enough to last a good long time.

I reached over the wall and parted some banana leaves. The kids were playing in the backyard. They laughed and giggled and frolicked without a care in the world, the way children were supposed to grow up. The sight made my heart soar. Dad watched from a hammock, asleep. Of course, if you ever asked him, he never slept while charged with the children's care.

I mentally counted, like I always did, just to be sure. Eight of them: Rick and Toby Bixler, brothers burned in the failed PCP lab. They would have gone back to the same hazardous and toxic environment had we not intervened. Sonny Taylor, the cute, hungry little kid who ate his mother's meth and then, after the judge gave him back, his mother locked him in a closet. What chance did he have? Marvin Kelso, his mom's boyfriend the molester—I couldn't even think about that horrible scenario. Randy Lugo, with five broken bones; how long before it would have been his neck? Wally Kim's mother died a prostitute wedded to the glass pipe. Tommy Bascombe, his mother was a speed freak and took Tommy to the most dangerous parts of LA to score dope. She had even traded him off for a while, but always got him back in time for social services to do their home inspection. She wasn't going to miss out on her welfare check. And Alonzo, my grandson. All present, I breathed easier.

Alonzo and Albert had been the catalyst that started my rapid descent into lawlessness. Three years ago, my son-in-law killed little Albert, my grandson, Alonzo's twin. My hatred went so deep I could not, would not, remember the son-in-law's name.

The justice system gave the son-in-law a pass. I wouldn't. I went against all I had stood for in law and order, and stepped outside the moral ambiguity of the law. I hunted him down and shot him dead. Went to prison for it, only to come out and find the court had given Alonzo back to the son-in-law's parents.

The same abusive family that had raised the son in-law to be a murderer.

I watched from the tree a moment longer, jumped down, and went to the front wrought-iron entry. Tomorrow we'd no longer have Wally Kim's smiling face and bright eyes to warm our souls. I didn't want to give him up but it was the right thing to do. Wally would be better off with his natural father, to be raised in his country with his culture and traditions.

I went in quietly through the front door. The hacienda stayed cool during the day, with thick walls and wide paver tiles. In the kitchen I kept busy preparing Marie's favorite dinner, homemade enchiladas à la Bruno. I set the table and lit two candles, and made sangria with fresh fruit submerged and floating on top in a cold ceramic pitcher.

Without any warning, the herd from outside burst into the house with Dad trailing along, their afternoon playtime over. He didn't look as healthy as when he lived in Compton. In his youth he'd been a strong man, the strongest I ever knew, and kept me safe while growing up in a dangerous neighborhood. He worked forty years as a mail carrier, never missing a single day from being sick. His shoulders were slumped now, his once glistening black hair was snow white, and his brown eyes were occluded by cataracts.

The kids swarmed around my legs. I picked up Alonzo and swung him high. He giggled. I tried not to show favoritism around the other children, but I naturally gravitated to my grandson.

"What's with the special dinner tonight?" asked Dad. "Did I forget some important anniversary or something?"

"Nope. Can you keep the kids in the game room tonight, feed them dinner in there, and put them down at the usual time?"

"You know I can." He kept his smile, but the light in his eyes dropped below a twinkle. He gathered the noisy kids with a gentle touch to their backs. "Come on, story time, let's go, story time."

Alonzo wiggled to get down. He loved me without reservation. *"Bronze Bow,* Granpap?" he asked.

"That's right, we're reading *The Bronze Bow*. Come on now."
When he had them all headed in the right direction, he stopped
and nodded toward the table and candles. "Is this something I
should know about?"

"I really need to talk with Marie about it first. I owe her that
much."

"Whatever it is, Bruno, don't do it. I'm telling you right now,
don't do it. Nothing's worth risking what you have here. And I
mean nothing. You know that. You can see it. I know you can."
He kept on moving down the hall.

I'd disappointed him. He'd called me Bruno instead of Son.
He only did it when he was serious and wanted me to pay close
attention to something important he'd said.

I looked up at the ceiling and shook my head. Of course he
was right. But what was I supposed to do? *What about little Sandy Williams and Elena Cortez?*

Their images crept in. Images of them all trussed up, twine
biting into their soft flesh, their eyes and mouth taped with duct
tape. Anxiety rose in me, my hands and feet fidgeted, and it
quickly shifted to anger.

I sat in the flickering candlelight waiting for Marie and wondered: How could Jonas Mabry have devolved into such an animal? Maybe it wasn't true. Maybe Barbara Wicks had it wrong.
That option didn't make sense. Barbara, the consummate professional, wouldn't make a mistake of that magnitude.

Outside, the wrought-iron gate clanged. Marie was home.
The quiet and the calm, soon to be broken when she found out.

The usual sounds reached out to the dining room. Her san-
dals slipped off, her purse hung up. She padded on small feet
down the hall. She was a fiery Puerto Rican woman with green
eyes. I held my breath. Every time I saw her, I felt the same all over
again. Her beauty, her smile, and simply her presence made any
problem dissolve away. I wanted to hug and kiss her.

This time, the problem would not go away.

She entered the dining room. The soft glow from the candles

caressed her smile as she took in the scene. Her gaze fell upon mine. She read my expression, the emotion plain on my face. Her smile disappeared. She pulled out a chair and eased down.

"Oh, Bruno, no. Please, no."

CHAPTER NINE

Marie watched me pour her a tall glass of the purple-red sangria. She took a sip. "It's Wally, isn't it?"

"What?"

I had not told her about my negotiations with the South Korean deputy ambassador, the conduit to Wally's father, Mr. Kim. With this other problem, I'd forgotten all about that issue. I nodded.

Tears filled her eyes. She came over and sat in my lap, buried her face, warm and wet, against my neck. I held on, relishing her touch, knowing the risk that in a few minutes she might pull away and never again would I have this same wonderful feeling. Her accelerated heartbeat transmitted through to my hands on her back. She kept her face hidden.

She ignored my question, asking one of her own. "When?"

"Tomorrow morning."

She jerked away enough to look into my eyes. "So soon? Why so soon? That's not fair."

"We've talked about this. It's the right thing to do."

"I know that. I know, but so soon? Come on, Bruno, can't we wait a month?"

"It's better this way."

She nodded and laid her cheek down on my shoulder. I rocked her gently back and forth as she stroked my hair. After a moment she said, "I smell perfume on you."

I nodded.

"Did Angelina Jolie come to The Margarite and mistake you for Denzel Washington and give you a big wet kiss?"

I'd made that story up one night not long ago when she'd asked me what had happened at work. Nothing ever happened and I made up stories.

I shook my head 'no' and croaked out the words in a half-whisper. Words I did not want to share. "It's from Barbara Wicks."

She leaped off my lap, her eyes wide, her mouth agape.

I couldn't get words to come out, trapped in a roadblock at the top of my throat. I hated more than anything in the world to hurt Marie.

She grabbed a linen napkin from the table and wiped her eyes to see me better. Not good enough, she skipped-hopped over to the wall and turned on the light. I squinted.

She said, "No, you aren't going back." She'd put it together just that fast from the name. Why else would Barbara be down here? Marie had always been the sharper of the two of us.

Her expression wrinkled up. "I know what she wants. I saw the news—" More tears. It hurt worse, ripped my guts out.

"I...I saw those poor little girls taken from their homes and I thought...I mean, I know this is selfish, and...and piggish of me, but I thought, 'I hope Bruno doesn't see this. He'll jump on his horse and go galloping off, and no way will I be able to stop him.'"

Her face smoothed out as she shifted to anger. She quick-stepped over, balled a little fist, and socked me as hard as she could in the chest. I sat still.

"You promised me, Bruno. You promised me that after we got down here—" She broke down and brought her hands up to cover her face. She was torn, I could see it. She couldn't live with herself if she talked me out of going and something worse happened to Sandy Williams and Elena Cortez, something that could have been avoided had I intervened. The truly sad part, we both knew, was that whether I went or not, something bad was likely to happen to those little girls. Historical statistics were not on their side. Now all that mattered was how much I could tip the balance in their favor.

"It's not what you think. I'm the only one who can help these little girls."

She pointed her finger at me and opened her mouth to speak.

I raised my hand. "Wait, please wait and let me explain." I swallowed hard. I didn't like reliving the story of the Mabry family and the house that bled. In all the years after the event, I'd never told anyone the story except Marie. One hot summer night while lying with Marie on damp sheets, my need to share overwhelmed my need to keep the images, pain, and emotions buried. Her hot body up against mine, her head resting on my shoulder, I told her the entire story. Her breath increased, her body tensed. When I finished, she said, "I am so very sorry, Bruno." She, too, had been outraged by the brutality, the cold insensitivity. The evil. We never spoke of the event again.

"I have to go, because it's Jonas Mabry who has the children. He took them in order to get me to come back to the States."

Her hand flew to her mouth. Her eyes went wide as tears filled them again.

I pulled her into me. After a time, still in the embrace, I asked, "You hungry? I am." I really wasn't, but wanted her to eat something.

"You're wanted," she said in a quieter tone. "The odds are not in your favor. They catch you, I'll never see you again."

"Baby, I have to go. I'll be all right. I promise you, it'll be all right. No one's going to catch me. I'll get in, find out what this is all about, find the two little girls, and get right out. One day, two at the most."

She wouldn't look at me and pulled away. She plopped down on the chair, tears streaming down her cheeks, her eyes aflame with anger. A reaction to be expected under the circumstances.

"What about the next time? Huh? What about the next time, Bruno 'the Bad Boy' Johnson?" For emphasis, she'd used an old street moniker the guys on the Violent Crimes Team had labeled me.

I spoke in a lowered voice, words I wanted to be true more than anything else. "There won't be a next time, because there is only one Jonas Mabry."

She searched my eyes for truth and nodded.

I went over and turned the light off. In the dim light from the candles, I went back and picked her up the same as I would a child, blew out the candles, and carried her to the bedroom. I was hungry for her, all of her. The ache I would have being away from her was already there. I wanted to savor every second of our time together.

I laid her gently on the bed and kissed her long and deep. I unbuttoned the top button to her blouse and she grabbed my hand. She got up on her knees and pulled my shirt off over my head, kissing my neck and chest. I slipped her blouse over her head and unhooked her bra so her breasts fell loose. We lay down, went slow, stretched time, tried to pretend we could make it last forever.

***

The next morning, Marie put on a fake smile as she loaded a bag of Wally's clothes and toys and books. Dad and Marie turned away to wipe tears as they said good-bye. The kids were confused, but most of all, four-year-old Wally. *Kids are so intuitive.*

We made it out the door, me carrying Wally close, even though he could walk. In an hour I would never see him again. The thought snatched my breath. I suppressed it.

I walked straight to the center of town where the 200-year-old, five-tier fountain provided a watering hole for birds from miles around. We sat on the edge and tossed dried bread to the bold pigeons. Wally giggled and chased after them. The birds flew and came right back, more intent on filling their stomachs than concern for their safety.

Right on time, a white stretch limo pulled around the cobbled street that encircled the fountain. I fought an urge to change my mind, scoop up Wally, and run like hell.

This was the first time Mr. Kim had even met his son. He'd come to Los Angeles for a world summit five years ago, to exchange ideas regarding the use of land mines in No Man's Land between North and South Korea. He'd met a younger, prettier version of Wally's mother, who had just started working the high-end convention center hotels, plying her trade. Before she'd given it all up for the glass maiden. They conceived Wally without Mr. Kim's knowledge. Later, she contacted Mr. Kim and told him about his son, said for $100,000 he could have his son, no strings attached. Marie and I hadn't been aware of any father when we took him from his mother, who was so sketched out and goggle-eyed with cocaine paranoia that she didn't know what day it was. The mother later died of an overdose. Mr. Kim had been looking for Wally ever since.

Mr. Kim was smart. He stopped on the other side of the circle. Approaching on foot would be far less intimidating. Two thick-necked bodyguards with sunglasses got out first, their shaved heads rotating from side to side searching for any threat. Mr. Kim, smaller, dressed in white linen pants and a cream silk shirt, emerged. He saw Wally and his face went from all business to a megawatt smile.

Relief flooded me. Giving Wally up to this man was going to be all right. Any doubt that this man was Wally's father, wasn't there now. Wally had his chin and jaw line.

Mr. Kim hesitated and then headed over. His bodyguards followed and he waved them off.

I said, "Wally, son, come here." The child stopped chasing the pigeons and hurried back. I hugged him and kissed the top of his head. I picked him up and sat him on my lap as Mr. Kim walked up. He took off his sunglasses and we locked eyes. He bowed and then extended his hand. I took it, fighting tears. He sat down next to us. He knew not to rush the exchange, not with a small child.

"Thank you for calling," he said. "I have been frantic to find him. Thank you for taking care of him and keeping him safe. I understand your motives and how it happened, and I can never repay you."

I had a large rock in my throat and found it difficult to reply. And even though this was the best deal for Wally, I still transferred some anger to Mr. Kim for making us go through this. The emotion wasn't logical, but I understood its basis.

"Wally," I said, "I want you to meet a good friend of mine."

"Who? Who's this?" For a brief second, Wally lost his smile. That intuition thing again.

"He's a good friend, and—"

Mr. Kim again proved this was the right decision. He pulled out three Tootsie Pops from his pocket. Wally's face lit up. He wiggled down off my lap and went over to his father, an action that displayed a child's natural vulnerability. Mr. Kim didn't try to pick him up. He took his time. "Hello, Wally." He handed over the chocolate sucker, the one Wally pointed to. Mr. Kim smiled and a tear ran down his cheek. He helped Wally unwrap his Tootsie Pop. Wally stuck it in his mouth and immediately tried to come back to the safety of my lap.

I held Wally off. "Wally, do you want to know a secret?"

He nodded, too involved in his sucker to take it from his mouth to talk.

"Mr. Kim, my very good friend here, is going to Disneyland and wants to take a little boy with him. Do you want to see Dumbo and Mickey Mouse?"

Wally looked at Mr. Kim then back at me as he thought about this offer. He shook his head "no," and tried a little harder to get back in my lap.

Mr. Kim looked scared. "Wally, I have some toys in my car right over there."

"What kind of toys?"

"A bright red fire truck and some race cars."

I hoped for Wally's sake that Mr. Kim really did have the toys in the car. Wally was going to be scared enough.

Wally hesitated, then again shook his head "no." Mr. Kim couldn't resist himself and gently stroked Wally's hair. This spooked Wally and he wiggled harder. I let him get back up in my lap as I tried to think of what else would work, short of physically forcing him. Mr. Kim looked back at the limo. If he was going to call the car, this was going to turn emotional for all three of us.

I turned Wally around to face me. "I guess you don't want to go with Mr. Kim, do you?"

This time he pulled the sucker from his mouth. "No."

"Okay, too bad, you're really going to miss out."

"Miss out on what?"

"Oh, Mr. Kim is on his way to buy a puppy."

Wally's head whipped around. "A puppy?"

Mr. Kim laughed. "That's right, a puppy. Do you want a puppy?"

Wally nodded his head "yes," wiggled down off my lap, and went over to Mr. Kim. "Let's go. Let's go get a puppy."

Mr. Kim wiped the tears from his face. He extended his other hand. "Thank you again, Mr.—"

I took his hand and shook, "Luther, John Luther."

We each took one of Wally's hands and walked him to the limo.

"I know you told the Korean embassy that you would not take the million-dollar reward. Please, the money means nothing to me, not compared to what you have done."

Marie and I hadn't done it for the money, and taking it would somehow trivialize our acts, all of them.

"I won't take the money, but there is something you can do for me."

CHAPTER TEN

Later that same night we stood in the open front door. At our feet sat a beat-up, black leather valise packed with one change of clothes and $20,000 from our savings. Money to get the job done and money to get me home. In a kidnapping, the first twelve hours are the most crucial; after that, the odds of a favorable outcome diminish to single digits. I wasn't going to be gone long.

I'd said my good-byes to the kids when I put them to bed. I held Marie in my arms, my face resting on the top of her head. Her hair smelled of green apples. I imprinted her scent in my memory. We stood quietly with the knowledge the trip would begin once the limo from the embassy pulled up out front. I didn't want to go.

Marie had said little throughout the evening. Now she spoke. "I need to tell you something."

I didn't move. In an instant my mind spun out a thousand scenarios, the most obvious from similar B-movie situations: *I won't be here when you get back.* But Marie would never pin an *or else* on this trip, not with these stakes.

After I squirmed a little, she said, "I fought with myself over whether or not to tell you. You have so much on your mind already. But I decided you'd be mad if I didn't."

"What is it? Tell me, please."

"I don't want you to worry while you're gone. You have enough—"

"Marie." I tried to pull her away to see her eyes. She clung to me.

"He told me not to tell you."

"Who, Dad? What is it?"

"There's something wrong with him."

This time I wouldn't let her get away with it. I pulled her back and watched her expression. "What are you talking about?"

"Your dad's sick. I don't know what it is. He won't go to the clinic."

"Cancer? Is it cancer?"

"I can't tell. No one can until there are tests. It could be anything."

My knees went weak. "How long have you noticed the symptoms?"

"He hasn't been eating right for a while and, when he does, it's a little at a time. Haven't you noticed his weight loss? I've been trying to get him to go to the clinic for about two weeks now. I was about to tell you, then all this mess happened. He's going to be real mad I told you. He said that if I didn't tell you, he'd go to the clinic tomorrow after you left."

I nodded, taking in this news and weighing it against canceling the trip. What price did one have to pay to do the right thing? This one could come with a heavy toll. "How bad do you think it is?"

She put her head back on my chest. "Bruno, don't worry about it. There's nothing to worry about until there are tests. Odds are, this is something minor."

The limo pulled up out front, the headlights illuminating the trees and other houses in diffused blacks and grays.

Decision time.

She said, "I didn't want you to go without knowing. It's probably nothing. Tomorrow we'll know more after he sees a doctor. I'll call you first thing, I promise." She reached down and picked up the valise. "Come on."

She wasn't going, but carried the valise to show me in some small way she approved of the trip. She went out the door into the night. I could do nothing else but follow along like a wayward orphan.

The walk down the flagstone entry to the street went on and on as I fought the desire to stay behind, to let someone else handle the problem thousands of miles away, a problem that had the potential to impact our lives to an unimaginable degree.

Over the six months before we'd left the States, Dad had aged twice as fast. He'd literally wilted right before my eyes. I assumed that the stress from hiding the kids caused this damage. Cancer studies have proven that stress is a serious causation factor. I couldn't have deterred him from getting involved with bringing the children to Central America. He'd always been a protector of the neighborhood.

But this wasn't necessarily cancer. I had to keep telling myself this wasn't cancer, this was something minor, like an intestinal virus.

Marie, slightly ahead, passed through our ornate wrought-iron gate. "Look at this."

Her words pulled me out of my conflicted thoughts. On the sidewalk, large painted white letters reflected the limo lights. "I KNOW WHERE YOU LIVE, YOU BLACK RAT BASTARD."

What else could go wrong? I muttered, "Shit."

She squatted, touched two fingers to the paint. "It's still tacky. Who did this?"

"I know who it is."

"Who?"

"You know how I've been trying to get the guys at the bar to tell me why they're here?"

"You mean outing your friends? I told you that was a bad idea. Wait, there was only one left. Don't tell me this is that crusty old man, Jake Donaldson?"

"Yeah, ol' Jake Donaldson. And you were right, I probably shouldn't have been trying to find out their dirty little secrets. Turns out, he's a murderer on the lam. He's no one to mess with. He saw me with Barbara. He thinks I ratted him out and Barbara is here to take him back. Now he wants to get even."

"Don't worry," she said. "He comes around here again, I'll

take a ball bat to him, make him wish he was back in the States on death row." She wasn't just saying this to make me feel better; she really would take a bat to him.

I remembered the story about him, how he'd shot and killed a black kid out on the sidewalk, and now he'd tagged me on my sidewalk. I wasn't going to feel right leaving with this hanging. Although, he wanted me, not Marie or the children. He wouldn't necessarily go after them, not when I was the target. In fact, not being around might even be better. I preferred deluding myself. Crazies were unpredictable.

Marie read my thoughts. "Trust me, I can handle this."

Her tone changed back to the familiar Marie and made it easier for me to get in the limo. I stepped up to the back door. The driver got out, came around, and opened it for me.

"What's with the limo? Wait, I don't want to know. Save it for when you get back, and then you can tell me the whole story." She went up on tiptoes to peck me on the cheek. Not good enough. I took hold of her and kissed her hot and wet and deep until we both gasped for breath when we broke. I hugged her and whispered, "I love you more than you know."

"Ditto. You just come back safe, you hear me, Bruno Johnson?"

My throat closed up. I could only nod. I let go and shot into the limo before I changed my mind. The door closed with the finality of a jail door clanging shut.

CHAPTER ELEVEN

I had expected the driver, an embassy employee, to look like Odd-job from the 007 movies, close-shaved hair, shoulders humped with muscle, without a visible neck. Instead, Mr. Kim sent a young, slightly built Korean man dressed in an expensive suit. He watched the mirror as we pulled away from the curb.

"Can we please make a detour?" I asked.

"Of course, I have been told to help in any way possible." His English came with a hint of East Coast accent, my guess, somewhere close to Boston.

"Calle Buena Vista. The salmon-colored hacienda. You can't miss it."

"Yes, sir."

I mulled over the options. Within ten minutes, the driver pulled up to the intercom recessed into a cairn of flagstone rocks. I rolled down the window and pushed the button. Nothing. I pushed the button again and held it down.

"Jesus, Bruno, is that you?"

I stuck my head out the window so the hidden camera got a better angle.

The large heavy gate slowly swung open. The driver continued up the drive and pulled through the porte cochere and stopped by the open front door. Ansel stood in the doorway in a kelly-green silk robe. I didn't get out. I wanted him to come to me. He hesitated, and then came down the steps.

"What the hell, Bruno, a limo?" He ventured closer, holding his robe together in a feminine way with both hands. His normally curly red hair was combed off to one side and mussed. His freckled face creased by a pillow.

I said, "I need a favor."

He looked up and down the limo. "Sure, pal, anything you need."

"I...ah... got called back to the States on business and..."

He leaned in closer, lowered his voice. "You can't go back. You're like the rest of us. They'll nail your black ass to the wall for mortgage fraud."

I hadn't told the guys about the children, the real reason I came to "The Rica." Instead, I had told them that I had fled the US just ahead of a major indictment for identity theft. I told them that I had created a gallery of fake persons with their own histories, and refinanced lots of homes at the peak of the market. According to the cover story, I had fled with twenty million.

"Trust me," I said, "I know what I'm doing and I have no choice. I have to go."

"Sure, sure pal, what do you need me to do?"

"You know that thing with Jake Donaldson?"

Ansel slapped the sill of the door. "Sure, that was really something, wasn't it? Who would have thought, huh?"

"You saw how he pointed his finger at me when he walked away?"

"You know, Jake, he was just mad. He'll be back at the bar like nothing happened. Trust me on this, I know people."

"He painted a threat on the sidewalk out in front of my house."

"You're kidding me, right? No shit?"

"Yeah, and I don't think anything will happen, and I don't expect to be gone that long, but, could you—"

"You got it, pal, anything you need."

"Let me finish. I want you to hire some local help. I want my place watched twenty-four seven."

"Oooh, that's going to be expensive."

"You're really going to strong arm me like this when my back's to the wall?"

He shrugged.

I couldn't expect him to foot the bill. "You cover it and I'll catch you when I get back."

"Ah, Bruno, not to be a wet blanket—but, what if you don't come back?"

He was right. I could get arrested and never see daylight ever again. I reached into the valise and peeled off one of the four bundles. "Here's five grand."

He took it, thumbed the bills. "With the prices down here, this will probably last you three or four weeks. But what about my, ah, handling fee?"

I glared at him for a long second hoping his conscience would kick in. He'd taken a movie star's entire savings and fled the country without so much as a rotten night's sleep.

I took out another bundle and tossed it to him. "I hope I'll be able to do you a favor someday."

His eyes turned greedy as he thumbed the cash. "I told you, I'm here to help."

I rolled up the window. The driver had heard the entire conversation, knew the meeting had ended, and drove off. I didn't know why Ansel's slimy behavior bothered me. You lie down with thieves, what do you expect? I guess I had just considered him a friend, and it hurt to find out otherwise.

**

The sleek white jet set down at a seldom-used General Aviation Center in San Bernardino, Southern California. Every detail of the trip had been prearranged by Mr. Kim. Customs came on board through the front door as I went out the back with the catering elevator truck. Just that easy. Crossed my mind that if a South Korean diplomat could orchestrate a human smuggling operation in a few short hours and pull it off, why couldn't North Korea smuggle in a tactical nuke and ruin everyone in the world's life with one press of a button?

At four o'clock in the morning, the catering truck let me off at the Quick Stop Market, an all-night convenience store in the city of San Bernardino. I purchased two disposable phones and called the number Barbara Wicks had given me. After one ring a male picked up on the other end. "You here? Where?"

"Corner of Waterman and Baseline in—"

The line went dead.

I bought a coffee and two packages of Hostess Sno Balls, the half-round balls of soft chocolate cake and marshmallow covered in pink coconut. I could never eat them around Marie. She said Hostess baked goods had too many poisons, processed sugars, and flours, and enough preservatives to give them a "half-shelf life of fifty-six years, three months and two days." She had a habit of over-embellishing statistics when she wanted me to understand something was serious. I already missed her.

I sat on the concrete with my back to the Quick Stop, to the left of the front door, drank my coffee and ate the first package of Sno Balls. I didn't need the second one. My stomach stretched tight, but I hadn't had them in nine months and stared at the last forlorn pair.

The dew hung in the dark night air, creating a yellow halo around the streetlight out past the parking lot. My heart leapt up into my throat. A black-and-white police car pulled in—a sleek predator, a shark. The cop car came right up to me, the blinding headlights no more than three feet way. I brought up my arm to shield my eyes. The car stopped close enough for me to feel the warm breath from its radiator. I fought down my panic. I didn't have any ID. If they ran me in and took my prints, they'd find the murder warrant. I'd be through before I even got started.

Options: I could stand, casually brush off my hands, and walk away. If they tried to jam me, I'd run. I didn't know the area, and they'd call in a helicopter and other units to seal off the area. What other option did I have? I could just sit, wave as they went on by. What would I do if I were these cops and still working the streets? Would I jam someone like me?

Hell, yes.

I rose, my old joints popping, picked up my Sno Ball trash, and walked to the trash can, away from my valise. Two cops got out and talked. They'd pulled in for the same as me, coffee and a snack. The driver stood six inches taller than the shorter, stout passenger. Both sported buzz cuts, their scalps gleaming in the light from the store. Their pressed blue uniforms, polished leather and shoes indicated new guys, not tired old veterans who might have been more interested in the coffee than jamming up some Sno Ball-eating black man sitting in front of a Quick Stop at four in the morning. Just my luck.

Fifteen feet perpendicular to the cop car, the parking lot ended in a wall of ebony darkness and temporary safety. I headed that way.

One of the cops said, "Hey!"

I kept walking, one foot in front of the other. Don't panic, be cool. Be cool.

"Hey, stop, old man."

I froze, and didn't turn around right way as I fought the urge to bolt. Their shoes scuffed as they moved up behind, one off to the side in a flanking maneuver. Good procedure.

"What's your name?"

I turned, the decision made to play it out. "Walter Shiftly. Why, have I done something wrong, Officer?"

"It's kind of late to be out sitting in front of a store."

I flashed my best smile. "Or early, depending, I guess. I couldn't sleep and thought I'd get me something to eat before work." I held up the unopened Sno Ball two-to-a-pack and the coffee cup.

Both stood in good interrogation stances ready for anything. "That your bag?" asked the short one.

I glanced over at the bag. Ten thousand in cash in this neighborhood said dope dealer. "Nope, that bag was sittin' right there when I walked up." The words sounded stupid even to me as they spewed out uncontrolled. Nothing else I could have said.

The tall one scoffed. "Right, you hear that, partner? He sat right down next to that bag, didn't open it, and didn't take it with him. I'm calling bullshit on this one."

The short one moved over to the bag. "If this isn't yours, then you wouldn't mind me looking in it, would you?"

I looked from one to the other as I took in a deep breath, preparing to bolt. I only hoped these two weren't crazy enough to shoot me in the back.

At the street, a dark green Ford Thunderbird bounced into the parking lot at high speed, drove over, and stopped beside the cop. Out stepped John Mack.

He stood six feet with 190 pounds of muscle. He wore his hair in a flattop, and the tattoo on a thick bicep that peeked out from under his t-shirt sleeve read: "BMF."

"I'm a detective with the Los Angeles County Sheriff's Department," said Mack. "Congratulations, boys, you got him, you really got him. Cuff him before he gets away. He's got a federal fugitive warrant for 187."

The two cops jumped me and took me to the ground. They slammed me down on the dirty, hard concrete and wrestled my hands behind my back. The coffee cup broke open. Hot wetness burned my legs. John Mack walked up, his feet inches away. Had this whole thing been a conspiracy between Mack and Barbara Wicks to get me back into the States to throw me in prison for the rest of my life?

CHAPTER TWELVE

Once cuffed, the two cops manhandled me to my feet and shuffle-dragged me to the back door of the black-and-white. "No shit, a federal fugitive wanted for murder—excellent!" said the tall one.

They tossed me in the backseat like a sack of potatoes and then got in the front. This wasn't my first time in the backseat and I hated it just the same, the confinement, the inability to make simple choices. Through the black metal screen that separated the back from the front, the short passenger cop asked, "What's your name?"

I didn't answer and watched Mack go into the Quick Stop with my Sno Balls in one hand. He went to the coffee kiosk, poured a cup, and walked back by the clerk, whose lips moved as he commented. Mack said something in return and stuck his hip up to make sure the clerk saw his sheriff's star clipped to his belt. Just like Mack, he didn't want to pay for the coffee. Mack stood out in front by the door, eating my Sno Balls and drinking free, steaming coffee.

"Ask that dude what this dude's name is, he knows him," said the tall police officer in the driver's seat.

The short cop got out. "Hey, man, what's this guy's name? He won't tell us."

Mack spoke around marshmallow cake covered in pink coconut. "That there is Leon Byron Johnson."

I let out a long breath and relaxed. That wasn't my real name. The tall cop mistook my relief for guilt. "Yeah, that's his name."

"Thanks, man, we owe you," said the short cop. He got back in and started typing the new information into the computer.

Mack sauntered over to the open window of the driver. "You take the 10 Freeway all the way into Los Angeles. It's about fifty miles, get off at Grand, hang a left and—"

The short cop had the valise on his lap, trying to open the latch. "Wait, hold up. What are you talking about?"

Mack pasted on a confused expression. "You fellas got yourself a federal fugitive. He has to be taken forthwith to appear before a federal magistrate. You're kidding, right? You really didn't know that? Well, you can't book him in just any jail. Get your watch commander to clear it and make a run to LA, no problem." Mack started to walk off.

The driver jumped out. "Hey, hey. You shittin' me?"

"Call the jail if you don't believe it."

The short cop muttered, "Bullshit, we are not going to LA, not this late in the shift." He jumped out. "Hey, you want him? You're the one who actually ID'd him. We didn't. He's really your arrest."

"Really? You boys'll give him to me, just like that?"

I sat in the backseat as it all played out, stunned at Mack's arrogance and bravado. *Mack, you son of a bitch. You better not overplay your silly little game.*

"I've been up all night on a surveillance. Just stopped in for some coffee to keep me awake on the ride home," said Mack.

The tall cop turned to his partner. "I don't want to give up a federal fugitive arrest. We don't get them very often."

The short one replied, loud enough only for his partner and not Mack to hear. "We get off in an hour, and I'm taking my wife and kids and my boat to Silverwood Lake. I'm not going all the way into LA. Fifty miles there and fifty back, that's a hundred miles. No way. And on top of that, who knows how long we'll be there booking this mope in?" He left his open door and came around to where his partner stood talking to Mack, their words too low to hear.

Mack shook his head, playing it to the hilt. He spoke louder than the others, loud enough for me to hear. "But I just came from LA, I don't want to drive all the way back there." He leaned over to the side and smiled at me. The two blue suits talked to him some more. The short one, talking fast using his hands, took some money from his uniform shirt pocket and handed it to Mack.

"Okay, I'll run him in, but you guys are going to owe me," said Mack.

The two cops came over, opened the back door. I slid out. They took off their cuffs and put on the ones Mack handed them. They escorted me over to Mack's Thunderbird and slid me into the front seat. Mack stood by the open front door, sipping his coffee, and whispered, "You can thank me later for saving your ass."

"Don't let them look in my valise."

Mack threw down the coffee. "Shit." He walked fast over to the cop car. "Hey, what about his bag?"

The short cop had the valise out of the car on the hood, trying to jimmy the latch with a double-edged knife. Mack made it to his side and took hold of the handle. "I got this."

"Wait a minute," the short cop said. "What if there's a couple of kilos of coke in there? This is our bust, and if there's dope we can book him in our jail."

Mack didn't let go of the handle and stared down at the shorter man. "This isn't *Let's Make a Deal.* You only get to see what's behind door number one if you take the body with it. And you said you don't want to make the trip. So make your choice."

The short cop hesitated, then shoved the bag toward Mack. "See you guys," said Mack. He walked back to the car unrushed and got in. The two cops stood and watched. They had to be wondering if they'd made a mistake. Mack started up, dropped the handcuff keys in my lap, put it in drive, and pulled out onto the street.

I didn't like the feel of steel on my wrists, not one bit, and fumbled to get them off. Mack took my last Sno Ball sitting on the dash and bit into the soft cake. He laughed with his mouth open. "Man, Bruno, you should have seen the look on your face when I told those two blue-bellies you had a murder warrant. I thought I'd pee my—"

I reached over and shoved the Sno Ball in his face. He wasn't ready for the move. The car swerved and his head jerked around to look at me, flecks of coconut clung to his cheeks. I laughed. "Now that's funny."

He didn't miss a beat. He laughed louder and playfully backhanded my shoulder.

I said, "Leon Byron Johnson—LBJ—you really thought hard on that one."

"Hey, it was an impromptu thing." Now he laughed so hard that we swerved inside the lane.

The mirth died a natural death as the serious business at hand sauntered in and smothered us both. The thought of those two kids in the hands of a freak. We drove into the night, down Waterman, to westbound on the I-10, the San Bernardino Freeway.

Mack said, "I hope you don't have something I'm going to regret in that grip of yours."

"Does it matter? Your ass is already hung out a country mile for aiding and abetting a fugitive."

He shook his head. "Nope, I never ran you for warrants. I don't know that you're wanted. You're just an informant that Chief Wicks asked me to work with."

"Really? That's your defense? We get caught, you're going to burn along with all the rest of us chickens."

"Yeah, you're probably right."

"You have any line at all on Jonas Mabry? Has he been in contact other than that note?"

"Sorry, not yet. You have any ideas on where we can start to look while we wait for him to make contact?"

Outside the car the dark freeway zipped by. We were passing through Colton. "I've got a couple of ideas. My mind's mushy right now. I need a couple hours' sleep."

"You didn't sleep on the plane?"

I didn't answer. Who could sleep? I didn't know what I'd find when I walked off the plane. And even if I'd made it that far, how long could I possibly keep moving around SoCal, where there were thirty- to forty thousand cops?

"I have us a room at The Fontana Valley Suites," said Mack.

"I hope it's a nice place. I'm not up for some fleabag with a swayed mattress and bed bugs."

"It's on the county's dime, so you know it's not going to be a five-star joint."

"County's dime? Are you crazy? You don't want a record of me anywhere around you. If you have the county pay for it, it goes on the expense account report."

He took his eyes from the road for a second, long enough to pick off some larger chunks of Sno Ball from his shirt and stick them in his mouth. "'In for a penny, in for a pound,' my Aunt Millie used to say."

"You fall down and hit your head or something? You nuts?"

He put on the turn signal and changed lanes right over to the off ramp exiting at Citrus. At the bottom of the ramp he turned right and then left at the first light to Valley Boulevard. He made a left turn into The Fontana Valley Suites' parking lot. Dirty and dented cars predicted the décor I'd find in the room.

"Okay," he said, "I need you to follow my lead."

"Follow your lead? We're just going for a quick nap, right? It's four o'clock in the damn morning. What's going on, Mack?"

"Take it easy, big man. I got a handle on this. Here, put on this ball cap and these glasses."

I hated the Dodgers and he knew it. The glasses were stylish and clear. I checked the mirror behind the fold-down visor. The props did change my appearance. I looked a little like a stockbroker out for a weekend pretending to be a sports fan.

Mack pulled in and parked next to a black Toyota Camry with an Asian male sitting in the driver's seat. Mack shut off the T-Bird. "Come on, you can have a couple hours, then you're going to have to work some of this magic Wicks is talking about until Jonas contacts us."

Mack knew how I worked. I'd met him on the Ruben the Cuban murder investigation nine months ago. In fact, when he and I finally ran Ruben down, Ruben threw a can of gas on Mack and was about to light him off, turn Mack into chicken flambé, when I'd intervened. Mack would have been a piece of shriveled-up charcoal.

We got out. Mack went up to the driver's window of the Toyota. The window whirled down. Mack turned to me. "Leon, I'd like you to meet Special Agent Wu with the FBI."

CHAPTER THIRTEEN

FBI, really? My knees wobbled. I was too old and tired for this kind of bullshit. What the hell was Mack doing? Every FBI agent had to have seen my ugly mug on a wanted poster at one time or another. I put on my best game face, smiled, and reached out and shook Wu's hand proffered through the window. "Nice to meet you," said Wu.

"Likewise," I said, and kicked the back of Mack's leg.

"Ouch. Man, what was that for?"

"Sorry, didn't see you there."

Wu got out, stretched. "I see you guys have worked together before. So, Leon, you're just joining this investigation?"

Mack bent over, rubbed his leg. "No, he's been off with an injury," he said through clenched teeth. "You know the type. They get a hangnail and they take two weeks' sick."

Wu looked at me then at Mack, and nodded as if he did know the type.

"He's not here for the Karl Drago thing. He's jumpin' into the Sandy Williams and Elena Cortez snatch."

"Well, good luck with that. I heard tomorrow, or the day after at the latest, you guys don't get any results, we're comin' in to take it over."

Mack turned, walked away, and said over his shoulder, "You can have it, Wu. Catch ya later."

I hurried to catch up. "What the hell's going on here?"

Mack chuckled. "We've been working this Karl Drago thing, and we hadn't been set up here for eight hours when some mope burglarized one of the FBI cars, took a gun and a laptop with high priority info. They had to splinter off two agents on the down low just to chase down the—"

"No, you know what I'm talking about. Who's Karl Drago?"

He stopped at the motel room door marked 126, raised his hand as though poised to knock, and continued on as if he hadn't heard me. "To chase down the crooks who took their shit. Real embarrassing." He knocked on the door. "You know the FBI, they won't get burned again, so now they're taking turns watching their own cars in the parking lot. Your hard-earned tax dollars at work. Well, not yours, not anymore." He smiled.

"Who's Karl Drago?"

"I'm on the Violent Crimes Team, remember? The team was set up on Drago when all this other shit went down, the first kidnapping, then the second. They pulled me off Drago to work the kidnapping. I'm just using this as a home base because the room's already paid for."

"With the FBI in the next room? Are you crazy?"

The motel room door opened. A woman in denim pants and a long-sleeve blue shirt with a Glock in a black nylon shoulder holster smiled back. A gold FBI badge hung from a chain around her neck. She turned and walked back around a large screen. The screen, aluminum frame with black material, blocked anyone in the parking lot's view into the motel room. Mack stepped around it. Like the rabbit going down the hole, I followed.

All the furniture in the room had been moved, stacked, and shoved into one corner. Computer monitors sat on tables set up in a U-configuration. One computer screen, divided into a quad, depicted four different images: a car in a parking lot, a motel room door—not The Valley Suites at street view—the inside of a motel room, and a bed with someone sleeping in it. A large someone with just a sheet covering him. Two other computer screens showed maps with two little red dots, both on Valley Boulevard. As far as I could tell, the location was right down the street from where we stood. This had to be the Karl Drago thing he was talking about.

A black agent sat in a chair next to the woman who let us in. Both looked bored to death.

"Hey, you guys," said Mack, "this is Leon Johnson, the guy I told you about. Leon, this is Mary St. John, you can call her Mary Beth, and Willard Godfrey. You can call him Will, but he doesn't like it, prefers Willard, like the rat in the movie."

I shook their hands.

"If he's not part of this operation, then he shouldn't be in here," said Mary. "And if he is going to stay, he needs to have some ID displayed."

Mack reached into his pocket and pulled out a Los Angeles County Sheriff's badge already on a chain, and hung it around my neck. Heavy emotions welled up in me, clogged my throat. For two and a half decades, the sheriff's star had defined who I was, how I lived. For the briefest of seconds I was ready to forsake all else to get the star back, to wear the uniform again for real. Then the urge quelled as I remembered my family waiting for me. And most of all, the look in Marie's eyes when I'd left.

Mack was going way out on a limb to run with me as I impersonated something I wasn't.

Mack said, "Come on, Leon, I can tell when we're not wanted."

"Brilliant observation," said Mary. She smiled again at Mack, and this time I read the look. Her eyes said she possessed a desire she couldn't have. Mack had turned her down recently and she still felt the rejection. That wasn't like Mack, to bypass a pretty woman. Something was going on with him.

Willard, the rat man, said, "Don't go away mad, just go away."

Outside the motel room, we moved down the walk a few doors to Room 136. Mack took out a key and handed it to me. "This is you."

I took it and opened the door.

He said, "You have two hours, then I'll be back to pick up your happy ass."

I needed to know what was going on but was too tired to argue. I went in, closed the door, and fell on the bed.

Two minutes later I woke to pounding. I got up and stomped to the door. That sorry son of a bitch. Why did he have to play these silly, childish games? I opened the door to bright morning light and brought my arm up to shield it. John Mack shoved his way in. "I said two hours. That meant you were to be up, showered, and ready to go. I gave you an extra hour and this is the way you treat me?"

"Good morning to you too. Any contact yet?"

"No, I'll go get some coffee and doughnuts, you hop in the shower." He turned to leave.

"Hey," I said. He stopped.

"How come the FBI doesn't just set up another camera in this parking lot to watch their cars?"

Mack smiled. "And that's all you got after three hours of quiet time thinking about this case? I thought the great Bruno Johnson would have this thing solved by now."

I waited for the right answer.

"Okay, their boss is a real ballbuster and two agents on the team are off the grid, while the others cover their shifts. They're out there trying to track down their stuff so they won't have to formally report it to the ballbuster. Back in the day, you and I would have done the same thing. These guys aren't like the regular FBI. They're okay."

"You go get the coffee. I'll think on our case in the shower and have it solved by the time you get back."

He laughed. "You have any cash?"

"Come on?"

"No, really, I'm a little tapped out until next payday."

I pulled out a money clip, peeled off three twenties, and handed it to him.

He handed back two twenties. "No man, I said coffee, not the buffet at the Hilton."

Thirty-five minutes later, we rolled out of the parking lot in the T-Bird and onto Valley Boulevard. I opened the cup of coffee and sipped it. Mack handed me a paper bag. He'd picked up four Sno Balls. When I saw them, my stomach gave a little lurch. I needed some protein, not more sugar. "Can you drive through someplace and get me something healthy, like a fried egg sandwich with some of those deep-fried hash browns?"

I might as well live it up. When I returned to San José, Costa Rica, Marie would put me back on vegetables and fish.

Mack held up a Sno Ball. "You had these last night, I thought you liked 'em."

"Get back on the freeway and head east to Yucca Valley."

Mack shrugged. With his free hand, he tore open the Sno Balls and stuck half of one in his mouth and mumbled, "This one of those leads we're going to track down?"

I nodded. From Valley he turned south on Citrus and pulled into an independent taco place called Albertos. "This okay?"

Ten minutes later we hit the freeway, with the fat "kitchen sink" burrito in both hands. The beast had everything but the kitchen sink in it, double wrapped in tortillas, and large enough for two men and a boy. I took the first bite, closed my eyes, and savored the warm greasy taste.

I hadn't noticed the heat the day before. This was summer in SoCal and, at seven in the morning, the warm air blew in the open windows. In less than twenty minutes' time, we reached Whitewater, where windmills, scattered for miles across desert hilltops, rotated slowly in a warm, lazy breeze. I could only finish off a third of the burrito before my stomach surrendered. Too bad—the greasy food tasted fantastic and was now determined to make me sleepy. "Okay," I said, "tell me about this Karl Drago thing."

Mack shook his head. "First, tell me where we're goin'. Why Yucca Valley?"

"Barbara told me the suspect was Jonas Mabry."

"Yeah, we know that already, and we can't find him. You know where he is? Is he in Yucca Valley?"

"How do you guys know it's Mabry? Did you get confirmation on the note? How do you know for sure?"

"You're not going to answer any of my questions, are you?"

We were both alpha dominants vying for who would be in control of this little two-man operation, a game neither of us would win. The last time we'd worked together, I'd been in custody and in handcuffs as he drove us around searching for the murderer Ruben the Cuban. The circumstances differed this time. I waited for him to give in.

He finally smiled. "Both girls were snatched right out of their homes without one iota of evidence left behind. Nothing.

"Before the crime was discovered, and right after it happened, an LASO deputy made a car stop on a green Ford Escort a few blocks from the location. The driver handed the deputy ID in the name of Alex Jessups, City of Industry. A residence not all that far away from where Jessups was stopped. The car was immaculate, without one mechanical violation. The deputy filled out a field interrogation card and sent Jessups on his way. At the time, no one put it together. Later, after we got the traffic cam photo from the Montclair snatch, we figured Elena Cortez was in the trunk when the stop had been made.

"With Sandy Williams, the City of Montclair has a state-of-the-art traffic control system with cameras at every intersection. Three blocks from Sandy's house, at Central and Buena Vista, we got lucky. The cam caught the same green Escort. They isolated and enhanced the driver. They entered the photo in the facial recognition system and didn't get a hit. Then they tried it the old way and made copies and sent them around to every law enforcement agency. A parole agent in El Monte recognized Jonas Mabry."

Every time someone said that name it took a little chunk out of me. Could I have saved these two little girls all this hardship had I merely acted like a big brother to Jonas Mabry all those years ago? "He's on parole?" I didn't need to ask.

"Yeah, twenty-five years old and he's been to the joint twice. First time for two-to-four, out in four. The second time he got the aggravated term five-to-ten. He did seven."

My throat turned dry and made speaking difficult. "What for? What did he do his time for?"

"Violence. Four cases, the first two he was given probation. First incident, age twelve, he stabbed his foster father with a screwdriver he'd sharpened for just that purpose. Got his foster father five times quick, before the father turned around and clocked him, knocked little Jonas out."

"Do you have the file?"

"Sure, a copy's on the backseat."

"Why didn't you say so?"

"Take it easy, big fella. Sounds like you haven't had enough sleep."

"Sorry." I reached in the backseat and found a fat manila folder under a blue windbreaker. I pulled it up front and set it on my lap.

Before I opened it and got started, I needed to call Marie. I needed to hear her voice.

Mack said, "I doubt if you're going to find anything in there. A dozen detectives from three agencies have been through it, and every possible lead was run down. Now, you going to tell me why we're going to Yucca Valley?"

"Jonas Mabry's father lives out there."

Mack veered across two lanes, going over the painted divider to make the off ramp.

"What are you doing?"

"Old man Mabry's dead. It's in the file."

CHAPTER FOURTEEN

We sat on the off ramp as cars zipped by. The file on my lap resembled a murder book in a homicide investigation, but this one was for the kidnappings. All the supplemental reports to the investigation had been added, updated, and, within the last twelve hours, collated and indexed. I flipped to the tab marked "Jonas Mabry."

I read while Mack talked. "Mark Wayne, a box boy at the Mayfair Market, discovered Micah Mabry dead behind the wheel in the grocery store's parking lot in Montclair.

"Micah had dropped out of society and had been invisible for years. We couldn't find any property in his name, he didn't have a driver's license, no history in Social Security, which means he did not have a legal job. Nothing. A ghost."

It happened that way with folks who witnessed something so heinous that their minds can't comprehend life's complex and sometimes violent ways. He'd merely retracted from life, pulled away, and lived on the fringe of society.

"What now, oh great Carnac?" asked Mack.

"Keep going. Head out to Yucca Valley."

He jerked his head to the left to check for an opening in traffic. "Bruno, that's a long damn way to go for nothing. What's out there in that pisshole of a desert?"

"Maybe nothing, but we got nothing."

***

From the beginning, I had tried to forget about Micah, his family, and their house. All those years ago. Now, when his name had come up again, the time frame wasn't clear in my head. I'd gotten a postcard in the mail maybe two years after the event. The standard plain white card came to the Sheriff's main headquarters, and interoffice forwarded it onto Violent Crimes Division. In crooked little letters from a shaky hand, the card read:

I never had a chance to properly thank you. Please come and see me. Soon. It's real important.

Micah Mabry

The return address: 12635 Old Woman Springs Road, Landers, California.

All those years ago, I fought for weeks whether to go or not to go. The card remained on my clipboard in plain view, where I couldn't help but see it all day at work. At night, the card brought back nightmares of dead children in an ugly house that bled.

Without trying, I became obsessed. I didn't want to go. I wouldn't go under any circumstance. One night after the Violent Crimes Team took down a bank robbery in progress, we conducted our usual victory dance with lots of beer in the closest store parking lot. I drank more than normal and shouldn't have been driving. I drove in a trance, but snapped out of it as I transitioned from the 10 Freeway onto Highway 62, subconsciously making the drive to the desert. I checked the map book and found Landers, a little no-account town outside a larger one called Yucca Valley. I drove out Old Woman Springs Road as the sun peeked over the horizon to paint the desert hot in yellows and oranges. For as far as the eye could see, Landers and Johnson Valley rolled in empty desert, spotted with sage and Joshua trees and salt cedar and small, one-room shacks. I stopped a quarter mile down the dirt road and watched with binoculars.

Parked out in front of Micah Mabry's shack was a broken-down GMC pickup, the black and gray paint splotched and ruined from the unrelenting desert sun. I didn't put my Toyota Camry in park and kept my foot on the brake, ready to flee at any moment. I watched a long time until the muscles in my foot cramped, the car interior turned claustrophobic, and the sides and roof closed in. Still, I waited. Off in the corner of my mind, I realized I had a subpoena for court and was already late. Robby would be looking for me, calling, sending a cop car by my house to wake me up. When that didn't work, Robby would check the jails for a drunk driver. Then the hospitals.

And, still, I waited.

Sweat rolled down into my eyes, burning. I changed feet on the brake over and over. I tried to analyze why I didn't want to see him and came up with the only logical reason: I didn't want a reminder of what he and I had gone through. I didn't want images so difficult to suppress, again laid bare to raw, emotional wounds.

Three hours into my vigil, a decrepit old man, slump-shoul-dered, gray hair, eased out the door of the shack. A man without motivation, without spirit, nothing more than an empty husk. I recognized him and received a jolt of an image: this same man on his knees in bloody water holding a dead child as he keened in grief. He'd aged so much in such a short period of time. He'd given up on life and life had not hesitated to run him over.

My breath came quick. My stomach heaved. I let my foot off the brake and drove away.

***

My mind kicked back into reality and my attention returned to the car with Mack. Mack kept his foot on the accelerator, passing all the other cars. They'd found Micah dead in a car about eighteen years after I'd seen him out in front of that shack in the desert. Eighteen years without a spirit was a long time to spend in hell.

"You read this entire file? The car they found Micah in two years ago, was it a black and gray GMC?" My voice came out in a croak.

"Don't remember."

I went back into the file and found it. A rental. A cherry-red Rent-a-Wreck Toyota Corolla.

"He died two years ago of natural causes," Mack said, "cardiac infarction according to the medical examiner. Positive ID with fingerprints."

The man died of a broken heart.

"Don't you find it odd that the car was found in a grocery store parking lot in Montclair? The same city Sandy Williams was taken from?"

Mack took his eyes from the freeway and glanced at me. "Yeah, I guess you're right. Nobody thought to look into that. It was a natural death, for crying out loud." He took his foot off the accelerator, looking to change lanes, get off, and turn around to go back to Montclair.

"No," I said, "Keep going. We've come this far, let's check it out." He looked at me again, this time not questioning my judgment, and put his foot back on the gas pedal.

CHAPTER FIFTEEN

I took the cell out and dialed Barbara Wicks.

"What are you doing?" asked Mack.

"I'm going to get someone working on Micah's rental car."

"We can do that as soon as we finish this fool's errand out in the desert."

Mack still lived by the old team's doctrine created by Robby, who stole it from the FBI: Don't show anyone your cards. Don't give anyone any information or intelligence that will assist them in catching your crook. The Violent Crimes Team cracking the case first had forever remained the number one goal.

"Good morning, Leon," Barbara said, with a smile in her voice.

So, the 'Leon' moniker was prearranged.

"I'm just getting into this case, but I need to have someone track down—"

"Hold on, let me get a pen," she said. "Okay, go."

"Micah died of natural causes—"

She cut me off. "We already checked and rechecked that. Autopsy confirmed natural causes and positive ID with fingerprints—two years ago—it has nothing to do with our current situation."

The heavy fatigue gnawed down my patience to a ragged nub. I waited.

"Leon?" she said.

"Micah died in a car."

"And?"

"In a parking lot in Montclair."

"Shit."

"Have someone check out the rental car. Go back and see who rented it and get an address."

"Right. Son of a bitch. How did we miss that? I'm on it."

"It was two years ago, and sometimes the obvious hides in plain sight."

She lowered her tone. "Thanks, Bruno. Where are you guys?"

"It's probably a dead end, but we're almost there, so we're going to check on something. I'll keep you updated."

"And I'll let you know what this lead turns up."

Twenty minutes later, we rode the rolling Old Woman Springs Road with her gentle rise and fall. Mack let me have quiet time as I read some of the thick file. Outside, the passing terrain looked familiar and, at the same time, it didn't. The last time out here, I'd been too unfocused to take in any permanent landmarks. Until we came to the shack. "Right there, pull in right there."

"How do you know? There aren't any numbers I can see."

"That's Micah's truck parked out front." The truck didn't look as if it had moved in all those years, but it had. Mack zipped in. The undercarriage bounced and squeaked from the uneven dirt. He stopped behind the truck. A cloud of dust caught up and overtook us, turned the light dim for a second. Mack leaned over, opened the glove box, and took out a gun. He tried to give me the blue automatic, a Glock 9mm.

"No, I'm not going to shoot anyone here."

"How do you know?"

"How can I, if I don't have a gun?"

I got out as Mack shoved the extra gun under the seat and followed.

The stucco on the shack's exterior walls wore puke beige paint with little cracks turning to fissures that let the wind and cold and heat inside. The desiccated wood door hung on rusted hinges. The one window, thick with dust and grime, didn't allow visibility in either direction. The door opened before I knocked. An old crone of indeterminate age stood in a faded floral dress, ragged at the hem from dragging the ground. Her hair, wiry gray, stood out at all angles. Her tired eyes didn't care who visited. She said, "He's not here. He left a long time ago."

My hand instinctively went to the sheriff's badge on the chain around my neck. Before I could speak, Mack jumped in. "Sheriff's Department, ma'am, you mind if we ask you a few questions?"

She stepped out and closed the door behind her. Mack and I looked at each other. Her maneuver was common among crooks who didn't want their contraband discovered. Or wanted to hide kidnapped children inside. My heart rate increased. Not this easy, it couldn't be this easy.

"Are you talking about Micah Mabry?" I asked.

"Who else would I be talking about?"

Mack said, "We're looking for Jonas."

"What's *he* done?" she replied.

"Have you seen him recently?" I asked.

She looked from Mack back to me. "No, not for ages."

Mack started to say something. I held my hand up, stopped him, and asked, "What is your relationship to the Mabrys?"

"None of your damn business. Get off my property. There's nothing here for you. I told you he's not here."

I said, "Micah Mabry is dead."

She swayed a bit and put a hand out and grabbed the door frame for support. Her voice lost its force, "When...how?"

"I'm sorry," I said. "You didn't know. He died of natural causes two years ago."

"Come in, come in. I need to sit." She opened the door to a musty dimness the sunlight tried to penetrate. We followed her inside.

No children watched television or hung out waiting to be rescued. The square room's naked concrete floor contained a ratty couch, an easy chair, and a swayed, rope-slat bed. The place smelled of cinnamon and sweat. In one corner sat a dorm refrigerator with a hot plate on top. Tidy and organized, the shack held the bare minimum for survival, with nothing left for comfort or luxury. She went over to the easy chair, sat, and rocked and looked off into the distance.

"Ma'am?" Mack said. His cell rang. He stepped outside to answer it.

I got down on complaining knees and put my hand on hers. "How long have you and Micah lived here?"

"Twenty-odd years. Met him walking along the highway with a summer monsoon coming. I stopped for him." She brought her eyes down to mine. "He wouldn't take the ride, said he needed the time to walk, said he'd already walked a hundred miles. He looked like he'd come a hundred miles. I told him I lived down the road right here, another ten miles or so, and if he wanted to he could stop to rest and have some water. He looked real bad, about to collapse. Didn't think he'd make the ten miles. To tell you the truth, I thought he'd walk right off into oblivion."

I nodded. "What happened two years ago? Where did he go?"

"I thought he'd come back. I did. Still did, until just now, when you sauntered in fat and happy to ruin my life."

She rocked some more and I waited.

"Two years back, his son, the spittin' image of Micah, he come drivin' up in a fire-engine-red car without any warnin', nothing, not so much as a letter. Old Micah, he never talked about any family. Didn't know he had any. Said, 'May, this is my son.' The boy said something like, 'Yeah, nice to meet ya,' or something, and turned back to Micah, and said, 'Can I talk to you outside?' Rude little bastard. Maybe twenty, twenty-three, too old to be rude like that.

"Micah, he came back in and said he had ta go, said he'd be

back in a couple days. That's goin' on two years. Now you tell me he's not comin' back. I had a thing for that crotchety old man."

The weathered skin sagged under her eyes, giving her a hound dog appearance. "I'm real sorry for your loss, May. We're trying to find his son, and we could use your help."

"Nothin' I can do. I've had enough jabbering for one day. Now it's time for you to leave."

"Are there any of Micah's things here? Anything with an address on it?"

"He had nothin' when he got here, and he left with nothin.'"

"We're looking for you to tell us anything, anything at all that might help us."

She stopped rocking and looked right at me. "I can tell you that son of his was crazy."

"Why do you say that?"

"Saw it in his eyes. When you've lived as many years as I have, you can tell by the eyes."

"What did he look like? How did he wear his hair? Did he have any tattoos?"

"He had on a pair of nice trousers, the kind you wear with a suit, but he didn't have on the suit. He wore his white button-down shirt open, no t-shirt underneath, kind of uncouth. He had two tattoos, like you said. One was very odd, that's why I remember it. A heart with a lot of detail." She pointed to her chest over her own heart. "Only in the center, colored real bright, he had a little yellow light, and inside that was a lump of scar tissue. Right below, scrolled in nice letters, was the name 'Bella.'"

The wound in his chest, the place his mother had shot him. "And the second tattoo?"

"Big bold black letters across his stomach."

"What did it say?"

"Couldn't tell, his shirt flapped this way and that. And, to tell you the truth, I didn't really care. The look on my Micah's face...my Micah was hurting inside just looking at the boy. And that's not right. That's not right, I tell you. Not for a father to act that way toward his son."

***

Back outside of the dark interior, sunlight blinded me for a moment. Mack leaned on the T-Bird's fender, his arms crossed. "The old bag give up anything useful?"

"Not a thing."

"That phone call was from Chief Wicks. She wants us back ASAP. They just got a ransom call."

CHAPTER SIXTEEN

Headed toward Montclair, I put the car seat all the way back and closed my eyes. "The ransom call come from Jonas?"

"Don't know. No way to tell for sure."

"So we don't know if Jonas has help?"

"The call came in on the hotline. Wicks played it for me."

"And?"

"The person was all over the place, started off low and concise and worked up to manic and screaming at the end. Said, among other things, that he wants an even million. He said, 'Three hundred thousand a piece will do it, just make it an even million.'"

I sat up.

Mack said, "Yep, sounds like he's grabbed another kid, one we don't know about. A kid some parent hasn't reported yet."

"Three of them—those poor children," I said.

"Bruno?"

I looked at him. "Yeah."

"The FBI just came into it. They're taking over the investigation. We're on our way to talk to Wicks. She can't run cover for you with the Feds crawling all over the place. She's scared for you. She thinks you should head south where you belong. She thinks this was a mistake."

"What do you think?"

He shrugged, didn't take his eyes off the road. "You do have more skin in the game than anyone else, and for no real reason."

If he didn't understand, I wouldn't be able to explain it to him. "She get anything on the rental car?"

"Did you hear what I just said? The Feds are in this now. It's a different set of rules, all of them going against you."

"Yeah, yeah, did they get anything on the car?"

"I didn't ask her."

I nodded and went back to mulling over the new information. Something niggled in the back of my mind. I'd read everything in the file on Micah and Jonas, read the crime reports, the forensic reports on the kidnappings, but I had purposely been avoiding the children's profiles. I didn't want to put a face to them. I didn't want to make their lives any more real than they already were. I put my fingers on the tab marked "Elena Cortez" and knew what I would find before I flipped to her section. "What about Jonas' mother Bella?"

"She's in prison doing life times two. You think maybe Jonas went to visit her? Maybe he told her about his plans to snatch these kids? That's a long shot, but maybe."

I muttered, more to myself than to Mack, "Not unless he has a fake ID. Felons aren't allowed to visit." I continued to pinch the tab for Elena, too hard, not wanting to turn to the pages. Bella had shot herself in the chest, just as she had Jonas, with a .22, a small-caliber pistol that deflected off her breastbone. Like Jonas, she had come close to dying, but survived. Mack dialed his phone as he drove, got Wicks back on the line. "Hey, it's me again," Mack said. "You might have someone go visit Bella Mabry in the joint to check and see if Jonas came to see her."

The rest of their conversation faded into the background of the passing cars, the miles of salt cedar that lined the freeway on the south side, and the rolling sand dunes. I flipped the tab and read.

Eight-year-old Elena was a foster child named Ellen Sims before adoption to the Cortez family, who legally changed her name. The Cortez family became the second family to adopt her. The first adoptive parent, Martin McGraw, molested her.

My stomach rolled and twisted in a knot. Who could this helpless little girl trust? Now, heaped upon poor Ellen's trials—add kidnapped by a psychopath. She'd only been with the Cortez family a short time after the adoption was finalized before Jonas had grabbed her.

I flipped over to "Sandy Williams" for further confirmation. Sandy's life did not read much better. Sandy Collins came to the Williams family only six months prior. Sandy, only seven, testified against her father, who had killed her mother with a knife, all but beheading the mother right in front of her. After the horrific incident, Sandy never spoke again. Her testimony in court relied on two flash cards, one "yes" and one "no." A mute unable to, if the opportunity presented itself while kidnapped, ask anyone for help.

I looked at the pictures of the little girls and knew I was right. "Tell Wicks it's a little boy. She should be looking for a missing little boy, not another girl."

"She wants to know how you know that?"

"Tell her she can raise the money for the exchange, but it's not about the money. He doesn't intend to give the kids back. He's going to take the money and run."

Mack looked back at the road and said to Wicks into the cell, "What? You're kidding. All right. All right. We're about thirty minutes out."

"Right."

He hung up, reached under the dash, and switched on the lights and siren. He moved over into the emergency lane and passed cars, the T-Bird doing 100 with little room between the K-rail.

Age had mellowed and smoothed off my rough edges. This reckless maneuver scared the hell out of me. I couldn't read the file anymore. I pushed my imaginary brake into the floor and held on to the door and dash. Over the loud din, I asked, "What's changed? What's happened?"

Mack kept both hands on the wheel, his eyes straight ahead, "The FBI just walked into the incident command center and took over, relieved Wicks of command and control."

"Why is that so bad? They have the resources and the man-power to put the boots on the ground, which is what this investigation needs."

"The Feebies have been playing hide-and-seek with their information."

"Nothing new with that. What do they have? Why are we hauling ass?"

"They've got an eye on Jonas Mabry. They're following him right now."

CHAPTER SEVENTEEN

I raised my voice over the siren, "You know, if the FBI grabs Jonas and he doesn't tell them where the kids are, they don't have the ability to compel him to talk, not with a triple kidnap charge hanging over his head. He's got nothing to lose."

Mack leaned forward a little, his eyes intent on the task at hand. "Yeah, yeah, I know. What do you want *me* to do about it?"

"I'm just thinking out loud."

"All they can offer Jonas is a lighter sentence on the three counts of kidnapping, but if we never find the kids, we don't have the kidnapping to offer the lower sentences on. He keeps his mouth shut, he walks."

"And unless Jonas has someone helping him, the kids will wither and die wherever they are. Mack, those kids are all alone with no one—"

"I know, I know. You got any ideas?"

"I do."

"What? Spill it, because I got nothing." The freeway opened up for several miles ahead, and he pulled into the number one lane closest to the center divider. I breathed a little easier. He shut down the siren and kept the red light to the front, kept the speed at 100.

"There's really only one option," I said.

He took his eyes off the road for a long, dangerous second and looked at me. He jerked his head back and shook it from side to side. "You're crazier than a shithouse mouse, you know that?"

"There's no other option."

His Adam's apple rose up and fell as he swallowed hard. "Okay, I'm with you, but we leave Wicks out of it. We do this, just you and me."

"I agree."

We rode in silence. "Couple of BMFs doing what's right?" he asked.

I understood what he said, a way of justifying our actions, ones that ventured far beyond where the Violent Crimes Team used to work in the gray area. We intended going deep into the black, the dark on the other side of the law, and, if caught, neither of us would see daylight the rest of our days. We used to have a saying for when crooks took this path: running head-on into "the other side of forever."

Mack said, "First, we'll need to stop at the Valley Suites and pick up a couple FBI radios."

I nodded as my mind tried to ferret out an option where I didn't have to involve Mack. I needed a diversion, a good one. I couldn't wait for an opportunity to pop up. I had to create my own.

"Talk to me, Bruno, what are you thinking? I know what you're thinking—you're thinking of leaving me holding my dick in my hand and doing this thing on your own."

When you worked the same job using the same tactics for so long, reading a partner's mind came natural. "Tell me about Karl Drago," I said.

Up ahead in the fast lane, we quickly approached a slower-moving black BMW. Mack changed lanes without signaling, passed the BMW, and changed back to the fast lane. Mack asked, "What? Who?"

"Karl Drago, the guy—"

"I know Karl Drago. He's the guy we were set up on when the kidnappings went down and I got pulled off. He's got nothing to do with this."

I needed Mack thinking in a different direction, a diversion, however minor. And maybe one we could rally into a larger one later on. I said, "The FBI's going to be spread thin working a mobile surveillance on Jonas, hunting for that third kid, and trying to keep an eye on Karl Drago. They'll put every available agent out in the field."

"I agree," he said, "but how does that help us?"

"We might be able to use Karl Drago as a diversion, to pull away manpower."

Mack slowly nodded as he wrapped his mind around a tactic with little validity. "All right, but I don't know how we'd use him."

"I don't either, until I have more information."

"Drago did two tours in the California prison system for murder. Did twenty-five to life on both. This was before 'three strikes' came in. He did twelve-and-a-half years, got out on parole, killed again, and got another twenty-five to life. Did another twelve and a half years, and just now got out again. The second victim killed wasn't a taxpayer. The only reason we're on him twenty-four seven is because if he kills a third time, it's going to make a lot of people look like buffoons."

"Why are the Feds involved if this is a straight murder and nothing else? The state has jurisdiction."

Mack smiled, still watching the road. "Twenty-five years ago, before every business on the street put in surveillance cameras, Drago and his crew pulled an armored car heist where Drago walked up behind an armored car guard named Willy Frakes, who was unloading plastic-wrapped blocks of currency. Right out in the open, in front of a bank, stuck a gun to his head, killed him, and took the money. No witnesses. You believe it? No one saw him do it. You can't get luckier than that.

"Someone called in an anonymous tip and the cops picked up Drago. The prosecution didn't have any witnesses and only a little circumstantial evidence. Drago only had a public defender, who talked him into taking a lesser charge on a plea for killing the guard. When he got out twelve years later, the speculation is that he killed the guy who ratted him out on the guard killing, a guy named Stanley Grandville, who was also thought to be in on the heist, but never proven. Grandville being in on the heist was just a working theory for motivation in the murder. Drago killed him for being a rat and went in again for another twelve."

I finished it for him. "The money was federally insured, which brings in the Feds."

"Exactly. We follow him long enough, he'll take us to the rest of his crew and violate his parole before he kills someone else."

My phone rang. Marie. I'd forgotten to call Marie. "Hello, babe." I missed her something fierce.

"Bruno, are you okay? You didn't call when you were supposed to."

"Everything's good. How are the kids? How's Dad?"

"Kids are great. They miss Wally, of course. I miss Wally."

"And Dad?"

She paused, time hanging in a large fat bubble. "He's..." Her voice cracked a little. "He's got stomach cancer."

CHAPTER EIGHTEEN

Mom came down with cancer while I attended elementary school. Marie had warned me before I left she thought Dad might be sick. I'd hung too much hope on the *might* part. The memory of Mom forever remained an open emotional sore. And now Dad.

In the front seat of the speeding car, thousands of miles away, I was unable to help him, to console him, tell him I was there for him. All of a sudden, I found it difficult to breathe. I needed to get back as soon as possible.

"I'm sorry, Bruno. I love you."

"I love you too."

"They're starting his treatment tomorrow, a consultation with the surgeon. Surgery and then chemo. As a last resort, radiation."

I closed my eyes tight and whispered, "How bad?"

Another long pause. "I did some research. His age is a big factor. It works against him. But he is in great shape physically, which is in his favor."

"Babe, please."

"Fifty-fifty. Bruno, I'm sorry, fifty-fifty."

I slid down in the seat and laid my head against the door's window. Marie would sugarcoat it for me, which meant the odds would be closer to sixty-forty, or worse.

"They have great docs here and top-notch hospitals. He's got a good chance."

At best, a good chance meant a coin toss.

"Have you found the kids?" she asked. She didn't want to load me up with any more pressure and asked an indirect question to find out when I was coming home. For the same reason she didn't want to mention Jonas Mabry's name.

"No." Now the conflict to stay or head home pulled harder than ever.

"Are you close?" Her voice broke; she couldn't hold her emotions together any longer. She needed me.

"Not really. Well, maybe."

Her voice came back strong. I visualized her posture going straight, her eyes narrowing as the need to nurture took over. "What's wrong? Tell me."

"I have the case file, and I think I've figured out Jonas. I know what he's doing. The three kids—"

She asked, "Three? There are three taken now?"

"That's right, and he's asked for money. A million dollars. I think after he gets the money, he plans to hurt them." I looked at Mack who stared at me, back and forth from the road.

"Why? How did you figure that out?"

I closed my eyes. "Because I think they're replacements for him and his sisters, the sisters his mother killed twenty years ago." The word "killed" caught in my throat like a sideways chicken bone. I half-whispered the rest. "Jonas never thought his mother should've gone to prison and blames me. In some screwed-up, psychotic way, he intends on re-creating the house that bled, to finish what his mother started and, at the same time, punish me for intervening. He'll kill Elena, Sandy, and the third child to teach me a lesson for intervening and ruining his mother's life and, in turn, allowing him—forcing him—to continue to live in a world he wanted nothing to do with. A life without his mother and two sisters."

"Oh, Bruno, are you okay? Really, are you okay? Geez, that's absolutely awful. You okay, Bruno?"

"Yeah."

"No, you're not. I can tell by your voice. You're not okay.

Are you with Mack? Let me talk to Mack." Marie knew the story about Jonas and the house that bled. I'd told her shortly after we met. She said a number of times she thought I had post-traumatic stress disorder and wanted me to seek help. And maybe I did have PTSD. I just never found the time to go have my head shrunk by a head shrinker. I opened my eyes and looked at Mack. I had not told him the theory about the kids. At the moment, I couldn't read Mack.

"Bruno, hand Mack the phone right this minute. I mean it, Bruno, do it now, mister."

I handed Mack the phone. He took it without question. He listened and watched the road as we sped along at 100 weaving in and out of cars.

He said, "No, that was the first I heard of it. Yeah. Now that he pointed it out, I think he's right. No, he's only been here one day and he's gotten us further along than seventy investigators from three agencies. Yes, I understand. I understand, Marie." He handed the phone back, shaking his head.

Marie said to me, "I'm coming."

I sat forward. "No, you can't. You're wanted just like I am."

"Exactly, just like you are, and you're there. There isn't a difference, is there, mister?" She always threw in a "mister" when she wanted to make her point.

"You're wrong, there is a difference. The kids. If we both get grabbed, who's going to take care of the kids? Who's going to take care of Dad? I'm sorry I'm saddling you with all of this, but you know I'm right."

She didn't say anything for a moment. Then, "Bruno, I know you. This is tearing you up inside. I need to be there with you."

When I worked the street, I remember being strong, physically and mentally. I had the ability to put heavy emotional issues away behind a door in my mind and not think about them. Most of them. Not this one. And age had weakened all of me. Tears burned my eyes. I didn't care if Mack saw them.

"This is going to be over quickly," I said. "We have a plan that will work. I'll be on a plane in two days, three at most. That's a promise."

"You're lying to make me feel better."

"No, we have a plan."

"Give the phone to Mack."

I handed the phone to Mack. He waved his hand, "Oh no, I'm not talking to that fiery wench again, no way. She scares the hell outta me, man."

"Please?" I held the phone out to him. As I waited for him to take it. Marie's voice came out small and tinny, dissipating into the warm desert air.

"All right," he said, "only because we're brothers separated at birth." He took the phone and put it to his ear. Now I was going to owe him big.

He nodded his head again and again. "Yes, we have a plan and it's a good one. No, it's not going to put our asses in a crack. No, I promise." He lied to Marie. He'd be okay as long as she never found out.

Mack had done enough lying for the both of us. I took the phone back. "Honey, it's me. I promise you, I'm okay. Listen, listen to me for one minute, okay?" She'd closed me out. I needed to change the subject. "Have you seen Jake Donaldson hanging around?"

She knew the game I'd shifted to and let the silence hang. "No, I haven't seen Jake Donaldson, but I have seen different men watching the house."

"Good. Don't worry about them. I hired Ansel to supervise some protection while I'm gone, just in case. Now, babe, we're pulling into a place where we're going to be exposed if I don't get out of the car. I love you, babe, more than you know. I'll be home soon."

"I love you too, Bruno. You come home safe. And you don't worry about anything on this end, I got it covered."

"I know you do. See you soon."

We drove in silence. "That's a helluva theory about the replacements," Mack said. "I think you're probably right."

I looked at him. "My father has stomach cancer."

He looked at me for a second, his mouth agape. Then he turned back and hit the steering wheel with the heel of his hand. "Shit."

CHAPTER NINETEEN

The Valley Suites parking lot contained fewer cars. No one stood watch. All the FBI agents who'd stood by for movement on the Karl Drago surveillance had left, reassigned to find the identity of the third child or to follow Jonas Mabry.

Mack knocked on the door to Room 126. Mary Beth answered and plopped back into a chair in front of her surveillance screens. She wore the same denim pants, a long-sleeve shirt with the FBI badge suspended from her neck, and an angry scowl. She'd been left behind to mind the store, now the sole gatekeeper of the evil that was Karl Drago.

On the screen, Drago, a huge fat man in only an oversized pair of striped boxer shorts, moved around in his motel room down the street. Black-inked tattoos littered his pale skin without pattern or scheme. On his back, from shoulder to shoulder, an ugly Viking with a metal-coned helmet and horns looked at us every time Drago turned his back. By his hips, a thick-bodied anaconda wrapped round his obese torso. His arms, sleeved with tattoos from his shoulders down, had been checkered with too much ink, and blended into nearly indiscernible images of naked women and mayhem. On the front of his thighs, when his knees came together, Jesus was on the right, eyes closed, and, on the left, his hands clasped in prayer. Jesus' face bulged with chubbiness. Drago had put on some pounds since the body art. He paced the room like a pent-up cat in the zoo.

Mack said, "We're going to jump into the surveillance of Jonas Mabry and we need a couple of your radios."

Mary Beth waved her hand in consent. Mack didn't move and said, "You have a cover team in case this turd goes mobile?"

Mary Beth stared at the screens. "Nope."

"What's the sense in watching him, then?"

"Exactly." She waited a beat then said, "He leaves his motel room, I'm to run out, jump in my car, haul ass down the two blocks to his motel, and hope I catch him pulling out. Then I'm to conduct a passive surveillance with observation only."

"A single car surveillance?" I asked.

"Exactly. But it doesn't really matter, because he's waiting for something. He hasn't left his motel room except for groceries in the last three days. And he eats mostly delivered pizza and Chinese."

Drago went into his bathroom, out of view.

Mack sat down in the chair next to Mary Beth. "You on a twelve-hour shift? You getting any relief at all?"

"Nope."

Mack put his hand on her shoulder. "They can't do that."

Mary Beth didn't seem to mind the touch. "Are you kidding? With the Bureau working a triple kidnapping? The SAC told me I didn't have to watch the screens constantly and could take a nap 'when needed.' Right, and if he slips out, it's my ass."

The obese Drago came out of the can naked. Tattooed across his chest were the words "Aryan Brotherhood Forever," and, below that, a Norse battle-axe dripping blood. Horns of a ram curled on both hips and the snout of the ram inked down the length of his penis.

Mary Beth didn't appear uncomfortable with Drago's full exposure. She said to me, "This dipshit's a white supremacist. You wouldn't do too well going around him, Leon. Or maybe it would be just what we need. Drago goes off on Leon, attacks him, and we got Drago on a felony. Back in the can he goes."

She sounded too hopeful. Back in the day, that would have

been a viable plan, but not with my current status as persona non grata—a wanted man can't testify with any credibility.

"Hey, Leon," said Mack, "can you grab those radios and wait in the car for me?"

Mary Beth took Mack's hand and shrugged it off. He nodded for me to do it anyway.

I got the radios and held out my hand. "The keys. I don't want to stand out by the car waiting on you like you're some soccer mom and I'm the delinquent kid."

He'd moved his chair closer to Mary Beth's and said to her, "I'll come back and relieve you at midnight so you can get some sleep." He handed me the keys.

"You'd really do that?" she asked.

"Of course I will," he said.

I left them to it, walked out to the car, got in, and drove away.

***

Taking the car without Mack had not been the plan and added a twinge of guilt on top of everything else. Mack had inadvertently given me the opportunity needed to evade him. He'd be onto me soon. He knew my destination and he was going to be mad. Once, not all that long ago, I had been on the receiving end of his anger, and it wasn't pretty.

Based on the radio traffic, the FBI referred to Jonas as "Chicken Hawk" and had followed him to the Carousel Mall in San Bernardino. The FBI had taken over but other agencies still assisted, so I could blend right in. I came up on the frequency and asked directions.

No one except Special Agent Wu knew what I looked like. I only needed to avoid Wu. I reached under the seat and found the gun Mack had put there while out in front of the house in Landers. A Glock. As I drove, I checked the loads and shoved the pistol into my waistband.

One city away, at the mall, agents and task force officers kept an eye on Jonas as he went from shop to shop. The tricky part came next. I had to ferret Jonas away under the watching eyes of trained professionals.

I cruised around the mall putting a plan together, memorizing street names and directions. According to the radio traffic, Jonas had just gotten in line in the food court at El Gato Taco. I parked and walked in. I kept the gun under my shirt and the radio out in plain view, but held close to my leg. I spotted the agents, white guys in windbreakers to cover their gear. Wu was there too. He sat in front of a cell phone store reading the paper. None of them blended well into the mostly black and Hispanic patrons. I stood by a pillar and picked out their target, Jonas Mabry, who sat among a throng of people, quietly eating from an enchilada plate. I hadn't seen Jonas for close to two decades. I froze at the sight of him. Jonas Mabry had morphed from a cute, wounded child to an adult with a shaved head covered in tattoos. His appearance, the way he handled himself, his eyes, most of all his eyes—he'd morphed into a predator, the kind I used to chase. The kind who, like on a number of occasions in the past, if given the opportunity, I would put down no different than I would a rabid dog.

People in the food court gravitated away from him. Moms pulled their children in close when they passed by him.

Jonas left half his enchiladas on the table, got up, and walked away, as if some unknown source had given him directions to do so. He moved in and out of the folks pushing strollers and carrying shopping bags, oblivious to the federal agents all around him. What was he doing? Playing a normal person in a mall when he had three children hidden away somewhere? Anger rose inside me. I tamped it down.

He stopped at a home decoration store and looked in the window, feigning interest. From a decorative mirror in the window display, he watched the people pass behind and farther out in the mall.

Jonas knew about the surveillance. He stood there cool as you please. *This guy was more dangerous than I had thought.*

I sat down on a bench next to an indoor fountain, leaned over, feigning tying a shoe, and used Mack's radio call sign. "Zebra-eight, he's made the tail. He's watching you guys. Back off, I got the eye."

Wu came up on the radio. "Mack, he's made us? You sure? If he's made us, we need to take him down right now."

I lied. "He hasn't made us yet, but he's going to, if you guys don't give him some breathing room."

"Okay, you got the eye, we're backing off."

The real Mack came up on the radio, his voice rushed, "Leon, where are you?"

I didn't answer. I didn't have much time left.

Jonas went on the move.

"Okay, he's moving, I got him," I said.

Jonas went along the shops until he came to one with a sales rack out front slashed to fifty percent off and strolled in. He moved through the store and stopped at a rack with western long-sleeve shirts. But he wasn't interested in western shirts. Not now, not ever.

I stepped just inside the store out of view from the mall and keyed up the radio. "Chicken Hawk bolted. He's on the run. He's going out the back. All units deploy to the east side, take up positions outside the mall on the east side. I got him. I got him from here."

Jonas stood casually, going from shirt to shirt.

Mack came up on the frequency. "Leon, talk to me. Where are you?" He'd figured out my game, but couldn't put it out on the radio without burning down my operation.

"Chicken Hawk's out," I said. "He's outside cutting across the parking lot. He came out on the east side through an employee access. Anybody out here with us? Anybody out here to help?"

Wu said, "He's made us. He's made us. Take him down. Mack, don't let him get away, take him down, now!"

"He's running east on Third," I said. "Get your cars and get on him. Get a bird in the air." I turned the radio down low and moved deeper into the store, right up next to Jonas. Jonas looked up, his blue-gray eyes vacant. "Hello, Bruno, long time no see. I almost didn't recognize you with that ball cap and glasses."

No way could he possibly remember me.

He smiled, showing he lacked two upper teeth right in front, making a black hole that whistled a little when he spoke. The radio in my hand went crazy with agents and detectives scrambling to get in their cars to cover streets, their voices small now. I turned the volume down even more. I said to Jonas, "You've been waiting for me?"

"Yes."

"How did you recognize me?"

"Oh, you've been the topic of many conversations between me and my mom."

He lied. Convicted felons were not allowed to visit in prisons, and he'd have felon written all over him. And Bella would never get out.

"I have your money, that's why I'm here," I said. "It's out in the car." I held my hand out, guiding the way.

"No, it's not," he said. "No way do you have the money. But I'll play your stupid little game, just because I know we have to in order to get past this part, so we can move on."

He came along quietly. His unruffled demeanor set off warning signals. My instinct said to move with extreme caution. In all my years of chasing heavyweight predators, I had never come across one about to go to prison, as quiet and calm as Jonas. Something was up.

CHAPTER TWENTY

Mack would have heard on the radio traffic that I had directed everyone to the east side of the mall, and he would have known for sure I wouldn't be on that side. He had to choose from three other directions to catch me. I had a one-out-of-three chance to avoid him. I led Jonas to the right toward the south side. If I were Mack, I would figure I would take the side farthest away from the east. Mack should be going to the west side.

I stayed an arm's length away from Jonas. I hadn't patted him down for weapons, and I was still too close if he wanted to pull a knife. I'd be gutted and left writhing on the floor before I had time to react. But I didn't want him too far away in case he bolted. Too much depended on me doing this right. The lives of two little girls and probably a boy.

On his front hairline above his forehead, going back on his shaved scalp, Jonas had tattooed devil horns. Combined with his blue-gray eyes, he portrayed an aura of evil. How had Jonas devolved to such a monster? My thoughts naturally fled to our kids back home in Costa Rica. I wanted to run to the nearest plane, fly back, take them in my arms, and never let them go. The social welfare system had failed Jonas Mabry. I would not fail my kids.

The handheld FBI radio traffic intensified as the task force officers failed to pick up their target. When I wouldn't acknowledge their requests for updates, they became more frantic with the prospect of an officer down. I had little time left.

Jonas stepped through the doors first, with me close behind. I expected to see Mack leaning against Mary Beth's car, arms crossed with an angry, smug expression. I didn't see anyone who'd give us trouble. I guided us over to Mack's Thunderbird, stuck my hand under my shirt, took a couple of steps back, and tossed Jonas the keys. "Open the trunk and get in it or I will shoot you down like a dog."

A smile slowly crept across his face, his lips parting to darkness where his teeth should have been. "You wouldn't shoot me, Bruno. You saved my life. You wouldn't take a life you've saved. That would be foolish. I owe you a life and I'm here to pay it back. That's what this is all about. Well, a small part of it, anyway."

I thought I had figured out his game, and yet his words, when brought out into the world, shook me to the core. My mouth went dry. I struggled for the right words. "I know...I know all about the kids, the type of kids. They're replacements, aren't they? Get your ass in the trunk. Do it right now, or I'll shoot you in the knee and put you in there myself. Because you *are* going in the trunk one way or the other." I held those strange eyes and couldn't look away if I'd wanted to.

He kept his smile. "That's right, me and Bella took those kids so you'd figure it out and come running. Bella thought of it. She wants to talk to you one last time. She was right, you're so predictable, Deputy Johnson." He bent over and picked up the keys. "I'll get in the trunk. But this part is a waste of time. You will eventually do what we want you do to do." He unlocked the trunk, left the keys in the lock, and got in, his movements more robotic than human. Drugs. He had to be taking some sort of downer, maybe even angel dust, PCP. I slammed the trunk deck and, for the first time, looked around. Luck still hung with me. Or had it? I now had the devil locked in my trunk and would eventually have to let him out.

I had not thought any further than grabbing Jonas. Maybe I didn't think I'd get that far. Now I needed a quiet, secluded place to chat with him. Only I couldn't think straight. What Jonas had said rolled through my thoughts, over and over. Had coming back to the States and grabbing him really been a part of *his* plan? He'd asked for me in his note. He was obviously deranged and delusional talking about Bella, so the rest of what he said could be discounted as well.

I drove out to Waterman Avenue and headed north. In the trunk, Jonas was quiet, no kicking or yelling. Waterman went straight up into the foothills, and farther up into the mountains. I drove up into the mountains to a wide dirt turn-out that led to a fire road blocked with a locked, metal-arm barricade. Others had gone around in four-wheel drive vehicles and knocked down a semi-path. I took Mack's Thunderbird around. The undercarriage banged and bumped. Still, not a whimper from the trunk. I would have liked it better if he had complained.

The dirt road had developed rain-eroded trenches that grew deeper the farther I ascended. I came to a point where the risk of getting stuck overruled any further travel. We'd gone far enough, no one would hear this far into the hills. I put the car in park right in the dirt path and got out. I stood at the back of the car and tried to get up my nerve to do what had to be done. Three years earlier, before I'd gone to prison, when I still worked with Robby Wicks on the Sheriff's Violent Crimes Team, this would have been standard operating procedure. I could hear Robby now behind me whispering in my ear: "What's the matter, pussy? You turn soft? You want your daddy to do this for you? Stand aside, you pussy, I'm only going to show you one more time."

In the end, Robby had turned into a narcissistic asshole, but I still wished him to appear and help me with this unholy task.

I tried to keep out the image of the child, Jonas Mabry, bleeding in my arms as I rolled code three up Atlantic Avenue, the other deputies risking punishment to blockade the intersections. I shook those images off and pulled the Glock from my waistband, unlocked the trunk, and stepped back.

The trunk deck popped open. I half-expected an evil clown to bob up like a jack-in-the-box.

Jonas didn't move. Maybe when we bumped across those deep divots he banged his head. Maybe he was knocked out and needed emergency aid. I took a step forward to peer in and caught myself. Don't fall for a simple trick like that. I stepped back and leveled the gun at the opening. "Come out."

CHAPTER TWENTY-ONE

From in the trunk: "What's the matter, big man? You *a scared* of a skinny, pencil-necked geek like me?" His voice mimicked a small child.

"Come on out or I'll shoot some rounds right through the side."

His hand appeared over the bottom lip of the trunk. "Hold your water, big man. I'm coming out. But we both know you won't shoot. I'm too important to you right now." His face appeared next, his smile full with the black hole. He swung his leg out. "You know this is all a waste of time. We should just skip this part and move on to the next." He climbed out. "You know you can't make me tell you what you want. You can't threaten me with death. That's a bite without teeth. You can't kill me. You'll never find those cute little children. And, of course, the big factor with you is that I have super powers. You see, you'd never take a life that you saved, you'd never do it."

I needed to take back control of the situation. "Turn around and assume the position."

He held up his hands. "Or what, big man? What are you going to do?"

I rose up and kicked him right in the chest. He flew back. His head banged into the trunk deck as the rest of his body folded into the trunk.

"You aren't listening to me, are you? I said get out of there. Now."

He gave a wilted cackle as he again climbed from the trunk, one hand holding his head. He stood on shaky legs and pulled a bloodied hand away from his head. Blood covered his hand and rolled down his wrist.

Scalp wounds bleed a lot.

"Now," I said, "turn around and put your hands on the car. I'm going to pat you down for weapons."

"Little late for that, don't you think? You asshole."

Finally, some emotion. He turned slowly. I helped out, kicked him again in the ass. He flew forward and banged his forehead on the open edge to the trunk deck. Another laceration. Blood ran down the side of his face.

His injuries didn't bother me, and I only had the urge to beat the shit out of him more as my anger rose. I had to control my emotions. I grabbed the back of his shirt. With my other hand I put the gun in the back of my waistband and patted him down.

Under his sock, taped to his leg, I found a dirk, a double-edged knife. A felony. Taped to the small of his back I found a .44 derringer. Two felonies. I tore it off. He had nothing else, no wallet, no bits of paper, just some money and a prescription bottle with four Demerol tabs.

I stepped back and looked at the gun in my hand, a reminder he'd made me nothing more than a pawn in his game. I hadn't played this smart. I should've patted him down before he went in. If he'd wanted to kill me, he could've had the gun ready when I opened the trunk. I thought of Marie and the kids back home. I kicked him from behind, right between the legs. He fell to the ground. His bloody head flopped in the dirt as he writhed in pain, his hands clutching his crotch.

"You going to tell me, or are we going to keep this little game of pain going until you're nothing but a bloody lump of flesh?" I asked.

He gasped. "You're an asshole, Deputy Johnson. And you're going to pay for everything you do here today. So think carefully." He coughed and spit, got up on his hands and knees, his head lolling, dripping blood. "I'm not telling you a thing. Think about it. Do you think I haven't mentally prepared for this? Do you think we've come this far for me to simply roll over and beg forgiveness? We want the money. You owe my mom and me a million dollars. Not money from the FBI. And not money from some person concerned over the little brats, but money from you. It has to come from you. Call it poetic justice."

My anger rose up again, and I kicked him in the ribs. The air blew out of him in a huff. "I'm the asshole? I'm not the one who's kidnapped three helpless little children, huh? And, putting all that morally corrupt mess aside, how, exactly, how do you figure I owe you a million dollars?"

He coughed and choked and let out a crazed laugh. "You know, asshole, you know."

"I don't, so tell me."

He looked up, blood running in his eye. "Because you had to be a big man that day. You had to kick our door in. If you'd have done your job the way you were supposed to, you should've just walked away. But no, you had to be the big man and kick the door in. We would've died like we were supposed to, me and Bella. Me and my mom would've died with my sisters like we were supposed to. Instead...instead look at me. You created me. You're a son of a bitch, a monster maker." He kicked out and missed.

I took a step back, awed at the intensity of his insanity.

Another piece to the crazy puzzle fell into place: Micah Mabry. The only person who could've told him about that day, about kicking in the door when I didn't have to, was his father. I said, "Did you kill your father?" Micah Mabry was old and could have succumbed to age. The government had not done an autopsy.

Jonas rolled over onto his back, chest heaving. "I would've killed my old man, believe me. I would have. I planned on torturing him, just like you're doing right now. Only he told me about you without any prompting at all. He told me what you'd done, the whole dumb-assed story. Then I told him what I was going to do to you for what you did to me and Mom. He died right there, grabbed his chest and keeled over like some kinda weak pussy, asshole."

"That was two years ago. Why did you wait two years to do this?"

"What? Wait a second, you don't know, do you?" He threw his head back and laughed. "Oh, that's a good one. Believe me when I tell you, that's really a good one. You're not only an asshole, you're a big dumb asshole. Come on, big man, break me up a little more, let's get on with this little dance. Figure out that I'm not going to tell you shit about those cute little children so we can get this thing going."

He'd been planning this for two years. I didn't know the significance of those two years, what they had to do with his plan, but it showed his resolve. I realized he wasn't going to give up the information. The sun beat down, draining my strength. Hopelessness crept in. What was I going to do now?

Jonas saw the shift in my resolve. "We done here? What a pussy. That's the best you can do? I expected a lot worse from you, of all people, a BMF, a Brutal Mother Fucker. That's right, I did my research."

His words made the BMF tattoo on my shoulder burn and tingle. Mistakes and poor judgment would haunt me the rest of my life. I could've had the tattoo removed, but left it as a reminder.

He used that word again, the one Robby would have used: pussy. I walked over and shot him in the foot.

He screamed and rolled around in the dirt. The dirt stuck to him like a Foster Farms chicken, dusted in flour before Dad dropped it into the hot grease.

I tried one last time. "You going to take me to those children?"

He groaned and continued to flop around. I dragged him back over to the car and shoved him into the passenger seat. What choice did I have?

He tossed around in the seat, fumbled with his prescription bottle, and popped two Demerols into his mouth. I headed down off the mountain. In ten minutes his agitation calmed. "Take me to Mission, west of Central in Montclair," he said.

"Why? Do you think I'm done with you? I could be taking you to the FBI."

"Really? We going to keep playing this game?"

"I don't want you to hurt those children."

"You do what you're supposed to do and I promise you—I give you my word—nothing will happen to them."

No way did I believe him.

We drove on for a few minutes. He wiggled until he got his foot up onto the seat. He gently peeled off his Nike. Blood was everywhere and his foot looked horrible. I felt bad and regretted the course of action I had taken. He took off his shirt and tied it around his foot. The tattoo the old crone from Landers had described, the heart with the bullet scar in the center, covered his left breast. As he moved, I spotted a larger tattoo in Gothic lettering across his abdomen: "Mama Tried." Right below that: "Patricide, try it."

"Please, tell me why you're doing this?" I asked.

His eyelids drooped from the narcotic, the muscles in his face slack. "You're a smart guy, you'll figure it out."

"Tell me."

Out the window he watched the passing landscape. "I need the money. I need the money because you ruined my life."

That logic, of course, didn't make sense. I had saved his life. "How can you be mad over what I did?"

He turned and looked at me, his mouth agape. His missing teeth gave an illusion that his hole went on forever. "We're done talking." He laid back and closed his eyes. "Take the freeway to Central, get off and go south to Mission, hang a right then a left on Kadota. Wake me when we get there."

"Wait. Tell me the name of the boy."

He opened one eye. "I don't know why I should. It won't help you."

I said nothing.

"Eddie Crane."

He closed his eye. "From Bell Gardens."

I drove and looked at him, again and again. I found it difficult to take my eyes from him. I didn't want to, but I did. I regretted the day I had saved his life. He slept with his mouth open, the eyes behind his closed lids moving constantly as if he was watching a lively tennis match.

Twenty minutes later I turned onto Kadota. I slowed. "Jonas." He didn't stir. I reached over and shook him, his skin cold to the touch like a cadaver. He roused, slow, coming up out of a sound sleep, even with a bullet through his foot. He lifted his head, looked around, and waved for me to continue. I drove until he held up his hand and I stopped the car.

He got out with a limp. "Wait a minute." He went across the sidewalk, through a fence and into a yard with a car parked on the dirt in front of the house, a broken-down, faded-green '84 Grand Marquis. The house looked abandoned, a derelict. He reached into the Grand Marquis and came back to the street, leaving a bloody snail trail. He tossed a brown paper bag into my car window. "Call me when you have the money. You have one day."

"One day isn't enough. How am I supposed to come up with a million dollars?"

"Not my problem. Do what you gotta do. Rob a bank if you gotta. Twenty-four hours."

I opened the bag and found a disposable phone. I looked back at him, then at the house behind him to memorize it for later.

He smiled a droopy smile. "Won't do you any good. I covered my tracks. You won't find a lead here. I'm to meet a doctor of questionable ability, who's been disbarred or whatever you call it for doctors. He'll fix me up. But I gotta tell ya, I warned him I'd be a lot worse than this. I've been hurt worse falling off my tricycle as a kid. I hope this isn't an example of the kind of work you do. If it is, I guess I'll never see my money. You have a nice day, Deputy Johnson." He turned and hobbled back into the yard.

"You'll always leave a trail," I said.

He turned and scowled and shook his head. I pointed to the bloody path he'd left.

"You're a fool," he said.

I drove away. *Maybe I was.*

CHAPTER TWENTY-TWO

I woke when the motel door slammed shut with enough violence to shake the walls and rattle the gloomy painting above the bed. If the cops had come for me, they'd have busted down the door. They wouldn't close it behind them. I put the pillow over my head. I needed to squeeze out another minute or two of sleep. I was so damn tired. Some of the fatigue came from depression, the hopelessness of the situation, the fact the kids had not been rescued and continued to be in serious jeopardy. I brought the illuminated dial of my watch up close to my eyes; I'd dropped Jonas off only three hours earlier.

"Come on," Mack said, "Get your sorry ass up. Where is he? What'd you do with Mabry?" Mack grabbed my foot and twisted it.

I kicked free, rolled over, and sat on the edge of the bed, my head hanging in my hands as I tried to wake up. The room was dim without the lights on. "I know you're mad. I just didn't want to involve you."

"I know all that. Skip to where you got him on ice. Where is he?"

"We need to get the money. Mabry's not going to do anything until he gets the money. I'm convinced of that now. Only then will we have a move to make. If we don't get the money, we don't have a chance. He'll give up the children if he gets the money."

"You squeezed him? You really put the boot to him, and he still wouldn't give it up?"

"Yeah, that's right."

"I guess you didn't do it good enough, did you, good buddy? Shit." He kicked the bed, then sat down next to me. I rubbed my face.

"I'm sorry for leaving you hanging like that," I said.

He didn't acknowledge the apology and lowered his tone. "You know how this works—the money's no guarantee. In fact, the odds in this kind of thing go against the kids if we do give him the money."

"I know, but in this case, I think he'll give us the kids once he gets the money. I really do. I'll do the exchange myself, and won't give up the money without proof of life."

I wasn't sure about the kids coming back safe. But I was sure about one aspect of Mabry's game: He wanted to hurt me any way he could, and I was somehow in his plan to do just that.

"This caper, coming out good, with the kids safe and the asshole dead, is only wishful thinking. You really did your best, beating this asshole?"

He knew better then to ask me that.

With my head still in my hands, I turned and looked at him. "Yeah, I did."

"You try putting his nuts in a vise and twisting?"

"No, I left my medieval torturing devices in Central America."

He reached over, took my right hand, and checked my knuckles. I jerked my hand away. "Stop it. We need to get the money."

Someone knocked at the door. I jumped up and headed for the bathroom to hide. "You expecting anyone?"

Mack went to the door. "Chill out man, it's only Barbara. When I saw my car—the one you parked right out front like some kind of in-your-face-asshole move—I called her. That was real ballsy, coming back here with the FBI a few doors down."

I wanted to ask how it was different from when he did so, but didn't have the energy.

He peeked out the window and then opened the door. Barbara Wicks slipped in. She spun around right into Mack's arms as he closed the door. He hugged her as if one of them had been stranded for years on a desert island.

I backed up and sat back on the bed. I hadn't seen them as a couple; it'd never crossed my mind. *The irony.* Not nine months prior, Mack had gunned down her husband, Robby Wicks, with an Ithaca Deerslayer 12-gauge shotgun. Mack kissed her like a ravenous lion, three days without food. She returned the same intensity. I needed to call Marie. I needed to talk to Marie. "You two want some privacy?" I asked.

They broke and half-turned away from one another, heads down a little, embarrassed. I no longer wondered how Barbara weaseled the information about where I had taken up residency in Costa Rica.

Barbara straightened her blouse and composed herself. She turned professional. "Sorry. Where are the kids?"

Mack answered for me. "He didn't get them. Mabry still has them."

Her eyes widened. "What? You *had Mabry*, what the hell happened, Bruno?"

"He tried, he really tried," said Mack. "Mabry wouldn't give up the kids."

She looked at Mack, her eyes narrowed. "Let *him* talk."

"We need to get the money," I said. "He'll give the children up once we get the money, I'm sure of it."

"You're sure of it?" she asked. "You're sure of it? You know what the stats say about giving up the money?"

She'd turned her eyes to full intensity. I pulled the bed sheet over to cover my nakedness; I wore only BVDs. "What did I bring you here for?" she asked. "Didn't we discuss this?"

Anger rose instantly. I stood and let the sheet fall. "Yeah, we discussed this, but I'm here to tell you, he wasn't going to give the children up. I tried."

"Bruno, how could you have tried if your hands are clean?" asked Mack.

"I used a gun."

"You shot him?" asked Barbara.

I sat back down, ashamed of what I had done. "Yeah, I shot him."

I told them all that had happened from the beginning and finished with, "And then he had me drop him off at a place he said was prearranged with a doctor waiting, some sort of underground doctor, off the radar. You see, he wasn't going to talk. He had drugged himself with some sort of analgesic, to help him knuckle through the pain. He knew exactly what he was doing."

By this time, Barbara had sat down on the bed next to me, Mack on the other side, like a couple of bookends, me in my BVDs.

Silence ruled the moment. Barbara finally said, "It's not about the money, not entirely."

"How do you know?" I asked.

"The FBI has your picture," she said. "They got it from the parking lot videocam at the mall. They got you holding a gun on Mabry and forcing him into the trunk. They now think you're the main player. That you, not Mabry, took the kids. And that Mabry is your shill to take the heat."

I stood and half-stumbled across to the bathroom, using the doorframe for support. I'd been set up—hard and deep.

CHAPTER TWENTY-THREE

Jonas had organized and planned his crimes with me as the epicenter. He'd somehow stayed several steps ahead of us. No matter what we tried, he had been able to predict our every move. Jonas came out of the penal system as a graduate with honors. No one I had ever chased had this intricate form of advanced planning. Up in the mountains he kept using "we." Someone else had to be helping him.

Jonas had used my background against me. I was wanted for rescuing abused children from toxic homes and taking them to a safe haven down in Costa Rica. Now he'd made it appear as if I'd come back for more kids. He set the trap so the entire kidnap scenario fell back onto me. If successful, he could take the money, walk away, and leave me holding the bag of crimes against these children.

I had to get the children away from him. The big question: If the option arose, if I could get the children back unharmed, would I, in exchange for their freedom, go to prison? A large hole opened in my gut, cold and empty. I thought I would go to prison if it came right down to that horrible choice.

Barbara brought me out of my funk. "No way will they give him the money. If they can set up that scenario, the FBI might front a fake bag of money to take him down. But no way will they let a million walk. No way."

Of course she was right. At least two of the kids were foster children recently adopted to middle-class parents without the means to raise tens of thousands, let alone a million.

"Jonas knows we can't raise the money," I said. "That's why he said he wanted me to rob a bank. He's either toying with me, or he wants to force me to commit felonies in the hopes I'll get caught. But one thing is for sure, violent crimes are a component of his plan before he ends this."

"He wants you to fail so you'll go to prison," Mack said. "That's what this game is all about. He wants you in the joint forever."

I nodded.

The way Jonas had set up the kidnapping and exchange left only one option for me. I needed the money to show to him. Then I'd force him to show me the kids before I handed over the money.

He wanted a million dollars in twenty-four hours. Where could I lay my hands on that kind of money in twenty-four hours? Money taken in a bank robbery averaged fifteen to twenty thousand from the tellers' windows. Twenty thousand at a whack would take fifty banks. To get the big money all at once, you had to hit the vaults. To take down a vault, you needed a lot of advanced planning and a team. I had neither.

"You're not going to do anything stupid to get the money," Mack said. "You're not going to play his game. Hello?" Mack got up, walked over and snapped his fingers in front of my face. "Earth to Bruno, earth to Bruno, are you in there? We'll give him a fake drop, a fake bag of money, and follow him. It's the only choice we have."

"I'm sorry, what?"

"I think John's right," said Barbara. "You're going to have to stay put for now. You can't risk getting picked up. When you talked to him, did you at least get the name of the third child?"

"Eddie Crane. Jonas told me Eddie Crane, from Bell Gardens."

Barbara took out her cell, speed-dialed, and waited. She said, "This is Chief Wicks, let me talk to the ASAC."

We waited a few seconds, then she said into the phone, "Hi,

Dan, the child's name is Eddie Crane. Start off checking Bell Gardens. No, I can't tell you where I got the information. I'm on my way to the ICC right now. Yes, all right. Thanks."

"What's the plan?" asked Mack.

Barbara looked at me. "How are you to contact Chicken Hawk when you have the money?" She'd taken to using the name designation assigned to Mabry by the FBI. I resisted the urge to look over at the drop phone Jonas handed me before we parted ways, the phone that now sat on the nightstand next to the one I'd purchased.

I lied. "He told me a pay phone to stand next to, tomorrow night at nine."

"Are there still pay phones out there?" asked Mack.

Barbara set up her cell to type in the information. "Okay, give me the location and number if you have it."

I recited the only pay phone number I could remember. "It's on Atlantic Avenue in Compton." I didn't know if the phone was still there. A twinge of guilt rose up to ruin my day just that much more. I hated lying to friends. But I needed time to think, to make a plan. And to sleep. If I could only get a little sleep, I knew I could figure this thing out. Jonas had left little time to do either. I'm sure he'd factored my fatigue into this part of his plan.

I flopped down on the bed and closed my eyes. The answer hovered overhead, just out of reach. I could feel it. Gauzy fatigue masked visibility and any attempt to clear the air.

"Bruno, what's the address where you dropped him?" asked Barbara. "I want you and Mack to go there and try to pick up his trail."

"First you want me to stay here out of sight, now you want me to go? It's on Kadota, off Mission. On Kadota, five houses south of Mission, on the right. There's a chain-link fence with an old Mercury Marquis sitting in the front yard. No numbers on the house. I'm staying here. I have to close my eyes for a few minutes or my mind's going to melt down."

I looked at Barbara, her expression stunned, as I described the house.

"That's Montclair, that's back in *my* city."

A new chief of police, and the kidnapping again pointed back to her jurisdiction. Not good.

Mack grabbed my foot and shook. "Come on, old man, there's plenty of time to rest when you're dead." Another maxim left over from Robby. Like a bad omen, Robby's ghost tainted this entire caper.

"Jonas is going to be long gone from the Kadota address, and he won't have left the smallest crumb to follow," I said. "Haven't you two been listening? He's planned this whole thing out to a gnat's ass. He's had two years to do it. Your time would be better served figuring out why the two years."

"All right, but I'm still going," said Mack. "You get some sleep. I'll be back."

I again closed my eyes and waved my hand in the air. Wet smacking filled the silence as Mack and Barbara kissed and whispered. Seconds later, the door opened and closed as they left.

I rolled over and tried to sleep. No good.

I picked up the phone and dialed Tara, the name for our house in Costa Rica. Dad had named our rental home Tara after the plantation in *Gone with the Wind*. He thought the house and grounds were huge, the largest he'd ever seen. Of course, not as large as a plantation, but a huge house on a land-scaped acre could fool an old man from South Central Los Angeles.

The call to Costa Rica went through surprisingly easy. Technology. The phone on the other end rang.

Someone picked up and said, "Hello?"

"Dad, where's Marie?" I checked my watch and computed the time difference. Marie should have been home for two hours.

"You okay, son? Everything all right?"

"Yeah, sure is. I won't be much longer. I've got everything in hand here, don't you worry about me. Where's Marie?"

"I don't know what you're up to, son, and I'm sorry you felt you couldn't trust me to tell me about it."

"There just wasn't a lot of time, Dad."

"And, you thought I'd try and talk you out of it."

"There is that."

"Damn right, 'there is that.' I taught you better, son."

"I said I was sorry." I wanted to tell him that *he* had not told me about *his* illness, but that wouldn't have been fair, not with what he now faced. "How are you feeling?"

"Fine. Some crazy old white man came by here today looking for you."

Jake Donaldson. I tried to restrain my anxiety. "What did he say? What did he want?"

"Said he was comin' back tonight and you had better be home or, and I quote, 'there'll be hell to pay.'"

"When? What time did he say he was coming back?"

"Long about now, I suspect. Yep, right about now." Dad must have checked his watch.

I tried to think. What could I do? I couldn't do anything from where I stood. I wanted to scream. "Listen, Dad, have you seen any men, any other men hanging around out front?"

"No, can't say that I have." His tone changed to firm, aggressive. "Why? What's going on? Does this have to do with you going back?"

"Dad, that man that came over today, he's a little off the deep end, if you know what I mean."

"Yes, of course I do. I saw that in him. I worked as a mail carrier for forty years, don't forget, and I learned a thing or two about people. Where do you think 'going postal' came from? Huh?"

"This guy's dangerous. He has priors for violence. Where's Marie? Is Marie okay?"

"I'll show that rude son of a buck violence if that's what he wants to bring. I have the kids' ball bat right here."

The door chime rang in the background. "Bet that's the son of a buck now."

"Dad?"

"Don't you worry, son. I'll be nice right up until the moment when he decides he wants to hurt my kids, then, God help him."

"Dad, don't you open that door." In the background, the sound indicated he was moving, walking across the tile pavers toward the door.

"Don't be silly. We lived in one of the worst parts of LA for years. This isn't a big deal, son, least not one I can't handle."

"Dad, he's killed two people already!" The noise of him moving stopped.

"What in the hell's he coming here for?"

Now I'd gone and done it. When Dad got mad he didn't always think logically. "Dad, wait, don't open the door, please."

CHAPTER TWENTY-FOUR

The door creaked open. Dad said, "Get off my property you son of a—"

Boom. Boom.

Gunshots.

"Dad?"

"DAD?"

Yelling in the background. More guns went off, this time more distant.

Scuffling.

Moaning.

"Dad? Talk to me. Dad?"

Someone else picked up the phone. "Hello? Who is this?"

"Is my father okay?"

"Hold on." The man spoke with a slight Spanish accent, Costa Rican. In the background, the man's voice more distant. "Sir, are you shot? Have you been shot?"

I couldn't breathe. I wanted to run, to do something, but stood there helpless.

The man came back on the phone, "Yes, he appears to be fine. We will have him checked out with the medics. To whom am I speaking?"

"Oh, thank God. I am the man's son. Are you the men working for Ansel Tomkins?"

"That is correct, sir."

"What just happened there?"

"I must apologize for our slow response. We had no reason to believe the man who came to visit would pull a gun. But he did, he pulled a large pistol. My partner, José Rivera, shot him from across the street. This wounded man ran through the house, out the back and over the fence. I don't know how he accomplished this feat, as he appeared to be elderly, and then you add the gunshot wound. This was quite remarkable. He left a blood trail."

This man, cool and calm, handled himself and spoke like no professional I had ever worked with, not one who had just been in a shooting. The money I gave Ansel bought the best. I shouldn't have ever questioned Ansel's integrity.

"Thank you. Thank you so much. Are you sure my father is okay? Can you put him on?"

"Yes, one moment, please."

"Hello?"

"Dad, are you okay?"

"Yes, of course, what a silly question. That son of a buck pulled a gun. Didn't say a word, just pulled it out. He was gonna shoot me in the face. I saw it in his eyes. I never met the man before today, and he was just going to shoot me for answering my own damn door."

Anger rose in Dad's tone as he regained his composure.

"I clubbed him over the head with the ball bat, but he fell forward into me. He should have fallen away from me. I think someone from the street shot him in the back." Dad's voice grew distant as he asked the man standing by him, protecting him, protecting the children. "Who are you? What are you doing here?"

"Dad, where's Marie. Is Marie okay?"

Back into the phone, he said, "How should I know? She's on her way to see you. To help you. I don't feel so well." He let out a groan. In all the time I had lived with him, he'd never showed pain or discomfort. He always hid his ailing, looked at it as a personal trial. This was bad.

"What? Wait, are you sure about Marie?" Sirens came over the phone and made hearing difficult.

"I have to go, son, it's getting busy here. Call me back later."

"Where did Marie say she was going to meet me?"

Dad clicked off. I whispered to no one, "Take care of yourself, Dad."

***

Why had Marie felt a need to come help? How did she think she'd help out? And the bigger question, how did she think she would contact me? I tried to control my breathing and laid down. The sudden adrenaline overload made my body quake.

I closed my eyes. Marie wasn't a fugitive. I didn't think she was, anyway. She was wanted for questioning, but, as far as I knew, there wasn't a warrant for her. She could get on any regular airliner and enter the US with her passport. She would be okay. Sure, she would. But how would she find me? I hadn't told her where I was staying.

Mack. She'd call Mack. I swung my legs over the edge of the bed, grabbed the phone, and dialed.

Mack picked up right away. "Thought you'd be asleep."

"Where are you?"

"Why?"

"Did Marie call you?"

Silence.

"You're picking her up at the airport, aren't you?"

"Now, Bruno, you know Marie better than I do. I didn't want to be on her bad side. She told me not to tell you. She wanted it to be a surprise."

"What kind of an idiot are you? Can't you see how this complicates matters?"

"Don't call me an idiot. And of course I do. She didn't ask me, she told me she was coming. *She* told *me*. What was I going to do, huh?"

"All right, all right, put her up in a nice hotel. I'll deal with her when I have time."

"When you have time? All you're doing now, good buddy, is

catching some Zs, and waiting for tomorrow night. Right, Bruno? That's right, isn't it, Bruno? You're not going out in public, that's crazy. You need to stay put."

"Yeah, well, that sleeping thing just changed. I need to get this caper done and over so we can get home. Dad's alone with the kids and shit's happening down there."

"What moves do you have to make? There aren't any. We have to wait for that phone call tomorrow night to set up a meet with this asshole. Bruno, whatta you got going? You're not going to do something crazy, like rob a bank? Bruno?"

"Just do me a favor. Get Marie to a nice hotel, okay?"

"Can't do it, old buddy. Tell me what you're going to do."

I clicked off.

The answer I'd been mulling over, how to come up with the money, chose that moment to flutter down out of the gauzy fatigue.

Of course, how simple.

CHAPTER TWENTY-FIVE

I shimmied into my pants, put on shoes, grabbed my shirt, and headed for the door. I went back for the two cell phones and the Glock under the pillow. I needed the gun. What I needed more was to slow down and think. When fatigued, I made too many mistakes. I stuck the dirk in my sock and the derringer in my back pocket.

My mind automatically shifted to the problem at hand. If Mack drove to LAX to pick up Marie, the fifty-minute drive there added to the fifty-minute drive back—that's if she waited at the curb when he got there—gave me an hour and forty minutes. Plenty of time to do what needed to be done and get away. I stopped at the door. But if Marie flew into Ontario, that was fifteen minutes there and fifteen back.

I opened the door to darkness. Where had the time gone? When you wanted time to slowly ooze through your fingers it never obliged, and when you wanted time to hurry on past it—

Out in the parking lot, a Yellow Cab pulled up and stopped. Marie stepped out. She saw me. Her face broke into a huge smile.

I'd been cut short on my plan. At the moment, I didn't care one whit. I caught her contagious smile and smiled back. Hers glowed warm with affection. We had not been apart one day in the last nine months. I had missed her terribly, and didn't realize how much until I saw that smile. I met her halfway, picked her up, and twirled her around. I kissed her long and deep.

I set her down and held on.

She looked up with her green eyes telling me how much she

loved me. "What?" she said. "Did you stop off at the deli to get a turd sandwich? Because your breath smells like it."

Her way of saying she was mad for flying thousands of miles to save my ass, but at the same time didn't want to scold me.

"Hey," I said, "I'm the one that should be mad. You were supposed to stay home with the kids and take care of Dad."

She socked me in the shoulder and smiled. "Things like these are fluid, you have to roll with it." Words I'd given her in the past, ricocheting back.

"I guess I have to quit telling you the details of my old capers and how they worked."

"You better not. And the kids are fine, and so is your dad."

"When's the last time you talked to them?"

"Why? What's happened?" She'd read my tone.

"Nothing. Everything's fine."

Wu walked up. "Hey, Leon, how come you're not out working, chasin' down leads on the third kid?"

He must have been out of the information loop. He hadn't heard about or seen the mall cam video where I grabbed Jonas. Or that the shot-callers in the FBI wanted the blunder kept under wraps. The well-being of the children stood in the balance. Sure, that had to be the reason, or he would have thrown down on me and taken me into custody. This time luck had landed firmly on my side of the fence. I had to be more careful. I should've visually cleared the parking lot before going out. I wouldn't get many more chances. I leaned over Marie and fought the urge to turn around. Without the ball cap and glasses, Wu might recognize me anyway. "Just taking a break to be with my girl," I said.

"I can see that," he said to my back. "What is it, that 'three-week thing'? You two only been together for three weeks, or something like that? Still in that mushy love phase?"

"That's right," Marie said. She'd caught on to my fear and held me close.

Wu came closer, only to get a better look at Marie. I spun her around on the outside closest to Wu and headed to the room. Marie had the curves in all the right places, and Wu would be not be looking at me.

We'd made it to the door when Wu said, "Hey, we're putting a bag together with a GPS for the drop tomorrow night. There's a briefing in forty minutes at Montclair PD."

I waved my hand over my head and, with the other, I unlocked the door. Wu said, "Make it a quickie, huh? From here, it's a twenty-minute drive to Montclair."

Marie turned. "That leaves us twenty minutes, enough to do it three times."

Wu yelled as I closed the door. "For sure, that's the three-week thing talkin' right there. You lucky bastard."

I got the door open and the both of us inside. I flipped on the light. Marie kissed me again, reached around and flipped the light back off. The threat of a lifetime in prison tended to intensify emotions, particularly love. We tore at each other's clothes. Once naked we heated up the sheets, took a break, breathing hard, and then heated them up again. We didn't have the time. Wu might be briefed at any second and say, "Hey, I just saw him going into a motel room." The FBI could be surrounding the place any minute. Or, they might wait for the outcome of the children, keep my involvement as an ace in the hole, a scapegoat to blame along with all my other alleged crimes.

I dressed quickly in the dark as the sweat cooled and dried on my skin. I reached over and turned on the bed stand light to see my lovely girl. She stared up at me with adoration, something I couldn't comprehend. I was nothing special to look at. I didn't know what I did to deserve her. "I have to get out of here."

"Where are we going?"

I stopped tying my shoe, reached over and put the back of my hand gently against her cheek. "I have something I have to do."

She read into my words and sat up, her eyes turning from sated to concerned. "I'm going with you, and you know that."

I shook my head and looked away.

"Bruno, I didn't come all this way for you to hide me away in some sleazy motel room. I'm here and I'm going to help." She held her finger up, "And that's it, end of discussion."

"Okay, get dressed." She jumped up and slid into her clothes almost as fast as she'd taken them off. I watched for the opportunity and stuck the Glock in the back of my waistband when she wasn't looking.

She had her back to me as she tucked her breasts into her bra and hooked it in the back. "I saw that. Why do we need a gun?" She turned around to look me in the eyes. No one could tell me women didn't have eyes in the back of their heads. I took the Los Angeles County Sheriff's badge off the nightstand and hung it around her neck. The gold star hung down over the cleft of her breasts and came off strangely erotic. I put my hands on her shoulders. "You can't come with me, but I can't do this thing without your help."

"Oh, no, I am coming with you."

She saw the shift in my eyes, held up her finger. "Bruno, no."

I leaned down and kissed her naked shoulder. She arched her back. I gently turned her around and unhooked her bra. "Bruno, no." This time, her "no" lost its finality. We commenced to reheat the sheets. Halfway through, she whispered in my ear, "It must be that three-week thing."

CHAPTER TWENTY-SIX

I cut the electrical cords from the lamps in the room, wound them up and shoved them in my pocket, while Marie asked, "Are you sure this is the only way? This idea is really crazy. I mean, really crazy."

I took her in my arms, kissed the top of her head, and hugged her tight. "We have less than twenty-four hours. Can you think of any other way to get a million dollars? No way is Jonas going to fall for that fake bag trick. He'll be watching for it. He's been way out ahead of us every step of the way. Our only chance is for *me* to show him the money, just a taste, and then I trade the children for the money."

"I would rather you have the FBI handle it with the fake bag."

No she didn't, not really. She wanted the best chance for the children. I pulled her away and looked into her eyes. She nodded as she fumbled with the sheriff's star hanging around her neck. I let her go with no illusions, maybe for the last time ever, and went out the door to the parking lot, head down under the ball cap, walking fast.

I needed a car, one that fit in with the places I needed to go, and I didn't have time to be picky. From deep in the parking lot I chose a beat-up, midnight-blue minivan, the model without the side windows. In the dark, the banged-up paint looked black. The door wasn't locked and the ignition had already been punched. The car had been stolen in the past and the owner, believing the van worthless, had not made the repair. Two seats up front. The back, designed for cargo, was littered with fast food wrappers and empty 40-ounce Olde English 800 beer bottles. The motor coughed and sputtered and finally caught. I headed out of the Fontana Suites parking lot and hoped like hell I would be back.

I drove two long blocks, past an industrial section lit with sodium vapor lights, and turned into another motel parking lot. One built with two stories in an L-configuration. The place used to be part of a major chain and had since fallen into disrepair with a private owner who didn't believe in maintenance or trash pick-up. Every parking stall held a beater car like the one I boosted. The place did a booming business with the speed-freak crowd. I double parked, got out, and walked right to the door I wanted. I stood to the side and checked my watch. Marie and I had synchronized, and the time had started when I kissed her good-bye.

Right now, Marie, with the sheriff's badge hanging around her neck, would be knocking on Mary Beth's motel room door. Two minutes for Mary Beth to answer, another three minutes for Marie to explain that she was there to relieve Mary Beth, two more minutes for Mary Beth to grab her things and jam out of there.

Time.

I stepped back and kicked in the door. I ran in. The only light in the dark room spilled in from the parking lot. The beached whale of a man on the swayed bed grunted at the noise from the intrusion, took a half second to realize what had occurred, and reached for a weapon between the mattress. The Viking warrior tattoo stared up at me. I jumped on his back and thumped his melon with the butt of the Glock. No reaction. He came out with a long knife. I hit him two more times. The gun butt thunked hard against bone. Karl Drago went limp. I pulled out the lamp cords and tied his large chubby hands together.

I checked my watch. Thirty seconds. I had allowed three minutes total, just in case Marie had not been able to convince Mary Beth. If Mary Beth had seen me on the screen attacking Karl, she would be here within the three minutes it would take to run out to her car and drive the three blocks.

"Come on, get up. Get up now."

"Who the hell are you? What the fuck you want?"

I reached over and turned on the lamp. My other adrenaline-shielded senses kicked in. Sour odor of pepperoni and kung pao chicken wafted up from the floor. The room lay to waste, littered with empty pizza and Chinese takeout cartons. Karl Drago lay on the bed more ugly in person than when I had first seen him on the screen in the FBI surveillance room. He squinted, then opened his eyes. "Oh, perfect, I'm being robbed by an Anus Africanus. You made a big mistake, pal, taking down this place. I got nothing. I'm out on parole two weeks now, and I got nothing."

"Shut your pie hole and stand up."

"Huh, you have about three minutes, asshole, and then twenty FBI agents are going to swarm in here and shoot your sorry black ass."

I stopped. He knew about the surveillance. How did he know?

"No, they're not. I took care of that. Now stand up, or I'll shoot you in the foot."

"Kiss my white ass."

I put the Glock on his foot and looked him in the eyes. "Last chance."

"Okay, okay, hold it, don't shoot. Jesus, whatta testy lil' prick. I'm moving." He got up, his tattooed belly hanging over his dirty striped boxers. His fat rolled and shifted as he swung his leg in a roundhouse kick.

I blocked it, swung the Glock, and caught him across the temple. He staggered, but didn't go down. I stuck the gun under his chin and shoved hard.

"Let me make myself clear. I will shoot your sorry ass and leave you for dead if you do not do exactly as I say. Do you understand? Tell me you understand."

He nodded. Blood ran down into his eye from the laceration to his temple. My mind leapt to previous training about blood-borne pathogens. He'd been in the prison system for going on two decades. He could have hepatitis C or AIDS. Had I still been on the job, protocol would have dictated containment, paramedics, and the donning of rubber gloves and mask. He'd be treated like a hazardous waste dump. No time to ponder over spilt milk. I scooped up his clothes from the pile in the corner. I froze. Underneath sat a black nylon bag with bright white letters: "FBI." I pointed at the bag and said, "You didn't?"

"What's that?" he asked. "Oh no, that's not mine. *You* put that there. You're setting me up."

"This is the bag boosted from the FBI car."

"Don't know what you're talking about. I want my lawyer."

The FBI thought Karl Drago was their prey, when in reality he'd been playing them all along. Mary Beth said that Drago had been waiting in his room, not leaving for three days. He'd snuck over while the FBI supposedly watched him, broke into one of their cars, and took their gear. Not only a bold, in-your-face kind of move, but one well thought out and executed. I had to change my opinion about this guy and proceed with more caution than before.

I checked my watch. Two minutes, forty seconds had elapsed. We wouldn't make it to the van and out before the troops arrived if the ruse hadn't worked. Marie had to have convinced Mary Beth or I was in deep shit. I picked up the heavy FBI bag. "Come on, move your ass."

"Let me get dressed."

"Later, move."

He lumbered out, bumping his gums the whole way. "You're working for Clay Warfield, aren't you? Never thought he'd go to hiring a nig—I mean, a black gentleman—for something like this. Hey, whatever he's paying you, I'll double it. You know I'm good for it. That's why you're here, right? You know what time it is, don't you? Okay, triple, I'll triple whatever Clay's paying you."

I knew of Clay Warfield like every other cop in Southern California, every cop in all the US, for that matter. He was president of the Sons of Satan, the notorious outlaw motorcycle gang.

I shoved Drago in the ass with my foot to speed him up. I repelled off his bulk, and he didn't move any faster. His fat jiggled and rolled as he walked across the parking lot to the minivan, his big arms tied behind his back. As we approached, the van grew smaller and smaller compared to his bulk, when the effect should have been the other way around. Maybe I should've boosted a one-ton truck. I opened the back doors. "Get in."

"Okay, fuck you, take me to Clay. I'll talk him out of what he thinks he wants to do, then guess what, pal? He and I will take you apart, piece by piece. Trust me on this. That's the way it's going to go down. Maybe I'll use a blowtorch on you. You know who I am? You do, I know you do. You know I have priors with a blowtorch. You know what I'm sayin'?"

He never stopped talking, but he climbed in and flopped down on his belly. The wadded-up taco and hamburger wrappers and empty beer bottles splashed to the sides. The sight of him, with all his white skin, made me think that, tonight, I might be more like Captain Ahab.

I didn't really have time to tie his feet and, under normal circumstances, I would have waited until after I'd gotten far enough away. Even tired, I realized the potential for violence in the glob of immorality compressing the van's suspension. I risked the time, took out another cord, and secured his ankles.

I got in the van, started up, and wished I'd gagged him. The man never shut up.

CHAPTER TWENTY-SEVEN

I had only a couple of minutes to ponder the next problem: stop for Marie or leave her behind? The safe choice was to leave her. She'd be mad, real mad, but she'd get over it. However, without a doubt, I needed help to pull off this caper I'd planned. I would just have to keep her on the sideline as much as possible.

I pulled over to the curb on Valley Boulevard where we'd agreed to meet and waited. Street people moved in the dark shadows of the sidewalk, self-absorbed in their own skullduggery. Why wasn't she at the preplanned location? What happened to her? If only her shadow, I'd recognize her anywhere. Had the FBI tumbled to her game and grabbed her?

Karl Drago worsened my anxiety with his continual complaints. "Hey, dickhead," he said, "I can't feel my hands or my feet. Loosen these things up. I lose my hands and my feet, I'll kill ya with my teeth. You hear me? I'll tear a chunk outta your neck with my teeth. I got good teeth, courtesy of the California penal system. I'll rip out your throat and enjoy doing it."

"For the last time, shut up. And think about what you just said. How are you going to move around if you don't have any hands and feet, huh? I'll just have to listen for your electric wheelchair to know when you're coming." That shut him up. As he pondered this new problem, I caught a shadow in the rearview mirror dash across Valley. Marie. My tight breathing eased up a little. She came along the sidewalk. I leaned over and rolled down the window on the passenger side. "Right here."

She heard. Ran over, opened the door, and jumped in just as I pulled away from the curb. She peered into the back. "Everything go okay? This van smells like body odor and cat urine."

"Sure, we're cool. I told you it would work. How about you? You okay?"

"Yeah, I got in just like you said." She held up the badge that hung from the chain around her neck. "But I feel bad. Mary Beth's really nice, and she's going to be in a lot of trouble when her boss finds out I duped her."

"I know, but it can't be helped."

We came to the corner of Valley and Sierra Way, a major intersection. Light from all of the combined streetlights poured into the van. Marie looked back to see our cargo. Her hand flew to her mouth. "Oh my God!"

Her tone startled me. "What?" I looked back, thinking maybe Drago had morphed into some sort of demon, more of one than he already was. He hadn't moved, and I realized she'd reacted to the fat lump of wasted humanity, tattooed and semi-naked in his striped boxer shorts. I said, "Didn't you see him on the monitor when I took him out of the motel?"

"Yes, but, oh my God, Bruno."

I waited for the red signal to change so we could enter the San Bernardino Freeway. I looked back again. Drago raised his head and smiled at Marie. "What's the matter with your slit, hasn't she ever seen a real man in his underwear?"

Marie turned back in her seat face forward, reached over, and put her hand on my arm.

"How sweet, love among the animals," Drago said. He sniffed the air, made a show of it. "Fact is, I do smell some animal lovin'. You two been goin' at it? You two have been bumpin' uglies, right? I can smell it on you. Come on, give, tell me all the hot sweaty details."

"He's a real charmer, isn't he?" said Marie.

The signal changed, I proceeded to the freeway. "Now you see why I'm not going to mind what we're going to have to do to him." I'd said it more for Drago's benefit than for Marie's. He went quiet.

"Did you bring the garden shears?" Marie said, smooth as butter.

These words coming from my Marie's normally innocent mouth shocked even me.

She wasn't done. "I'm going to enjoy clipping off his toes one at a time. This little piggy went to market, this little piggy—well, you know the routine."

***

I'd never worked in San Bernardino County and didn't know the area. I drove to the only familiar place I knew. I got off at Waterman and headed north into the same mountains. Drago started up again: "How much is Warfield paying you? I told you, I'll double it. How'd you get me away from the FBI? That was no easy trick."

"Who's this Warfield he's talking about?" asked Marie.

I didn't answer her.

Drago said, "Right, like I'm going to believe you don't know the president of the Sons of Satan, Southern California."

Marie looked at me as I maneuvered the van in a long sweeping turn into the first switchback. She whispered, "Maybe we need to find out how this Warfield figures into this thing."

I nodded. "Maybe, but in the end, it's really not going to matter."

Drago said, "Like I'm gonna believe you don't know Warfield's a player in all this. Right. And I'm a Jewish pope. If by some crazy quirk of fate you really are dumber than dirt, and really don't know Clay Warfield, you two are walking dead. That's all I gotta say. You're walking dead, and don't even know it."

Drago kept up his verbal barrage until I turned off the asphalt onto the dirt road, then he went silent again. After a few minutes, I felt around for the interior light switch while negotiating the narrowing dirt path. I turned on the interior light. "Look, see if he's being good."

I didn't want two tons of trouble loose, not even for one second. Marie looked back. "Yeah, but his hands and feet are turning a little purple."

"Damn straight," Drago said, "I'm not gonna tell you again, loosen these up, or when I do get loose, I'm gonna rip both your heads off and shit down your necks."

"We're almost there," I said, "and if you don't tell us what we want to know, then it's not going to matter whether you have feet and hands."

"I'll save you two darkies the trouble. I didn't give it up in the joint where I was locked up with a thousand assholes all wanting what I got. Think about that a minute. You think you're going to be any different? You think you're going to be able to get me to talk? You're outta your little pea brains. I did twenty-five years in the joint without telling a soul. Don't you think I don't know what time it is? That once I tell you, Warfield told you to take me off the board? I'm no dummy. So you better listen, I'm not gonna tell a couple of Beavis and Buttheads like you one damn thing. You understand? I'll take it to my grave if I have to."

Marie pivoted in her seat. "Fair warning then, the trip to your grave's going to be ugly, painful, and very noisy with all your screams."

I leaned over close to her and whispered, "Jesus, Marie, where's this coming from?"

She didn't whisper back. "This pile of dog shit is all that's standing in the way of rescuing three little children and keeping me from getting home to my kids. Hand me those garden shears."

Who was this new Marie? I had gone bad early in life, broke the law, done things I regretted more and more as I got older. I came back from that place and improved my life. To think Marie was headed down a similar road made me ill. We had to get this thing done and over before she lost that innocence I held so dear. Before it became too late to turn back.

The van bounced as I went around the metal arm that blockaded the fire road. The headlights illuminated the 'No Trespassing' sign. One of my cell phones buzzed. I checked. Mack. I didn't want to talk to him. He could add nothing to what was about to happen. Something I no longer had the stomach for, especially not with my Marie present. Jonas proved that much when I had him out in the same place earlier. Stuck now, we had no choice, and had to play this scenario all the way out. The lack of options made me irritable. I stopped in the exact same place as before and shut off the van. With mountains all around, the darkness closed in. I couldn't help thinking that we were trapped in a metal box with a wild animal, and I welcomed the opportunity to get out.

Drago went quiet again in anticipation of the upcoming trauma to his body.

I focused and turned my voice serious. "Last chance, tell us where you hid the money, and we'll let you go."

CHAPTER TWENTY-EIGHT

I was unable to move from the van. Drago wasn't going to make this easy. I didn't want Marie to see what had to be done to save the children. I couldn't help thinking that Drago had been only eighteen, hardly more than a child, when he had committed the armored car robbery and killed the guard. Now, twenty-five years later, he lay in the back of the van, a dangerous product of our rehabilitation system. We'd failed Drago and society twice, once in child welfare, and once in the penal system. The same as Jonas Mabry.

I left Marie in the passenger seat and got out. Without a moon and no ambient city lights here in the mountains, we were in pure darkness. My skin itched with the thought of other Karl Dragos loose in the world.

I opened the back doors. Drago didn't move. I pulled out the dirk and slit the cord binding his ankles. His legs fell apart and he moved them to get back circulation.

"Come on, slide out."

He rolled over on his side and tried to inch out the back, difficult with his oversized belly, like a worm that had swallowed a Volkswagen Beetle. I reached in, took hold of his cold, bloated foot, and pulled, really putting my back into it. The man didn't budge.

"I think the only way this is gonna work is if you cut me loose," he said.

Marie appeared at my side. "Honey, I think he's right, otherwise we'd need a crane."

I slid open the side door and showed Drago the Glock. "I will shoot you, you understand?"

"No you won't, darkie. I know what you want, and you won't get the money if you do something stupid like that. You won't get the money for your little shit-assed kids. I heard you talking. You two are a couple of real tools. Cut me loose and let's talk turkey."

I didn't move. The 9mm Glock was large enough to drop a normal-sized running man, but might only piss off Drago. If I had to shoot him, I needed something larger, something more on the order of a Sharps .50-caliber buffalo rifle.

"Come on, man, cut me loose and let's get to negotiating. I needed some help to pull off what I got in mind anyway. I'll cut you two in for twenty-five percent. Twenty-five percent, that's more than fair."

How could we possibly align ourselves with the likes of Karl Drago?

Marie sensed the dilemma, gently put her hand on my shoulder, and with her other hand, took the dirk. She leaned in and cut Drago's hands loose.

"Ah, Jesus, that burns like a thousand fire ants eatin' my skin. It's on fire, I tell ya." He stayed on the floor of the van, rubbing his wrists. "Can't say that I blame you, it's a lot of dough we're talking about here. If you're not working for Clay, then you're just a couple of freelance operators. Okay, I get it."

I walked backwards to the rear of the van, keeping Marie behind me. We waited. I held the Glock at my side, prepared to raise it and dump all fifteen rounds in the magazine, center mass, right into his chest where his heart should be. If he had one.

Drago struggled up to his hands and knees and backed out of the van, bringing with him the pile of litter. Bottles and paper wrappers rattled and fell to the ground. The dark washed out all color, turning everything to different shades of grays and blacks. Drago blotted out the van's dark shape. His white-gray skin glowed, his eyes recessed in shadow, as he continued to rub his wrists. An ironic sight in his striped boxers. Had he not been so dangerous, he would have looked ridiculous.

"That took some real balls to grab me right under the nose of those Feds," he said.

Quick as a cat, he leapt at us.

I brought the gun up and fired, hitting him in the thigh. Marie yelped. Drago tumbled and rolled in the dirt as we backed away.

"You shot me. You son of bitch, you shot me."

I pulled Marie under my arm and held her there. She had never seen anyone shot. Sure, at the hospital she'd witnessed the aftermath, but that was different. Never right in front of her. Who could be prepared for the way the violence snapped? I was saddened for her, and again wished she had not been there to witness the unwelcome actions of the lowest sub-level of man.

She shivered. I hugged her hard for a long second, let go, and moved over to Drago. "Now, you ready to tell me what I want to know, or is the 'tool' standing here over you going to have to shoot you in the foot, in the shin, in the knee? Well, you get the idea."

He groaned and rolled back and forth. "Who are you, man? You're some kinda cold-hearted, black demon-asshole." He quick rolled toward me. His bloody hand reached out for my leg to pull me down. I jumped back and raised the Glock, taking aim at his foot.

Marie yelled, "Bruno, no."

I jumped back, pulling Marie out of reach with me.

Drago laughed. "I can see who wears the pants in—"

I shot a round next to his face. The bullet kicked up little rocks and dirt, peppering his skin. He flipped away, both hands to his face. "Jesus, are you crazy? Shit, are you outta your mind? You tried to shoot me in the head."

"If I wanted to shoot you in the head, you'd be dead right now. Where's the money?"

"Okay, okay. We can't get it until tomorrow."

"Not *we*, Drago."

He pulled his hands down from his bloodied face, his smile wide and scary. "You won't have a chance getting that money unless you take me along. Trust me on this one."

"Why not?" asked Marie.

"Because I hid it someplace, and it's going take all three of us to get to it."

I kept quiet. Marie did better with him, so I let her talk. "Where?"

"The Southern California clubhouse for the Sons of Satan."

CHAPTER TWENTY-NINE

Marie foraged around in the van and found a dirty Black Sabbath t-shirt. I tossed it to Drago, who sat on the bumper at the back of the van and tied up his thigh. The bullet had passed right through the tattoo of Jesus' praying hands and missed the bone. He had an overabundance of thigh flesh to spare. He'd lost a lot of blood, but he didn't look any more pasty for the loss.

"Why tomorrow?" I asked.

"Oh, no. We have to get the ground rules straight first."

I waved the Glock. "If you haven't figured it out, the only ground rules are the ones I make. And I'll make them as I see fit."

"No chance, it's not going to work that way. We work a deal right now, or you can go back to shootin' and torturing."

"We know where the money is now," said Marie.

"Good luck with that."

"So I'll ask you one more time, why tomorrow?"

"Seventy-thirty split. I'm the seventy, because I put in twenty-five years of my life waitin' for it. And what, you got about two minutes invested?"

"How can we make a deal with you?" asked Marie. "The first chance you get, you're going to try and hurt us again. You've already tried twice."

"Ask your man here why. He knows. I can tell he knows. He's been to the joint. I can smell it on him. In the joint there's a code we live by. I give you my word, I'm good for it."

Marie looked at me for confirmation. I nodded. "That's true to a point."

"I give you my word, it's my bond. You can ask anyone."

"Fifty-fifty," Marie insisted.

I waved the gun. "We're not here to negotiate. That's ridiculous. The amount's not going to matter. We need what we need to trade for the children. We don't need any more than that. So it doesn't matter what the split is."

"You're telling me you don't care about the money for yourselves? Is that right?"

"That's correct," Marie said.

"And you're doing this only to help out some little shit-assed kids?"

"Yes," she said.

"Okay, now we're getting somewhere. What's up with these kids? What do you need the money for?"

"Someone from my husband's past is trying some sort of revenge thing and has kidnapped three children," she said. "He won't give them back until we give him the money."

"Some piece of shit has kidnapped your kids? I wouldn't give him any money. I'd cut his nuts off and stuff them—"

"They're not our kids."

"Wait, they're not your kids, and you're doing all of this for someone else's kids?"

"That's right," I said.

Drago thought about that for a moment. "How much does this piece of shit want?"

"A million." The number came out low and without confidence. The amount sounded beyond absurd.

"A million dollars for three kids, are you shittin' me?"

How had our forward momentum been derailed and degenerated to talking our problem over with this prince of humanity?

"You don't have the million, do you?" asked Marie.

Drago looked at me, then at Marie. He offered his hand to

me, splotched with his drying blood, and held my gaze. Blood-borne pathogens came to mind again, but I didn't look away.

"You shake with me and make a deal before I go any further," Drago said. "Before I tell you any more."

"Don't do it—don't get that close to him," Marie said.

Drago didn't move, didn't say anything, and continued to stare.

"What's the deal?" I asked.

"Bruno Johnson," warned Marie. "You get close to him and I'll—"

Drago's mouth dropped open. "You're Bruno Johnson? You're *the* Bruno the Bad Boy Johnson?"

I wanted to look away, ashamed at my reputation, but continued to hold his gaze. "That's right."

"You did a couple of bullets up at San Quentin on B block."

I nodded. "No, only a year, then was transferred down to Chino."

"Yeah, yeah, but you're the guy. You're the guy who killed his son-in-law for killing your grandson, am I right? You're the guy who saved all those kids in Los Angeles. You're a friggin' legend, my man. You go to prison now, you'll reign as king. It might almost be worth it to go back to the joint for something like that."

In prison, and on the street, all criminals live by a code with few rules. Anything goes as far as crime, robbery, murder, and even mayhem. All except one. You don't mess with children. You don't harm or molest them, or you are automatically sought out and killed. And, if you, as a prison inmate, as a non-K-Nine, a non-keepaway, have the opportunity to kill a "baby raper" and don't, then you, too, are marked for termination. That's why "baby rapers"—the K-Nines—are kept segregated, lumped all together and kept away from the general population. Anyone who took aggressive action against those degenerates by enforcing that rule was considered a hero.

Drago held out his hand with sincere vigor. "I don't usually hold with no nig—I mean, well, you know what I mean, man. But I still want to shake your hand, bro."

I needed something from him, so I handed the Glock to Marie and stepped in close, bracing for the worst. He took my hand and shook it, strong and unyielding. Power and strength emanated from this guy, the most formidable person I'd ever come across. I would not stand a chance empty-handed against him. Not one chance in hell.

He let go. "Okay, here's the deal. You help me get the money, and then I'll help you get the kids back."

"That's not going to work," I said. "We need the money as flash—"

"There's not enough money, is there?" Marie asked again.

I stepped back with Marie. Drago looked at her, then back at me. He shook his head.

"How much is there?" I asked.

"I don't know."

"We've gone through all of this and you don't even know?"

He shook his head again.

Marie lowered her tone, just as scared as I was, her voice cracked. "How much did you get away with in the robbery?"

If this plan wasn't going to work, what other option did we have? I started thinking about how we could get him tied up again, and dropped off where the FBI could babysit him; keep an eye on him for the sake of the public's well-being. A lion loose among the lambs. Or a hyena.

"Three hundred thousand," Drago said.

CHAPTER THIRTY

In the joint, I had lived with lots of guys like Drago and had learned to get along with them, even got to like some of them. I needed to keep in mind that Drago had killed an armored car guard for the money we were now trying to obtain. Tainted money. Blood money. Drago fit the worst category of animal I used to chase while on the Violent Crimes Team. And yet here, I had begun to trust him, just a little. A bad move on my part? Even so, three hundred thousand dollars put in with cut-up paper might be enough to flash to Jonas Mabry. That much flash, presented properly, might give us just enough time. After all, Mabry's main objective was to get me to commit robbery and violent crimes, to further tarnish my moral compass, to get me put away in prison forever. His goal was now semi-accomplished by me kidnapping and shooting Karl Drago.

"Three hundred thousand is not nearly enough," Marie said.

"Why tomorrow?" I asked. "Tell me why this caper has to be tomorrow."

Drago nodded. "Like I said, I stashed it in the clubhouse, and tomorrow there's a local ride, the June ride for Toys for Tots. All the clubs in SoCal gather toys for the halfway point in the year. They do it again in December for the publicity, for all the TV cameras. Along with the toys from the June ride, they double up and look like stars, real pillars in the community. Bunch of bullshit."

"So the Sons of Satan clubhouse will be empty tomorrow?"

"Sort of, I guess."

Marie, with her clenched fists down at her side, took a step toward him. "Sort of? Sort of? It is or it isn't, mister. Which is it?"

"Ooh, girl, you need to take a chill pill." He smiled, trying to get her to smile back. When she didn't, he said, "They're never gonna leave the clubhouse unmanned. Never. There'll be a couple or three prospects and a couple old heads to supervise."

"Four or five then?" I asked.

"Yeah, four or five is all that's going to be there on Saturday."

"Saturday?" Marie screamed. "Are you kidding me?"

"What's wrong now?" Drago said.

"No, numbnuts, it's Thursday," Marie said. "Today's Thursday." She turned to me. "This isn't going to work. Nothing about this idea's going to work."

"It's all we got, it has to work," I said.

The Black Sabbath t-shirt wrapped tight around Drago's leg had turned darker, and blood ran in a little rivulet down his leg. He didn't show any sign of pain, nor did he seem to care any longer that he'd been shot.

"Are you a member of the SS?" I asked Drago.

"Hell no, man. Are you kidding? Those old boys are some crazy, violent assholes. So what if today is Thursday, what difference does it make?"

I didn't answer and asked, "If you're not a member, then how did you get into the clubhouse twenty-five years ago to stash the money? And how do you know it's still there?"

"Okay, what? You need the whole, sad story right here and now?"

"That's right, and we're running out of time, fatso, so get to it," said Marie.

"She's feisty. You shouldn't let her talk like that. Before too long, she'll be runnin' your game."

I didn't want to tell him she already did, and I liked it that way.

She reached for the Glock in my hand. I put my hand gently on her chest and moved her back a step. To Drago, I said, "So, how did you get in the clubhouse twenty-five years ago?"

"Back then, me and Clay Warfield was prospects, we were buds. *Back then.* Now he's the president of SS International. You believe it? President of the world. Man, did he get lucky or what?"

No luck had entered into Warfield's ascendancy to infamy. He rose in the ranks of the most dastardly outlaw motorcycle gang in the world through blackmail, tyranny, mayhem, and cold-blooded murder. The FBI wanted him worse than any other crook, almost more than the top man in Al Qaida.

Drago continued on, "Another buddy a mine, he worked for a big-time locksmith, an affiliate of the SS. I helped him install the clubhouse safe, this big double-door monster. Weighed at least two thousand pounds."

"You hid three hundred thousand dollars in the safe of the Sons of Satan clubhouse?" I asked.

"No, not exactly. Okay, look, I guess I'm gonna have to explain the whole thing." He paused, waiting for us to tell him to go on, to beg him.

Marie put her hands on her hips and turned and walked away a few steps to cool off.

"Come on, Drago, keep going," I said.

"What kinda bug flew up her ass?"

Marie spun around and pointed a finger at him. "I do not like this man."

"Drago."

"All right. All right. Look, I did the armored job with this other bud a mine. And later that same week he took a fall for his third B and E. I knew he was gonna flip and give me up. I knew I was goin' in for a good long jolt because of the thing with the guard. So I needed a safe place to hide the money, a place that was going to still be there when I got out. You ever see the movie *Thunderbolt and Lightfoot*? The dude hid the money in the wall of the old schoolhouse, and they moved the whole damn schoolhouse. You see that movie?"

"Drago."

"Man, you're worse than a woman on the rag. Okay, so I think, what better place to—"

Marie stepped back over. "We got all that. You hid it in the clubhouse safe, great. How do you know they haven't already found the money? Why wouldn't they find a big bag of money like that? This doesn't make any sense."

"The guy who helped you out on the armored car job," I said, "his name was Stanley Granville?"

"Yeah, that's right. How did you know?"

Granville, aka Big Grandy, had been Drago's second murder victim, the guy he killed his first time out on parole. "Go on," I said.

"I'm with ya about them finding the money, but not a chance in hell," said Drago. "They haven't found it, guaran-fucking-teed."

Marie shouted, "Why?"

Drago looked at her, paused, then said, "Because I thought this whole thing out, believe me. Listen to this, I bought gold with the money, melted it down into this big doughnut-ring-looking kinda thing, and painted it black so it looked like steel. My bud, who I helped put the safe in, didn't even know it was gold. No one knows it's gold. We had to anchor the safe to the floor, to these large bolts, preset in concrete. I told this bud o' mine that the doughnut was like a washer, a spacer kind of thing between the safe and the floor so the safe wouldn't rock. I did it with the SS standing right over us watching the whole time. The dumbasses."

The simplicity of his plan was brilliant and at the same time ballsy. No one in the world would find his stash. But what made it safe, made extraction a problem. Getting the doughnut out while keeping your skin. The caper's plan now went from a sneak and peek to running into a lion's den with five or six hungry lions in residence, grabbing a forty-pound haunch of lamb, and escaping without getting your ass eaten.

While I pondered Drago's grand design and the consequences of failure, my mind worked subconsciously. "Wait. Wait a minute," I said. "You bought gold twenty-five years ago? How much was it an ounce?"

"What? Hell, I don't know. I knew this fence who traded me gold for the cash. Gold melts real easy. I mean not real easy, but with not as much heat as you'd think you'd need. I used a blowtorch and poured it into a sand mold, little at a time. Took forever."

"How much? What was the weight?"

"Forty pounds. You'd have thought three hundred thousand would have bought more than a measly little forty pounds. You should have seen how small forty pounds was." He made a motion with his hands indicating a small pile. "It was sad, man, I'm telling you, a damn shame, really."

"So, this doughnut thing you smelted, it weighs forty pounds?"

"Yeah, that's right. What'd I just say? In fact, the fence discounted the money 'cause it was hot. He wouldn't give me the whole three hundred thousand in gold. He said the cash was hot. What a bunch of bullshit. But what could I do?"

Marie had caught on to where I was headed with my questions and jumped in. "So, you're sure about the forty pounds though, right?"

"What's the matter with you two idgits? That's what I said. Two hundred and sixty-two thousand dollars, after Mad Mike took his cut, got me right around forty pounds, give or take an ounce."

Marie looked away as her mind went to work. I stepped closer. Her brainpower far surpassed mine. So as not to disrupt her, I quietly said, "Sixteen ounces in a pound, how many ounces in forty pounds?"

"Six hundred and forty," she said. "What's the price per ounce today?"

"Seventeen-fifty."

When you lived with a bunch of expats who watched commodities like a kettle of hawks, you tended to pick up on that sort of mundane minutia.

Drago's voice went up to just short of a yell. "Wait. Wait. What's seventeen-fifty? No way. You're sayin' an ounce of gold is going for seventeen hundred and fifty dollars?"

Marie waved her hand for us to be quiet as she tried to compute the large figures in her head.

"I thought gold went up and down a little," Drago said, "but stayed pretty close to the same price. That's what Mad Mike Farris told me. He told me that twenty-five years ago when we made the deal, that gold stayed pretty steady."

"Sssh," I told Drago.

Marie looked up.

"Well?" I asked.

"One million, one hundred and twenty thousand."

CHAPTER THIRTY-ONE

"A million two?" Drago yelled. "You're shittin' me, right? That can't be right. A million two." He started to mutter to himself.

I pulled Marie far enough away from the van that Drago couldn't hear, but close enough to keep the Glock on him. "What do you think?"

"I'm no good at this kind of thing, Bruno. I don't know." She thought about it for a moment. "What was that thing about Granville? What was his first name?"

"Stanley Granville, Big Grandy. I didn't put it together until just now. I asked Mack why the Feds were involved in watching Drago. He said the money from the armored car was federally insured. That story didn't sound right, not for a twenty-five-year-old robbery, but I went with it. Granville pulled the job with Drago."

"At first Drago said a *bud,* and didn't give a name," said Marie.

"Right. He's trying to keep the details down on the fabricated part of the lie so it's easier to remember. Drago went in for twenty-five to life for the armored car robbery and got out on parole the first time after doing twelve years. He came out, killed Stanley Granville for ratting him out, and went back in for another twenty-five to life, did another twelve and got out this time."

"Okay, and?"

"Twelve years ago, Granville was the president of the SS."

"Honey, I know I'm missing something here, so just spell it out," Marie said.

"Drago was the FBI's staked goat. They were waiting for Clay

Warfield, current president of the SS, to order the hit on Drago for killing their past president and for the hit to be carried out. Then they would have a dead Drago, no loss there, and a conspiracy to commit murder with a RICO violation on the Sons of Satan. The FBI could dismantle a large chunk of the SS and make a huge splash in the news."

Everything fell into place. That was why they had kept Mary Beth in the surveillance room when everyone else had been reassigned. They didn't want her to follow Drago if he left. They wanted her as a witness to his death."

"How does this thing with Granville impact what we have going?" Marie asked.

"The SS will have a 'shoot on sight' order out on Drago. I don't know how he survived in prison this long. They must have kept him segregated for this very reason."

"I know how he survived, look at him," she said. "The man could pick up a small horse and dunk it in a basketball hoop without breaking a sweat."

Maybe a few years ago, but not now. Drago had gone to fat. No doubt, even shot, he was a formidable opponent, but not to the degree she thought.

We moved back closer to Drago. "You mentioned that we could help you get this golden doughnut," I said. "You have something in mind, don't you?"

Drago quit muttering. A large smile broke, filling his flat, pie-pan face. "I gotcha, don't I? You're gonna do it, aren't ya?"

Marie said, "Shut up, fatso, and answer him."

He eyed Marie a moment and said, "Your firecracker little bitch said the gold's worth one million, one hundred and twenty thousand. You need the million. I ain't gonna be good with no one hundred and twenty thousand for my end."

"We don't want any of the gold, none of it," I said. "We told you that. The deal here is that we help you get the gold. We take that risk. In exchange, you take the risk of possibly losing the gold when we trade it for the kids. On that end your risk is much smaller. We're dealing with one twenty-five-year-old psychotic, and not with an international urban terrorist organization. It's a fair trade."

Drago didn't say anything for a minute. "Okay, deal. But when it comes to makin' the trade—the gold for the kids—I get a say in how we handle it. You don't just get to piss away all my gold. I get to be part of the plan." He held out his hand. I took it and shook.

"Now, tell us this great and wonderful plan of yours," Marie said.

Drago slid off his perch from the back of the van, keeping his weight on his good leg. He hobbled around to the passenger side of the van, opened the door, and brought the FBI bag back around. He sat in the same place and said, "With this."

He unzipped the bag. His hand turned into a blur of speed and came out with a .40-caliber Sig Sauer pistol. He pointed it at me and smiled.

"You son of a bitch," said Marie.

I nudged her with an elbow. "Where'd you get this language? I don't like it."

"Yeah, well, dipshit's holding a gun on us and he's going to shoot us any second now, so I think I'm entitled to use any language I want."

"No, he's not," I said.

"I'm not, big man? Tell me why I'm not."

"Because you want us to dress up like FBI agents to infiltrate the clubhouse. You need us as much as we need you. You could never pull off looking like an FBI agent. And you need a partner to make it look legit." I'd figured out his plan as soon as he picked up the bag.

He chuckled. "That's right." He set the gun down on the floor beside him and pulled out a windbreaker and a vest, both dark blue with large white letters 'FBI' emblazoned on the front and back.

"You're pretty smart for an Anus Africanus."

"Don't you call him that," Marie said. "Next time you call him that, I'll take you down, you understand?"

He chuckled again. This time his whole body jiggled and rolled. "Looks like the first order of business is getting ol' Drago here some clothes."

"Toss me that gun," I said.

He eyed me as if trying to decide how far to push his newly found freedom. Then he picked up the gun and tossed it to me. I tossed it right back. He caught it, surprised. I took the loaded magazine out of my pocket, the one I'd taken out of the gun earlier, and tossed it to him. "The gun's no good without bullets."

He pointed his finger at me and smiled. He stuck the magazine back in the gun and pulled back the slide to charge the breech. "You know, I might have to change my mind about you Anus—"

"Don't do it," Marie said. "Don't you say it."

"Come on," I said, "we have to get some clothes and make a phone call."

CHAPTER THIRTY-TWO

I moved Drago up into the front seat next to me while I waited in the Walmart parking lot for Marie. No matter how hard I tried to put the feeling out of my head, I couldn't help but think this guy was going to make a move on me at any moment. In the front seat was bad enough; you add in leaving him unrestrained by hand-cuffs—that just went against the grain of twenty-five years chasing his type.

Marie carried the cash she'd brought from Costa Rica and size orders for clothes. She was also going to make a stop in the pharmacy area and pick up some supplies to treat the gunshot wound.

Having the lion sitting in the seat next to me kept my adrenaline pumping, which kept fatigue at bay, which kept my thoughts clear. Somewhat, at least.

"You know," I said, "this gold thing changes the scenario. We aren't going to have time to convert it to cash. I'm going to call Jonas and ask for a meet."

"Jonas is the one? This shitass punk who took these kids?"

"That's right."

"Good, maybe we can get your end of the deal settled right away before we even get to mine," Drago said.

"No, I don't want you to do anything, and I mean nothing at all to spook him. You understand? If this goes down the way I think it will, I just want you there to verify that we'll have the money coming, but in the form of gold. I want you to tell him the story you told us about how and what you did with the gold."

"Let me get my hands on him. Believe me when I tell you, he'll give up his grandma when I'm done with him."

"No, I've already tried that and it didn't work."

"What, you think you're *me*? You don't understand—"

"I want your word you won't try anything. This end of the deal is mine and mine alone to call."

He looked at me for a moment and then nodded.

"No, I want to hear it. Tell me I have your word."

"All right, ease up on it, homeboy. You got it. You have my word on it. And don't think for a minute that I believe that you and your slit don't want the money."

"Her name is Marie, and you will refer to her as such, or we are going to have a big problem."

"Yeah, yeah, I gotcha, I'm sorry. I didn't really say it on purpose, it just comes out. It's hard to talk different after twenty-five years in the can. *You* know what I'm talking about, right?"

I did know.

I hit the speed-dial number on the burner phone Jonas had given me. One ring and someone picked up. "Yeah?"

Drago leaned over to listen in, his breath sour and hot, with burnt pepperoni and kung pao chicken. I didn't like him that close, and involuntarily tensed in anticipation of a knife slipping in between my ribs.

"It's me," I said.

"I know, Deputy Johnson, no one else has this number. You're not supposed to call until you have the money. No way could you have the money, not this quick. Not unless you're working with the Feds with a phony bag. You working with the Feds, Deputy Johnson?"

"No. And I think you know me well enough that I wouldn't do that. All I want is to get those kids back safely. I'll give you the money, you give me the kids, and we are done with each other."

"Heh, heh, right. Who's to say we're done? What if I do this again?"

I didn't know the answer, the one he wanted, anyway. "I guess I'll have to deal with that problem if and when it comes up."

"So then, I'll ask you again, Deputy Johnson, why are you calling? Do you have the money?"

"No, I don't have the money, but I have something better."

"What?"

"Forty pounds of gold."

Jonas didn't say anything for a long moment. He was mad at the change of plan and was deciding if he would hang up, walk away from the whole deal, leave the children down in some hole to smother, alone and scared. My imagination ran full tilt. Sweat broke out on my brow.

"One million, one hundred and twenty thousand," he said.

His words sent a chill down my back. How had he computed that figure so quickly? He not only knew the price of gold, but he'd computed all of the figures in his head. Jonas Mabry was far more intelligent than I had thought. With intelligence came a higher risk assessment and threat level.

My voice cracked, "That's right."

"Gold will work. I'll call you back in an hour to tell you where to bring it."

"No, wait, don't hang up."

"What?"

"I'm calling because we don't have it. I know where to get it, but we need a little more time."

"Deputy Johnson, you don't know me, not at all. I don't play games, never have. I lost my childhood. It was stolen from me by you. But you know all about that, don't you, Deputy Bruno Johnson? I told you the time frame."

"I'm going to get the gold, I promise you that, and if you wait you can have an additional one hundred and twenty thousand. Hello? Hello."

Damn, he hung up.

I waited for him to call back. He'd only hung up to mess with my mind, and he was doing a great job.

"Yep, he's a punk ass for sure," Drago said. "I didn't really believe your bullshit story about the kidnapped kids. Now I do."

The phone rang, I answered.

"You can have twelve more hours," Jonas said.

"I need until Saturday night, that's forty-eight hours total. Twelve more hours in addition to what you just offered. That's not a lot, not really, not when you consider what's at stake." I hated to beg a criminal, any criminal.

Silence on the phone. He was thinking about the new offer. I said, "Gold works better for you, anyway, think about it. You can take gold into any jewelry store, a little at a time, and trade it for folding money. If I gave you cash, there would always be the threat of marked bills or wafer-thin tracking devices."

More silence.

I continued on, talking faster. "This is a good deal, much better than what you wanted."

Silence. Then, "How do I know this isn't some sort of game you're running on me?"

"I can prove it."

"How? What store or bank are you going to hit?"

I really didn't want to tell him the where and the how. "I have with me a guy who just got out on parole after twenty-five years. He did an armored car job twenty-five years ago and hid the proceeds after converting it to gold."

"Right. And he's going to just hand over the money to you, just like that?"

"No, not just like that, I had to persuade him."

"Like you persuaded me?"

"Yes, but I was more successful with this guy."

"Is he dead?"

"No."

"Bring him to me. I want to confirm it with him. I don't want you running some kind of stupid little game on me, Deputy Johnson."

"Fine—when and where?"

CHAPTER THIRTY-THREE

Marie came across the parking lot pushing a shopping cart. Items in the cart came up to the top rim. What had she purchased? I got out and checked around to see if anyone took particular notice. The cell in my pocket buzzed. I answered.

"Bruno?" Mack sounded peeved, as though speaking through clenched teeth to suppress his anger.

"Yeah, Mack, how's it going?" As I spoke, I opened the back of the van and helped Marie pile in her purchases, which, besides what she'd gone in for, included an empty five-gallon bucket, some tie-down straps, white grocery bags filled with different types of snacks, and other not readily identifiable items.

"You took Drago?" asked Mack. "Why'd you take Drago, Bruno?"

Mack wanted me on the phone to keep me talking, to ping the signal and home in on us. "I wanted to talk to Drago. When I saw him on the surveillance video, he seemed like a man in need of rehabilitation, and I thought that with my background I could—"

"Cut the bullshit. Why'd you take him?"

I closed up the back of the van with Marie inside, moved to the front driver's door and got in, scanning for cops the entire time. "I think you know why."

Mack lowered his voice. "He doesn't have the money anymore, and if he tells you he does, he's running a scam. He's making a chump out of you. Bring him back. It's more important than you know. There are other things in play here, Bruno, trust me on this. Think about it, even if you had the money, you can't trade it for the kids. It won't work. You know better. I know you know better. You don't have the resources to back your play. Come on in, Bruno, please."

I started up and drove slowly to the exit, pulled out onto the street, and headed east back to the desert. Drago might be one of the lowest forms of animal, but he didn't deserve to be staked out as bait and killed for no other purpose than to bring down a criminal organization. "I can't do that and you know why," I said.

"This is going to put us on the opposite sides of the fence."

"I'm sorry to hear that. I value you as a good friend."

"As a friend, I'm telling you, you're wrong going down this path. You're putting too much at stake. Way too much."

"What more can there be at stake than the lives of three children? I have to go, John, I know you're trying to keep me on the phone."

"No, not this time. This time was a free one."

"Tell Barbara I'm sorry it has to be this way, that when all this goes down, I'll try and call to give her a heads up. She'll be my first call. Tell her that. Good-bye, John." I handed the phone to Drago. He didn't need instruction. He broke it in half, stuck his hand out the window, and let the pieces drop to the passing concrete, to be run over and over again by freeway cars and trucks.

From behind, Marie put her hand on my shoulder. I turned to look. She'd turned the white bucket upside down to sit on it. She'd taken a thick, nylon tie-down strap and hooked it from one side of the van wall across to the other, and held on to help stabilize her ride. Smart girl. I didn't want her sitting in the back with all the garbage, but she'd said Drago couldn't, not with his open wound, her medical background overpowering her disgust for him.

We rode in silence for another thirty minutes. Fatigue crept in—the thick, heavy kind—the kind with wispy apparitions that appeared and disappeared at random, my body telling me I needed to sleep or it would sleep without permission from control central. I took the Whitewater offramp, stopped at the bottom, made a right, and continued on into empty darkness. Out here, headlights could be seen for miles and miles. I watched the odometer. Asphalt turned to dirt. And still I continued on. I stopped at seven miles, exactly as directed, the terrain at the edge too rough to continue. This place looked a lot like the one I'd chosen in the foothills to speak first with Jonas, then with Drago. If something violent occurred, nobody would find our bodies for days, or maybe not at all with all the coyotes and other scavengers.

The desolation and darkness worked in our favor. We'd see Jonas coming a long way off.

Marie slid open the side door, got out with her Walmart bag, and opened the passenger door. "Swing around, let me fix that leg. Bruno, come around and hold this flashlight." She'd also thought far enough ahead to purchase a flashlight. Drago and I both followed directions. For the last forty-five minutes of the drive, Drago had gone quiet. In the weak flashlight beam his skin reflected pale, pastier than before. His plain black tattoos were darker now in contrast, and more menacing. His eyelids drooped and his facial muscles didn't have the strength to hold up any sort of expression.

Marie took a bottle of Pedialyte from the bag, opened it, and handed it to him. "Here, drink this."

His hand came out of the dark in slow motion and took the bottle. "What is it?"

"Shut up and drink it."

"What's the matter with him?" I asked.

"Blood loss. Here, look."

I shined the light on her hand and followed where she pointed. Drago's gunshot wound had continued to leak. The bumpy road had not helped. Blood soaked the side of the seat and pooled at his feet in what might qualify as a small pond. She snapped on rubber gloves.

"He going to make it?"

She stopped and looked up at me. "What do you think? Wasn't

it you who told me that, with these guys, you had to cut the head off and bury it ten feet from the body in order to kill 'em?"

Drago's ashen face cracked a smile. "Hey, that's a good one."

She took out a large bottle of hydrogen peroxide, screwed off the top, and punched a hole in the foil seal with her nail. She dumped some on the wound. Pink and red foamed up and rolled off down his calf. She looked up, waiting for his reaction. He didn't move and stared at her. She waited until the foaming stopped, then did the same procedure again and again until the quart bottle emptied. Next, she took out a fat package of feminine sanitary napkins, daubed and dried, tossing the used ones into the back of the van. The wound looked like an angry eye socket minus the eye, with purple, puckered edges. I couldn't help thinking I was glad that wasn't on my leg.

Drago finished the electrolytes, burped, and tossed the bottle out on the ground. Marie stopped, went and picked up the bottle, and tossed it in the back of the van. "Pig."

"Thank you."

"It wasn't a compliment."

"You two need to play nice," I said.

She took out a large bottle of iodine. "This might sting a little." In the dim light she poured the red-black liquid and jumped back.

"Yaaaaa. Jesus, Keeyrist!" Drago bounced and jumped around in the seat, his eyes wide, his mouth a cavernous *O*.

"You shouldn't litter like that," she said.

"You're nothing but a cu—"

I leaned in and with one hand clamped his throat. "Don't you say it."

His words choked off. He gagged.

Marie and I jumped back as he projectile vomited all the liquid he'd just ingested. When finished, he groaned, put his head back on the seat, and closed his eyes.

"I'm sorry," Marie said. I put the light on her face, her expression one of true sorrow and pain. She took out a second bottle and opened it. "Here, drink this."

Drago waved his hand. "Can't, my stomach, I'm nauseous."

"You're going to have to sip this and keep it down, or we're going to the hospital. You understand?"

"Try to get me into a hospital, lady, just try it."

"It'll be easy once you're unconscious. And believe me when I say that I don't know why you're not already."

He hesitated, glaring at her. The large bottle looked tiny in his huge paw. He put it to his lips and took a drink.

"This time sip it, and keep sipping it. Don't stop."

She took out two more napkins and put one on each side, at the entrance and the exit. "Here, press firmly." Drago leaned over and would have kept going had I not put both hands on his shoulders and pushed him back in. He managed to hold onto the bottle and the napkin as Marie wrapped his leg again and again with a gauze roll. Next, she took out an elastic bandage, the kind for knee injuries, and tightly bound the wound. She handed him a bundle of bananas. "When you feel like it, eat these."

"I ain't no—"

She held up a gloved finger. He shut up. She took off the gloves and tossed them in the back. "We're going to have to torch this van when we're done. It's turned into a hazardous waste nightmare." She took something else out of her bag of tricks and handed the small package to Drago.

"What's this?"

"Breath mints. Do me the favor, would you?"

He smiled.

Bright light lit up the van from the side, blinding us.

"What a touching scene," Jonas Mabry said from afar.

CHAPTER THIRTY-FOUR

Jonas' car was backed into the sage. We hadn't seen him pull up, or more likely he'd been there waiting the entire time. He'd seen us doctoring Drago. I had one of the guns in my waistband. He had to have seen it by now. His bright lights washed out any possible target and worse, it illuminated and exposed my vulnerability.

Long shadows crossed the bright light as Jonas approached. His limp on a shot-up foot made his shadow dance. I turned away to let my eyes readjust. Drago sat in the van seat, head back, eyes closed, his pallor as waxy and gray as a cadaver. Had he gotten worse? We needed him.

Jonas stopped. His body blocked the light and, at the same time, kept him in a darkened relief. "You shot him like you shot me, only higher up. He doesn't look well, Deputy Johnson."

Marie stood tensely at my side.

"I want proof of life," I said.

"I knew you only wanted this meet for something like this."

"*You* asked for this meeting, not me. But while we're here, I need to know we're not going through all this for nothing."

He came closer, his diminishing shadow restoring the bright light. From behind, Drago said, "Man, he doesn't even have a gun. He ain't any bigger than my old dog Bo. Grab him, I'll make him talk."

"Shut up."

Jonas laughed. "You'll be lucky to live out the night with as much blood as you've lost. Here." He tossed me a bottle.

The burnt-orange prescription bottle no doubt contained

pain pills. Jonas wanted his gold, and the pain drugs might help keep the shock from creeping in on Drago.

I looked back at Drago. His eyes were fierce little beads as he obeyed Marie and sipped his life-replenishing drink. Jonas had given him the motivation to live. To crush, kill, and destroy another day.

"Let's get on with it," said Jonas. "I can see he's been shot. I don't think you went out and found some random person to shoot and bring here, so let's hear the rest of the story. How are you going to get the gold?"

Marie took a step forward. "No, not until you show us the children."

I put my hand on her shoulder and kept her from taking another step. I whispered, "It's better if you let me handle this."

"Is this the little woman? You did all right for yourself, Deputy Johnson. Little young for you but—"

I cut him off. "We didn't come here for small talk."

"No, we didn't." He stepped up the rest of the way, close, and held out a smart phone. "Here, see for yourself."

Someone on the other end had held up another phone and panned two little girls, about six or seven years old, and sent the video. They cuddled next to each other asleep in a nest of soft clean blankets. He took the phone back. "That's enough."

They were all right. The children were all right.

"How do we know that's their current situation?" I asked.

"I guess you'll have to take my word."

"Where's the boy?" asked Marie. "Where's little Eddie Crane?"

Jonas feigned surprise, and not very well. "What? He wasn't there? Well, I don't know what's happened to him." Jonas now stood close enough for me to see his ugly black-holed smile as he waved his hand. "You know, as it turns out, I wanted to give you a little bonus, a little motivator."

"That right?" I said. "We need to see Eddie."

"Yeah, the extra motivator is that I didn't take kids from good homes. I took them from homes where they were being molested and abused, just like you did before you fled the country."

Marie gasped and brought her hand up to her mouth.

"That's right," Jonas said. "I did my research, and knew you'd be even more likely to play along if the children were of a certain ilk. I thought you'd have found this out by now. Anyway, I need to help you along."

Certain ilk. That was not his vocabulary. He mimicked words someone had told him. They came out in rote. I didn't know if I believed him, but sensed he now told the truth. "Jonas, where's Eddie Crane?" I asked.

"That's all you get for now. Let's hear about this gold."

If the phone call wasn't recorded, and someone had just sent it to him, then Jonas had someone helping him for sure. Getting the kids back during the exchange just became that much more difficult.

I turned to the side. "This is Karl Drago."

Drago had put his back against the headrest, his eyes closed. He brought his hand up to sip from the plastic bottle, as if he couldn't care less about what went on in his world or anyone else's.

Jonas stood his ground. "I've heard of him. Aren't the Sons of Satan out to cut his nuts off? He's got a green light on him by everyone, including parolees and members or associates with the SS. It's not too healthy to stand close to this man, Deputy Johnson."

"I'd forgotten that you've been in the joint. So you know about the armored car robbery, then?"

"No, not the robbery. Where's this gold, and why is it going to take you until Saturday?"

"Drago took the money, converted it to gold, and hid it in the Sons of Satan clubhouse. All the Satans are going to be busy Saturday on the Toys for Tots run."

"Oh, that's a good one, absolutely priceless. The Sons of Satan clubhouse. Which one?"

"The international headquarters in San Bernardino. You going to give us the extra time?"

"I believe you now. You have until Saturday night, eight o'clock. That'll be right around sundown."

"Eddie Crane," Marie said. "We're not moving one inch until we know Eddie Crane's safe."

Jonas turned his head slowly to look at her. "Does she speak for you, Deputy Johnson?"

"That's right, she does."

"Heh, hch." He turned and headed back into the light. He said over his shoulder, "Little Eddie Crane, as you call him, was already medically compromised when I grabbed him. Remember that. I had nothing to do with his injuries."

"You son of a bitch," Marie said. I took hold of her shoulders as she made for Jonas. Jonas didn't turn around and kept walking.

"Let me go, let me go, I want a piece of that animal."

A loud explosion made us both jump out of the way. One of the headlights of Jonas' car winked out from the pistol shot. I turned and jerked the gun out of Drago's hand. I wanted to slug him in the mouth, but didn't.

Jonas' car door opened and closed. The engine started, the car backed up, tearing out sage and shrub, and then drove away in a cloud of dust.

The night's darkness slammed down upon us. I couldn't see, and a bit of claustrophobia snatched at my breath. You couldn't defend in darkness; control reverted to those who lurked.

"That guy's an asshole," Drago said.

"I told you. I told you not to get involved. You gave me your word."

He put his head back and closed his eyes. "I didn't get involved. I just shot out his headlight. No big deal. Gave him something to think about. Let him know he wasn't dealing with a couple of pansy-ass pussies."

"I'm glad he took a shot at that asshole," said Marie. "If I had a gun, I would've done the same."

"What's the matter with you two?" I said. "He's holding the kids. You can't shoot at him until we have the kids. Then have at it. But not until we have the kids."

Fatigue was turning my mind to mush, and I wasn't entirely

sure they'd been wrong. I should've known for sure, but nothing seemed black and white anymore. Everything disappeared in obscured shades of gray, with the truth hiding off in the distance. I needed to sleep. Before we did anything else, I needed at least four hours. "Come on. Get in and let's go."

Far out ahead, Jonas' single headlight bounced and jutted this way and that as he drove to the paved road. I was pretty sure the taillight pattern on the car was from a Toyota, but millions of Toyotas drove the streets of Southern California. We followed far behind. My vision blurred with fatigue, thoughts came and went unbidden. I slowed. "I can't drive. Honey, can you take over please?"

"Sure. Can you get us to the road first? It's not much farther and...Oh, my God, Bruno, stop. Stop."

My head whipped forward to see this new apparition, a hallucination. I slammed on the brakes. In the dirt path walked a small child, five or six years old. Tears streaked his dusty face, his eyes wide in terror.

CHAPTER THIRTY-FIVE

Marie slid open the side door and jumped out before the van came to a complete stop. She stumbled in the headlights and almost went down, righted, and made it to the child. She slowed and stopped, cooing, talking low to him, her words barely audible over the van's engine.

"It's okay, baby, it's okay, honey. No one's going to hurt you."

Drago muttered, "That son of a bitch, leaving a kid out here like that. Next time I won't be aiming at his headlight."

I couldn't deny him that. I wanted to do the same.

"Out here in the dark like this, we coulda run him over," Drago said. "The kid coulda wandered off. How'd he know we'd come across him? Kid's gotta be scared outta his wits. What a son of a bitch." Drago's rapid language acted as a cover for his fear and inadequacy. I recognized it in myself.

Drago got out on wobbly legs, stuck his arm in the van's open side door, and scooped all the refuse from the van's floor out onto the ground. He went around back, opened the doors, and did the same again. He closed the back doors and came around in time to help Marie and the child mount the van. I don't know where Drago found his reserve strength. These actions had to be beyond taxing. I should've gotten out to help but could hardly muster the energy to keep my eyes open. Adrenaline no longer worked.

Drago slid the side door shut, climbed back in, and closed his door.

Marie perched on the five-gallon bucket, the boy on her lap.

She let go of him, put her arms over the strap one at a time, so the strap went across her chest to stabilize them, and then took hold of the boy.

"Drive, Bruno." Her tone left no room for debate. "Drago, hold this flashlight."

I started the van moving and checked the rearview. Eddie Crane, who looked about five and small for his age, had sandy-brown hair that hung down in his hazel eyes. He wore denim pants and a long-sleeve shirt.

"It's okay, little man, no one's going to hurt you," said Marie. "You're okay now. You understand? You're okay now." To me, she said, "Bruno, watch where you're going."

I looked back just as the right side of the van veered off the narrow track into the sage. The van bumped and bounced in the air as I muscled us back into the rough track. How long had it been since I slept? Three days? Three and a half? I'd slept the night before I worked the cabana bar at The Margarite, the day all this had started. I tried to count the days and couldn't count past two. A bad sign. I focused everything I had on the task at hand, keeping the van on the road and my eyes open.

The boy had yet to make any sound at all.

Marie said, "There's a note pinned to his shirt pocket." Paper rattled. I focused on the road.

Marie read:

"My name is Eddie Crane. If found, return me to Deputy Bruno Johnson, California Rehabilitation Center, Chino. Ha, Ha.

PS. I didn't do that to his back. His new parents did. The boy won't talk, won't say a word. He's broken."

Over the van's engine, Marie's voice caught. I checked the mirror again, her sorrowful expression filled with tears. Checking the mirror proved one task too many for my fatigue-laden brain. I again veered and corrected.

"Bruno, please pay attention."

"It's okay, honey," she said to Eddie. "I'm a doctor. Let me look at your back."

Drago held the bouncing flashlight and, after a couple seconds, his tone came in a low whisper, "Oh my God. That son of a bitch. That cocksucker."

A large dose of adrenaline kicked in. I pulled over. "What?" I spun in the seat.

Marie wept openly and hugged Eddie, one hand on his bottom, one on his head, nestling it into her shoulder, her hands avoiding his back, as she whispered, "It's okay. It's okay now. No one's going to hurt you ever again." His back, crisscrossed with open wounds both scabbed and festering, indicated multiple events of abuse. I'd seen this too many times in the past while answering calls as a patrol deputy. Eddie Crane had been beaten with an electrical cord.

***

I woke in a strange bed. My whole body ached from the deep, coma-like sleep. With the curtains pulled, the motel room retained its innocence, concealing a fleabag appearance. The dimness, though, wasn't able to mask the smell, musty with a hint of sour and of the destitute. As my eyes adjusted, a small lump materialized in the twin bed next to mine. Then I remembered. Eddie Crane.

Where had Marie gone?

I swung my legs around and sat up. On the nightstand sat a carton of chocolate milk and a package of Sno Balls. My stomach growled. I guess, when away from home, junk food became an approved staple. I tore open the package and went to it. She hadn't been gone too long; the chocolate milk carton dripped with cold condensation. The rush of sugar woke me even more, and I groaned with pleasure at the combined luscious flavors.

Eddie's head came up out of the covers like a prairie dog, his eyes telegraphing fear.

"It's okay, Ed, I'm a friend. You don't have to worry about me. You want some of this?"

He shook his head "no." I held up a Sno Ball. "These are real good. You don't know what you're missing." I eased over and set

one on the edge of his bed. He didn't take his eyes off me. His
delicate emotional state would take lots of love and tenderness to
get him back on the road to trust.

The door opened. Bright light burst in and stole my vision.
Marie closed the door. "Ah, Rip Van Winkle has awakened." She
came over. "Hey, mister garbage disposal, those aren't for you."

"Oh, sorry."

She leaned down toward her wounded charge. "Hi, Eddie,
how are you feeling?" He looked up, half a smile snuck out. Marie
knew how to work wonders with at-risk children. She picked up
the lone Sno Ball on the bed's edge. "Here, it's okay, you can have
this." He snatched it from her hand and took a large bite. She
smiled. Her happiness made me smile, and my face flushed warm.

"It's okay, little boy," she said to me, "you can have your treats
too. I have more. How are *you* feeling?"

"Alive again."

"You were a walking zombie last night."

"Where'd you go?" I asked.

"The room next door. I changed Drago's bandage."

I wish she hadn't done that without me. The image of the
zookeeper going into the lion's cage without an assistant holding a
bazooka leapt out at me. "How's he doing?"

"I don't know why the man doesn't have an infection. I think
it's because he's not fully evolved and his relatives are direct de-
scendants of Cro-Magnon man. He's really bouncing back fast."

I nodded toward our latest charge devouring a Sno Ball, bits
of confection cake and pink coconut falling to the rumpled bed
sheets. "Have you thought about what we're going to do with him?"

She came over and sat next to me. "What do you think we're
going to do with him?"

"Yeah, I thought you were going to say something like that." I
took another bite of Sno Ball and guzzled the chocolate milk before she changed her mind and returned us all back to the dreaded health food mode.

"Do you disagree?" she asked.

Like dropping everything in Costa Rica, coming back to the States to chase down Jonas and the kids Jonas took had left us no choice. The same applied to Eddie Crane. He was out of options, as well. I shook my head "no."

She reached into a Walmart bag on the floor at our feet and took out a new burner phone. "Here, you need to call, tell them to quit looking for him. I don't want them wasting precious resources that they can divert back to searching for those two little girls."

"Can I at least get a shower first?"

She smiled, got up from Eddie's bed, leaned down, and kissed my forehead. "No."

I took the phone and dialed Mack's number. Barbara Wicks answered. "Bruno?"

"How did you know it was me?"

"Educated guess. It's a number John's phone didn't recognize, and I've been waiting for you to call."

"You answer John's phone a lot, do you?"

Neither of us said anything more in an uncomfortable, pregnant pause.

I finally said, "Last night, we got proof of life."

"What? That's great, Bruno." She paused again, then said, "But we're dead in the water here. You're communicating with him without our trace capability, without the manpower to run down the cell tower leads as they come in. Do you know what you're doing? Are you going to be able to live with yourself when this thing goes south on you?"

"I'm sorry you feel that way. I think this is the best chance we have to get the little girls back."

She didn't want to comment on my evaluation of the situation. "We've confirmed it, Eddie is number three."

"Barbara, we have Eddie. We got him back from Jonas last night."

"What! You're kidding. Bruno, that's fantastic. What's his status? Can you at least drop him at a fire station or clinic?"

I stood and walked into the bathroom and closed the door. "He can't go back to his adoptive parents."

Her tone changed from happy to stern and challenging. "Why?"

"They beat him with an electrical cord, one of the worst cases I have ever seen." The image from last night returned. My knees went weak, and I had to sit down on the toilet seat. She didn't say anything for a long moment. "How do we know Jonas didn't do it?"

"That's one reason why I'm calling. Jonas said that he did his research, and all three children were being abused by their adoptive parents."

"And you believe him?"

"Yes. He doesn't have any reason to lie. And with Eddie, the injuries are several days old, definitely before he was taken."

"Drop the child off, Bruno. Go to an ER somewhere, anywhere, go in and drop him off."

"Can you guarantee he won't go back to his adoptive parents?"

Silence. Of course she couldn't. In fact, she knew just like I did that, in all likelihood, Eddie would be placed back with the same abusive parents. That was the way social services worked. The judge would insist the father or mother, whoever had done the horrific abuse, attend a few weeks of therapy. Only a few weeks were never nearly enough to correct a sick mind, one who'd beat a helpless child bloody.

I had also put Barbara in an untenable situation. She couldn't tell anyone we had recovered Eddie, not without explaining how she had communicated with me, a wanted fugitive who was now thought to be complicit in the taking of all three children.

"What are you going to do with him?" she asked. Being so close to Mack, Barbara had to know about the children we took to South America.

"We're going to take care of him while we explore our options. What you can do is put a team on researching the background of the kids. Jonas says he knew about the abuse. He got the information somewhere, somehow. He didn't do the due diligence himself.

He's too memorable in his appearance. His partner in all this must have. You find the partner and you might get a good lead on the other two kids."

"Bruno, Jesus. Bruno, you can't save the world. You know that, don't you? You're going to have to leave something for the system to handle. I know it's broken, but there's going to come a point when you'll reach a maximum saturation level and sink to the bottom of the ocean, taking with you all those you're trying to help. You understand what I'm saying?"

I thought about her words while she remained silent. She was right. But how could I possibly walk away? Not without guilt that I could have done something positive when I had the chance.

After a long moment, she said, "I shouldn't tell you anything about what we have going on at this end, not after what you've done. You really stabbed me in the back here, Bruno. And I don't care so much about me, but you hurt John's feelings, and when you hurt John—well, don't do it again, don't put me in that position."

I waited for her to tell me what she was leading up to. How many times could I say I was sorry? "Barbara, you know if there was any other way—"

She ignored my entreaty. "We think we know who's helping Jonas."

I waited. Guilt wouldn't let me ask.

"It's Bella, Bruno, it's Bella Mabry. She's out on parole."

CHAPTER THIRTY-SIX

"No way, she can't be out," I said. "She got LWOP—Life Without the Possibility of Parole—for killing Betsy and Sally Mabry and for almost killing Jonas."

"She applied and received compassionate leave," Barbara said. "The California State Parole Board let her out."

"I'll ask it again, why?"

"She's dying of breast cancer."

I didn't like myself for thinking it, but she should have been left in prison to die. "Then she's the key to all of this. She's the catalyst that set off Jonas."

"That's what I figure. I separated from the FBI task force. They don't agree with me. They're still focusing on the kids. They think searching for Bella Mabry is senseless, without any productive value."

I gripped the phone tighter. "Why?"

"They have a report from the California State Parole that gives her state of health as grave, not likely to survive two weeks."

"They're fools."

"Yes, that's what I thought. I have all the personnel under my authority that I can divert looking for Bella."

"That hangs your career out a country mile. If the FBI succeeds and you don't—"

"Hang the career. At the end of the day I have to do what's right, or I can't look myself in the mirror."

I wanted to remind her that's exactly what I was doing but held my tongue.

"What you're doing's not the same," Barbara said. "You're not making the right choices."

She'd read my mind. I took a moment to reexamine the path I'd chosen and, with a refreshed thought process, I still came up with the same conclusion. "I know, and I'm sorry you feel that way."

Silence. Then she half-covered the phone and yelled, "Just a minute, John, I'll be right out."

"The reason I have John's phone is that he wants to throw in with you. He just doesn't know how to come down off his high horse to ask you. He won't beg."

"What I have planned, he doesn't want any part of."

"That's just it. He knows this is a renegade op you're planning, and he doesn't care. He's your friend and wants in. He doesn't want something to go wrong, something that, if he'd been a part of, he could have helped prevent. He wants in more than anything he's ever wanted. He's made the decision; he's willing to risk everything. He's really a bonehead for thinking this way. Don't let him, Bruno. If you care about him at all, if you care about me, don't you let him in."

"It's not only his career we're talking here, it's jail time," I said. "If this job goes bad, and it could very easily, it will be that other-side-of-forever kind of prison time."

Her voice caught. She was trying to stifle her tears. "He's aware of that, Bruno Johnson. He's not a fool. Don't you dare make him out to be a fool."

"I could never take on that kind of responsibility." A lump rose in my throat thinking about the sacrifice my friend, John, was prepared to make.

"Good," she said. "I knew that, I just had to hear it from you. You two are one and the same. That's why I have his phone without him knowing. That's why I was hoping you'd call." Her voice caught as she let her pent-up emotions go.

"Thanks for the information," I said. "I promise to keep

you posted on the money exchange with the children." I hung up.

I sat on the toilet, mulling, working and reworking the logistics. No scenario now worked, not with the added burden of Eddie's care and safety. Someone had to stay with him. We couldn't hire a babysitter. The risk the sitter would find his injuries and call the police was too great.

Marie knocked lightly on the door. "You okay in there?"

"Yeah, can you gimme a minute, please?"

"Let me in, Bruno. I want to talk it through with you." She'd been listening at the door.

No options remained, none at all. After fifteen minutes of internal debate, I hated to do it but had no choice. I flipped the phone open and hit redial on 'recent calls.'

"Bruno? Man, am I glad you called." John had his phone back.

"I need your help," I said.

John yelped. "Ouch. Come on, hon."

Barbara had socked him. She yelled, "I hate you, Bruno Johnson."

***

I set up the meet with John in two hours on Hospitality Lane in San Bernardino, about five miles from the Sons of Satan clubhouse. I closed the phone and fought the feeling that I had just betrayed two good friends. This caper had to work. I came out of the bathroom. Marie stood waiting. She saw my expression. She crossed her arms and shook her head. "Not gonna happen, Bruno. I'm not going back. I'm not leaving you here to do this thing by yourself, not without me, you're not."

"Hold on, babe. Wait, I agree with you."

She dropped her determined expression. "You do?"

"Sure, I have it all figured out."

"You do? What are we going to do with Eddie when you and I go into the Sons of Satan clubhouse?"

"It's not the best plan, but he's going to have to wait for us in the back of the van."

Her mouth dropped open. I held my hands wide and said, "What?"

She pulled back to sock me, caught herself, and looked over her shoulder at Eddie, who'd curled back up and slept the deep slumber of the despondent and the hopeless. She shoved me into the bathroom and closed the door. I held up my arms, a boxer covering for the incoming blows.

"Don't be silly," she said. "I'm not going to hit you, even though what you did out there was not my Bruno. That was the horse's-ass Bruno that you know I don't like."

I let my arms ease down and a tentative smile creep in. The smile took it one step too far.

"The hell I'm not," Marie said. She socked me hard in the stomach. With her small hands and delicate shoulders she didn't hurt me, couldn't hurt me if she wanted to, not physically. She knew it. I pulled her in and gently held her against my chest.

"I'm sorry," I said. "I love having you here, I do. But think about it, please think about it." She didn't move. Her chest rose and fell a little faster than mine, her warm breath on my chest. We stayed that way a long time.

I pulled away and gently kissed her neck and then nibbled her earlobe. Her arousal fueled mine. Her breathing came faster. I tugged at her shirt. With both hands she shoved me away, then pulled her top over her head. I came back in and kissed her like I had never kissed her before. Like a last kiss. She grabbed onto my head and held on tight. I never wanted to leave. I wanted to stay there for all eternity as we kissed deeper and deeper.

I pulled her bra straps off her shoulders. Then pulled the bra cups down. My hand came up and gently took hold of her breast, fondling her nipple. She broke the kiss and took in a huge breath. She again shoved me away and went for my pants button.

I helped her and shucked them as she pulled down hers. I picked her up and juggled her against the wall. As I penetrated her, we both gasped as we became one.

***

Afterward, both of us sweaty and spent, I set her on the sink and held her tenderly, my legs shaky from the exertion. My thoughts, like hers, couldn't stay in the moment any longer, and had to move on to planning, to getting on with it, to get it over and done with. We needed to—had to have this thing over. She whispered, "How will I get across the border?"

"The US doesn't care who goes south, and the Mexicans don't monitor that direction." She knew this; we'd crossed together nine months ago. She was scared having to do it again by herself and wanted reassurance. I didn't want her to go alone. But what other options did I have?

"So, I drive Eddie across and go down to Ensenada," she said.

"That's right, and you meet up with Larry Rupp, like before, and he'll make you the papers you need for Eddie."

"Then I wait for you there."

My head buried in her neck. I sniffed long and slow. Trying to memorize forevermore her beautiful scent, unique only to her. I shook my head "no." "You have to go on down to Costa Rica."

She shook her head. "I'm waiting for you in Ensenada, Bruno."

"Dad has cancer. He needs you."

"He can wait one more day. This is only going to take you one more day."

"No, Dad can't wait."

She read my tone, and pushed me back. "What happened?"

"Jake Donaldson came to the house with a gun and tried to shoot Dad because Jake's mad at me. Misplaced anger. He's not right in the head."

Her eyes went wild and she socked my shoulder. "And you didn't tell me?"

"I'm telling you now. You didn't need something else to worry about."

"The kids? Are the kids okay? Is your dad okay?"

"Yes, everything is fine. I had Ansel hire some folks, and they're watching the house. They're taking care of everything, but one of us needs to get back there."

"Is that asshole Donaldson in jail?"

I didn't want to tell her the details of the shooting; she'd find that out soon enough. "No, he got away."

She slipped off the sink and grabbed up her clothes, putting them on. "You're right. I need to get down there now, for the kids."

CHAPTER THIRTY-SEVEN

Marie took the van to a used car lot on Valley Boulevard, where she planned to park close by and walk up. She couldn't trade the van in; the beast had no value, or title, having been stolen.

I sat on the bed, dressed in the new clothes Marie had picked up while I slept, and returned Eddie's stare. "Can you talk?" I asked. "You going to say something soon?" He stared, his eyes big, gut-wrenching big, and filled with innocence. My own inadequacy hung thick in the air. I wanted in the worst way to do something for him now, not later. "You want to go on a trip?" He shook his head "no." "You wanna go on a trip with Marie?" Caution crept into his expression. He nodded "yes."

"Good man, so do I."

The knock at the door interrupted us. I opened the door a crack. A slice of sunlight cut across the room. I had one second to recognize Drago before he shoved his way into the room. "Wait, what are you doing?" I whispered. I didn't want him scaring Eddie. Drago scared *me,* and I'm not a traumatized little kid. "Hey, hey, I said you're gonna scare the kid." Eddie didn't cringe as I'd expected him to or crawl away. He sat unmoving, watching us.

"What? Scare this little guy?" Drago took two giant steps over and held up his fist. "Wus, up little bro?" Eddie didn't smile, but he held up his fist, and Drago knuckle bumped it with his. Drago said, "We're old pals. Aren't we, bro?" Drago held up his fist again, and Eddie tapped it again, his head tilted away in shyness.

I guess I had slept through a lot last night. Drago wore re-laxed denim pants with an obvious lump around his thigh from the bandage. A huge white and blue football jersey with the numbers "00" draped over his big belly. What else would have fit? The jersey, an improvement over all that pale white flesh with the disgusting tattoos, went a long way to mask his lack of sociability.

Drago stuck his nose in the air and sniffed. "I smell some-thing sweet."

Marie was right; Drago hadn't quite evolved from caveman knuckle-dragger to intellectual human. I picked up the bag on the floor and handed him some chocolate cakes and two chocolate milks.

He took them and sat on the bed, almost capsizing it. "Cool, man. Little Debbie cupcakes. Haven't had these in...in goin' on twelve years." He tore open the first one and shoved the whole thing in his mouth.

"You know, if you chew them a little, you might even be able to taste them," I said.

Drago stopped eating, and tearing open the next package, looked as if I'd slapped him. Eddie smiled, slid off the bed, and came over to me. He put his hand up and pulled down the goodie bag. He took out a Little Debbie cupcake, went back to his nest, and burrowed back in. Drago looked at Eddie then at me and smiled. He continued to munch as he opened the chocolate milk. He spoke around the now black load of mush in his cavernous mouth. "Hey, our job just got easier."

"What are you talking about now?"

"Talked to a bro of mine. He said the FBI has a pole camera pointed right at the front of the clubhouse. They're watchin' the SS, it's some kinda RICO investigation."

"Are you kidding me? How does that help us? It means the job's off. We can't go in with the FBI watching. And what are you doing calling friends and asking about the clubhouse? You tipped our hand."

Why had I not thought that the FBI would be watching the clubhouse? Of course they were. It's what I would've done had I wanted to use Drago as a staked goat.

"Man, you need to take a chill pill. Everything's cool, trust me."

I should never have lain down to sleep. In that short time the plan had gotten away from me. "Take a chill pill? Explain to me how you think this is going to go down with the Feds watching?"

Drago looked at Eddie. I stood there stunned that Drago had the sense to be concerned about the child in the room. More stunned that I hadn't seen the error before Drago had.

I nodded toward the bathroom. Drago struggled to his feet. The mattress righted itself but still had a huge dent where he'd been sitting. He took the goodie bag from me and led us the short distance into the bathroom. He filled the bathroom with his bulk, leaving little room for me. I had to shove in to get the door past me to close it. He took out a bag of Doritos Cool Ranch chips, tore them open, and dumped half in his mouth, spilling little shards down his front. I waited for the grinding machine to process the food before he could talk.

"I don't see how you think this is a bad thing," Drago said. "If the Feebies are watching the clubhouse, then the boys aren't going to pull any shit when we drive up." He stopped eating and sniffed the air, leaned over and sniffed me. He flashed a broad smile. "You two just don't give up, do you? Any chance you get, you just get after it, don't you? Man, I'm jealous."

I ignored that last part. "We? You're not going. You never were going." Originally, Marie and I were going to try and bluff our way in wearing the FBI insignia and yelling that we had a search warrant.

Drago opened his mouth wide, more bits of Doritos dropped onto his chest. "Whoa, there, my Negro cowboy. If Drago's not goin' in, then no one's goin' in."

"I'm confused here, my Aryan brother. How, in your pea brain, did you think you were goin' to make your Sons of Satan friends think you were an FBI agent?"

"They're not my friends."

But my question caught, made him think. I could see it in his eyes. "I could lay down in the backseat and—"

"And what, sneak in when no one's looking? No, the deal's cheesed, we're done."

Someone knocked on the bathroom door loud and high up. Not Eddie, for sure. I opened the door, expecting to see Marie.

John Mack had his hand in the air about to knock again.

CHAPTER THIRTY-EIGHT

Mack peeked around me at the hulk. "You two reliving a little bit of that prison love?"

I ventured out cautiously, half expecting to see a squad of cops behind Mack, ready to take down the federal fugitive who came back to kidnap more children and spark fear in every household in America. What was he doing here? How had he found us? He didn't know where we were. We were supposed to meet in two hours on Hospitality Lane.

"How did you find us?" I asked.

He slugged me in the stomach, hard. I bent over, choked and gasped and fought to keep down my Sno Balls and chocolate milk. Drago pushed by me, his big paws up, going for Mack's throat. Mack took several steps back, his legs parted in a strong horse stance, hands up, ready to take on the tsunami headed his way. No fear in his expression where there should have been one of impending doom. I rasped, "No, hold it. Don't."

They both froze, inches away from grappling. I coughed and choked. "Everyone take a breath and relax."

Mack leaned around Drago. "I owed you that one and you know it."

"That right?" Drago asked. "He owe you that?" I nodded.

"Karl Drago, meet Los Angeles County Sheriff's Detective John Mack."

Drago didn't hold out his hand. His eyes narrowed. "A cop?

A county cop? Are you kiddin' me? I hate cops. I mean, I really hate cops."

"He's a friend."

"No cop's a friend of mine."

I waddled over to the bed, cradling my stomach, and sat down. Eddie continued to eat his Little Debbie cupcakes as if he always watched adults play their stupid games.

"Where's Marie?" asked Mack.

"How did you get here?" I asked.

"Drove."

"Don't be a smart-ass, how did you find me?"

Mack didn't need to answer. In an instant, my mind had tracked backward until I came across what happened and realized I had probably subconsciously done it on purpose. I had called John with a burner phone and got Barbara. I didn't pull the battery or destroy the phone after the call. They had pinged me and got the coordinates. He came to the motel as a sign; he wanted to show me he could be trusted.

He shrugged and smiled.

"I'm sorry, John, the deal's off. We can't make a play on the Sons of Satan clubhouse."

The smile disappeared. "Why not? The SS clubhouse? Man, that's somethin', really somethin'. They have that kind of money in there?"

Drago came over and again sat on the other bed, compressing his end almost to the floor. "Bullshit, we go or I go by myself, but it's going to get done, believe me. It's going to get done."

"Watch your language," Mack said.

Any other time those words would have ended in a fight, but Drago looked at Eddie and nodded.

"Drago here tells me there's now a pole camera on the clubhouse, and the FBI's monitoring it."

"So?" Mack said.

Drago wanted his money enough to side with a county cop.

"Yeah, I'm with the dipshit. So?" Drago must've thought Mack a dirty cop and that Mack wanted in for a piece of the pie.

"I'm not going to tell you again about your language," said Mack.

"You're both a couple of fools," I said. "The plan was to pull up to the front of the clubhouse dressed in FBI windbreakers and use subterfuge to get in. How can we do that if the FBI's watching the place?"

Eddie didn't need to hear any more language that Drago couldn't control. "We're not going to talk about it now," I said. "We'll talk about it later. But I'm telling you, there isn't a scenario that's going to work, not under these conditions, not with these narrow parameters and the amount of prison time at risk."

Mack came over close to the bed I sat on with Eddie. He nodded. "Hey, kid, you got any more of those?"

Eddie held out the bag. Mack stuck his hand in and came out with another package of Sno Balls and the last carton of chocolate milk. "Thanks, kid, you're all right. You Eddie Crane?"

Eddie looked at me. I nodded, then Eddie nodded. I said, "Eddie isn't talking right now because he doesn't have anything to say. When he has something to say, he'll let us know. Right, Eddie?"

Eddie nodded and took another bite of his Little Debbie.

Mack opened his Sno Balls and shoved half of one into his mouth. He opened the chocolate milk and slurped some of it down. "Okay," he said, "I think this thing will still work."

This wasn't going to end easily. "Hold on," I said, "you two come with me." Mack and Drago followed me over to the bathroom. Drago and I went in. No room remained for Mack, and he stood at the threshold, his back to the room. I said, "Okay, go."

"What is this, the cone of silence or something?" asked Mack.

"The kid, you idgit," said Drago.

"Don't call me an idgit. And you're the one who can't control his pie hole."

"Children, play nice," I said. "What were you going to say, Mack?"

Mack took a drink of chocolate milk as he looked over the top of the carton, past me, at Drago. He swallowed and said, "FBI's spread too thin to be involved in the surveillance of the clubhouse. San Bernardino County Sheriff's Criminal Intelligence Unit is doing it for them in a joint operation."

"It doesn't matter; it's still being watched by cops."

"Look," Mack said, "It's not FBI, and that's all that matters. We...I go to the Sheriff's Criminal Intel guys and tell them we're going to do a 'knock and talk' as a ruse to get in to see who's inside. We tell them we have an informant who is going to lead us directly to some evidence that we've been looking for and haven't been able to find until now. And, that we took Lex Luthor here out of custody just for the ride over, and to do the knock and talk. Then he's going back to prison where he belongs."

"I done my time," Drago said. "I'm out free and clear."

"You're on parole, asshole."

"I'm an asshole?"

I held up my hands between them. "Stop it, right now." I thought about it for a minute. "That's no good."

"Damn straight, that's no good," Drago said. "You're not goin' in there without me."

"Dipshit, with my plan, you are going in."

"Huh?"

Mack raised his voice. "According to Bruno, you were never going in in the first place, fat boy. But this new way, you're going in, but you'll be handcuffed like our prisoner."

I shoved one man in the chest, then the other, to keep them separated. Who was I kidding? If Drago wanted to go through me, he needed only to raise up his size sixteen shoe and squash me like a bug. "It won't work, Mack, because you're putting yourself up front," I said. "When this thing goes down and they investigate, you're done. You'll be prosecuted. You'll lose your job and go to the joint."

Mack smiled. "For what?"

"Yeah, wait a minute, he's right, for what?" Drago said. "You think the SS are going to complain to the cops that someone snuck into their clubhouse and took a million in gold? Hell, we do it right, they won't even know what we took."

"A million in gold?" asked Mack.

"Forget about the gold, asshole, you're not getting an ounce, not even a gram," said Drago.

I'd told Mack on the phone that we were going in to get the money to pay the ransom, and didn't get into the long, drawn-out story of how the money had transformed from paper to mineral. "Okay," I said, "what about collusion, and aiding and abetting a known fugitive? I'll be on that surveillance tape with you."

"Not if you wear sunglasses and a baseball cap pulled down low. And if we get in and get out without causing a big scene, then no one on our side of the fence is even going to tumble to what happened and look closely at the tape."

"You don't think someone will recognize me on the video?" I asked.

Drago smirked. "I don't think so. You guys all look—"

I spun and stuck my finger right in his face. "Don't. Don't you even think about saying it."

CHAPTER THIRTY-NINE

Marie used the cash I'd given her for a nice little Honda Civic, dark blue with a sunroof. She pulled up right in front of the motel room door, sideways, taking up three spots, not intending on staying long. Once any plan was decided and in place, she went after the elements, one at a time, with the determination of a bulldog to complete the task at hand.

She came in and saw John. She smiled and jumped in his arms. He hugged her. "Hey, kid, how's it going?"

She took a step back to get a better look at him. "You look great. Wait just a minute. Your smile, the way you're standing all comfortable in your skin—you have a girlfriend, don't you?"

Both of our mouths dropped open. Mack looked to me. "You told her, didn't you?"

"I haven't had the time."

"That's kinda scary," said Mack.

I nodded. "You're tellin' me. I have to live with her." She laughed and gave me a playful sock.

"Who is she, and how long have you been going out?" asked Marie.

"About nine months or so now. Great gal." I had never seen Mack smile so hugely.

"I should've seen it coming," I said. "It's Barbara Wicks."

Marie laughed and hugged him again. "That's great, you deserve a good woman." Her expression turned solemn. "I'm glad you're here to help, but I'm worried you're going to get all caught up in this thing, especially if it goes bad."

John turned sheepish. "Naw, not with Bruno runnin' the op. And even if it does, I always wanted to see Costa Rica."

Marie gave a weakly motivated smile and then turned serious as she went into a flurry, grabbing things and shoving them into a cheap, rolling travel bag. I caught a glimpse of tears filling her eyes, and it hurt in the pit of my stomach. I wanted to tear off Jonas Mabry's head for putting us in this situation. All of us watched her, not knowing what to do. We were all men, and men couldn't comprehend or say the right things in moments like these.

She sniffled, wiped at her eyes. "Come on, Eddie, you ready to go on a trip?" He nodded. She took him by the hand and, with her other, grasped the handle to the roller bag.

"Let me put that in the car," said Mack. He grabbed the bag and went out.

Drago took the same cue and said, "I need to use the can." He went in the bathroom and closed the door.

I took Marie in my arms, buried my face in her neck, and said, "You be careful now, you hear?"

"Me? Bruno, I'm scared to death for you and what you're going to try and do."

"There's no trying about it, babe, I'm going to do it and be back home in twenty-four hours. You wait and see." I was trying for cocksure gangster, but it came out shaky and weak.

"You be careful."

"This is a piece of cake compared to those train heists I did for Jumbo." I spoke before thinking. Bad move with a hot-blooded Puerto Rican woman.

She pulled away from me. "Yeah, and if you'd told me what you were doing at the time, I'd have kicked your ass then."

I nodded to her and Eddie, who stood close, his hand still in hers.

"Sorry, Eddie, I promise to watch the language and to do better."

When she looked back at me, I kissed her again, long and deep. She broke our clinch with a sob. She pulled away and fled through the door. I couldn't watch her leave. The car started and pulled away from the motel.

***

Criminal Intelligence worked from a mobile trailer parked at the back of HQ, and I dropped Mack off at the gate. He walked the rest of the way in.

Drago and I waited in the maroon Crown Victoria on Third Street, just down from San Bernardino County Sheriff's Department Headquarters, waiting for Mack to return. I sat behind the wheel, Drago in the backseat, taking up the entire backseat sitting crossways, his back to the door, his feet touching the other. The car listed to one side.

My foot tapped incessantly with nervous energy from being so close to a hive of law enforcement officers, all of whom would be eager to take me down. Ugly thoughts wouldn't go away. The potential consequences for what we were about to do swirled in my head. This didn't feel like any other plan from my past life, first as a cop on the Violent Crimes Team, and then as a criminal committing thefts and taking children from abusive, toxic homes as I prepared to flee the country. This caper created a stronger feeling of foreboding and, strange as it sounded, left a metallic taste in my mouth.

All of a sudden I figured out what was missing. How simple. I lacked self-confidence, the most important element in any successful plan. Apparently, what I really needed was a porch, a rocking chair, and an afghan to cover my legs. The thought made me smile. Robby Wicks used to say, "Stay on the porch if you can't run with the big dogs." I should be fine, because I had the biggest dog I could find sitting in the backseat. Only I didn't have a choke chain to control him. Drago was truly the wild card in this operation.

"Hey, Dog," said Drago, "turn the radio to 620 AM, they're owned by the SS, and they're covering the Toys for Tots Run live."

I didn't need the noise and aggravation but tuned in anyway. Knowing what your opponent was doing was always a good thing. The announcer said, "A group of two hundred and fifty Sons of Satan are revving up their bikes as the long procession starts out the gate of Glen Helen Regional Park en route to the Los Angeles Convention Center. These humanitarians on two wheels will collect and secure plenty of toys today to ensure a happy Christmas for thousands of kids."

Down the street, Mack popped out of the gate at the back of the sheriff's headquarters and loped toward us. His running could draw undue attention. I looked around to see if anyone saw him. He made it to the car, came to the driver's door, and opened it. He waited for me to move over. I did and he got in. "Okay, we're live. Everything's set."

"Any activity at the clubhouse?" I asked.

"Nothing. Two hours ago at six thirty, the president, Clay Warfield, and the sergeant at arms, Sandman Colson, mounted up with a hundred and twelve other assholes and took off on their Harleys."

"The Sandman's out of prison?" asked Drago.

For the first time since I'd met Karl Drago, I detected a hint of fear in his tone. Faint, but there.

Mack looked in the rearview at Drago. "Yeah, why?"

"That guy's a stone-cold angel of death. He'll kill ya, cut your liver out, and grill it on the barbeque while he swills a beer. He'll do it like it was an everyday thing, casual like."

"You talk as if you've seen him do it," Mack said.

Drago shuddered. "Ruined me on beef liver, and I used to love liver with onions. My moms really knew how to cook it." We both stared at him.

"Then I guess it's a good thing old Sandman's out shagging toys for the tots," I said. Drago glared at me.

I turned back to Mack. "Does Intel have a count on how many are left?

"Two prospects, that's all." Mack smiled.

"Excellent, let's get this done."

CHAPTER FORTY

On the way to the sheriff's headquarters, we stopped off at Little Mountain Foreign Auto Repair. Drago knew the owner, Martin Hyde, and we picked up tools he needed to break into the safe. Odd, how the garage had specialty tools to crack a safe. The tools had been left out back by a dumpster, packed in two heavy canvas duffels. Drago had been planning this a long time, and had his prior contacts like Hyde all lined up.

With Drago in the backseat, and all the tools in the trunk, the Crown Vic sank dangerously low over the back tires, and made the front end rise higher than normal.

Mack pulled over to the curb. "Tell me one more time why we have to crack the safe if the gold is sitting underneath it?"

"Hey, we don't have time, we have to keep moving," I said.

Mack gave a look that said he was taking control of the caper, and that he needed all the information before we stuck his neck way out on the chopping block. Least that was the way I read him.

I turned to Drago. "Tell him, but the *Reader's Digest* version."

Drago used both hands to talk. "Look, it's simple. In theory, if you don't anchor a safe, the street urchins could simply come in and haul the whole thing off. Then they could open it at their leisure somewhere safe and where they'd have more time. So, when I helped put the safe in, we put four, three-quarter-inch bolts, preset in concrete where the safe was going to sit. We drilled four holes in the bottom of the safe so that these bolts could come up through the floor of the safe. Then we screwed them down with nuts."

"Okay, now I can visualize it," said Mack.

Drago went on anyway. "I told the old president that there was a gap under the safe that a thief with small hands could reach under and hacksaw the bolts."

Mack snapped his fingers. "So you told him you needed a washer to cover the bolts, hence the gold doughnut painted to look like lead."

"Give the dumbshit a prize," said Drago. "Now he's got it."

"Hey, take it easy, big man. When Bruno described it, he didn't go into details."

Mack pulled away from the curb and headed down the street.

"Now children, play nice," I said.

In too little time we made the last right turn onto the street to the clubhouse, still fifty yards down on the north side. For five decades the clubhouse had been a gathering place for the socially inept, the socially outcast, the brutal who practiced mayhem, and human corruption of the first order. Ironically, located just two blocks from a hospital.

For the tenth time, I tugged and pulled and adjusted the LA Dodgers cap down low over my eyes and checked the rearview mirror to see how the disguise fared. The hat and the sunglasses covered the distinguishable parts of my face. Maybe Mack was right, this *was* going to work. I had the Glock in a pancake holster out in plain view like an FBI agent would, and wore the navy blue windbreaker with "FBI" across the back. I was as ready as I would ever be.

Mack wore the tactical vest with the FBI letters. He again pulled over to the curb in front of a house. At the rate we were going, we were never going to get there.

"Put the cuffs on him," Mack said. "We have to make this look real."

Drago put his catcher's mitts up on the top edge of the back-seat. I tried to put the cuffs on, but his wrists were too thick for the cuffs to ratchet closed. "Hold them like this, so it looks like you're cuffed," I said.

"It's better this way," he said. "I don't wanna be cuffed, not now, not while walking into this greasy snake pit full of those back-stabbing assholes. Hey, gimme a gun, would ya?"

"Are you outta your mind," asked Mack. "Because we aren't outta ours. You forget, we're the sane ones."

"You might want to rethink that position," I said. "With what we're about to do, I'm no longer entirely sure that's true."

While I spoke, I slipped Drago the dirk I'd taken off Jonas. He nodded just enough for me to notice. The razor-sharp, doubled-edged knife disappeared, hidden somewhere in his bulk. I had the derringer I'd taken from him shoved down in my crotch. Physically uncomfortable, but it created a modicum of solace, no matter how meager. The discomfort was a constant reminder. Whenever I made the slightest move, the vest gun snagged and pinched delicate skin.

Mack grunted at me and took his foot off the brake. "Here we go." He drove the last few yards to our destination. "Look at it this way, we get into trouble, all we have to do is get out to the front yard and wave to the cops. They'll send in backup."

He'd read my mind. "Yeah, and then what?" I asked. "It'll take them five, ten minutes to get here. It only takes a second to pull a trigger, and about two minutes to beat a man to death."

"Nice talk," Mack said. "Don't jinx us."

"Hey, look, the gate's open," Drago said. "Those prospects'll get their asses kicked up between their shoulders, Clay finds out."

Mack pulled through an eight-foot, wrought-iron fence with spear-shaped, pointed tops, and right into the Sons of Satan clubhouse yard. The bikers didn't need a fence of any sort. No crook in his right mind would even think about pulling a burglary where he might end up in prison with a bunch of SSs already doing time for murder. Loyal and dedicated SSs with nothing else to lose.

The clubhouse was exactly that, a large single-story house

built at least fifty years ago, with painted gray stucco and a tar composition roof. All the wooden window frames were neatly painted with a contrasting white, and the glass panes covered in foil on the inside. The front exterior was immaculate and could have passed as a parking lot for a popular urban dentist. The shrubs were trimmed and the small patch of green grass was mowed to perfection. The SS kept a flagpole with a Sons of Satan flag on top and the American flag underneath, a violation of flag protocol, a subtle statement of biker values. To the side of the front door hung a huge Sons of Satan winged 'death head' plaque carved in hardwood with a high-gloss varnish. The death head, a perfect omen.

Mack pulled right up to the front of the clubhouse and parked. We got out. I expected something more, anything really, than the vacant parking lot. No one rushed out brandishing weapons to tell us to get the hell off the property. Mack turned and looked across the parking lot, through the bars of the eight-foot fence, and down the street as he tried to pick out the utility pole camera to let the sheriff's Intel boys see him, let them know we had arrived.

Drago, bold and without shame, walked toward the front door as if he belonged there. Maybe he did. The door swung open. Two shaved-head white males with fresh enflamed tattoos on exposed arms stood ready to repel any and all comers. The tattoos in black and red and white ink depicted Harley Davidson motorcycles and the Grim Reaper, various handguns and shotguns, and women with large naked breasts. This was more what I had expected. Both wore denim vests and black Dickie pants, a kind of uniform. Both looked close to the same age, about twenty-eight or thirty, their domes tatted. They displayed no emotion.

Mack caught up to Drago and whispered, "Stay with *us* asshole, you're not the leader here. You'll blow this whole deal."

I caught up and passed Drago and Mack on the front walk to the door. "FBI, we have a search warrant for the premises and we demand entry."

The two prospects looked at each other and then back at us. They didn't move and continued to stand shoulder-to-shoulder, blocking the door's entrance. The taller one with a smaller head said, "No one's comin' in here. I don't give a shit if you got CIA, the Secret Service, and the whole fucking army behind you. Which you don't. So you're not comin' in. So you can turn your ugly asses around and get the hell outta here."

From behind me, Drago chuckled. "These boys are prospects. If they let us in without having their asses kicked and stomped into the ground, when Sandman Colson gets back, he'll do it worse. Isn't that right, boys? And maybe Sandman will even lose it like Sandman tends to do. Then these here boys, their ugly corpses will be put in the back of a DeFrank's Plumbing truck, taken out to the Mojave, and shoved six feet under blow sand, Joshua trees, and jumpin' cholla. Am I right, boys?"

Drago had too much information on how this all worked.

The two prospects didn't look at one another. The shorter one said, "I don't give a shit what you say, you're not comin' in here."

The camera trained on the back of my neck made the hair stand and ripple. What were we going to do? The ruse was set up as a "knock and talk," a consensual contact with a consensual search, that's what Mack had told the sheriff's detectives. If we went western on these two, the detectives would roll in the backup. Ten cop cars with lights and sirens. We wouldn't know if the backup was called until they arrived on scene, and then it'd be too late to run. Back to prison forever. Sweat beaded my forehead.

Drago, with his mass, stepped around me, effectively blocking the view to the doorway by the sheriff's camera, big enough to block out the sun. "You boys think these guys are cops. They're not. They're with me."

I stepped to one side to see if his words had any effect. Neither said anything, neither moved, their expressions void of any emotion. I would've been hard pressed to hold my urine had Drago walked up cold to my house and wanted in.

"Do you know who I am?" asked Drago.

Again, no response.

"In the joint, they call me 'Meat.'"

The taller one's eyes twitched. "I heard of a dude named Meat. He's in the joint doin' life. Warfield tells us about him all the time, says we go to the joint, and we see this Meat dude, our 'prime directive' is to take him out any way possible. And if we don't, we get taken out."

"Prime directive?" Drago said. "You two hard-ons don't even know what that means, do ya? Clay tell ya what I look like?"

Neither answered.

Drago lifted his football jersey, exposing the tattoo Aryan Brotherhood Forever, with the battle axe dripping blood underneath. He rolled his belly fat. The axe made a small chopping motion. Both their mouths dropped open.

"And now watch this," said Drago. He shucked off the handcuffs and dropped them to the ground. Drago acted, pushing the edge he'd created, and took one giant step. He moved right up on them, took a throat in each hand, lifted, and walked into the clubhouse. The two biker prospects gasped and choked.

We'd made it inside easy enough. Now the trick would be getting what we came for and getting the hell out.

CHAPTER FORTY-ONE

The two prospects clutched at Drago's wrists as their toes left the ground.

Mack closed the door behind us. Drago heaved and the boys tumbled to the floor and scrambled about, trying to recover.

"That's good, boys," said Drago. "Just do what Uncle Meat tells you, and you might be able to keep your balls where they grew and not shoved down your throats."

The immaculate outside of the club, the false front for public consumption, did not match the inside. The place smelled of urine and beer, body odor, and thick, solidified cooking grease. Beer bottles littered the large open room that held five couches, facing each other like wagons circled to fight off Indians. There was nothing stylish about it.

Just like Drago's motel room, take-out from many different restaurants cluttered the floor, and had been waded through, stomped, and kicked about willy-nilly. A huge plasma screen television filled nearly one entire wall. One corner hung cocked lower and had been smashed in from a thrown bottle or a head rammed into it. It still worked. A show about an outlaw motorcycle gang, *Sons of Anarchy*, played silently, except where a cone of darkness from the damaged corner gradually shifted into color, moving upward where the show appeared around damage.

The boys tried to stand. Drago kicked at them. "Stay down there."

They stopped squirming. Drago pointed to the TV. "You

punks getting in a little training film, are ya?" He kicked one in the side. "What's your name, punk?"

The prospect didn't act intimidated. He was probably used to this sort of treatment. "They call me Slim Jim."

"What about your butt-buddy?"

The other one said, "My name is—"

Drago kicked at him, "I'm not talking to you, asshole." Drago looked at Slim Jim. "Well?"

"Roy Boy, they call him Roy Boy."

"Roy Boy, you go with this man," said Drago. He pointed to me. "Help him bring in some tools from the car. Don't do anything stupid, you understand?"

Roy Boy nodded as he got up.

I wasn't sure I liked the idea of Drago calling the shots, but, for the moment, I'd go along. He was getting things moving and we really needed things moving.

I spun Roy Boy around and patted him down. Clean, nothing on him.

"Huh," said Drago. "You, stand up." Drago searched Slim Jim. The same, nothing. "What? You boys haven't made your bones yet, so you can't pack, is that it?"

Neither spoke. Roy Boy looked at Slim Jim, but Slim Jim didn't look back at him.

I nudged Roy Boy and we went outside. Mack stood at the front door and hit the trunk release from the key fob. I let Roy Boy carry the two heavy canvas bags, a burden he could barely handle alone. I followed, scooped up Drago's cuffs, and closed the front door behind us. Oddly, I felt safer inside the lair than outside under the eyes of the cops who had the ability to put me in a concrete block for the rest of my life.

The false sense of security gave me pause. I thought about Marie and Eddie, who would just be crossing the border. In another hour she'd be in Ensenada.

I put one cuff on Slim Jim and the other on Roy Boy. While we were outside, Drago had found the fridge and had already guzzled half a 40-ounce Olde English beer. He picked up the canvas bags with one hand without relinquishing his hold on the forty. He kicked Slim Jim in the ass. The momentum jerked them both. "Let's go."

Slim Jim scowled. "Where to?"

"You know where, asshole. The president's office, where else?"

Mack remained by the window the entire time, watching the front through a crack in the curtains and a wedge he'd scraped out of the foil.

"You got this?" I asked Mack. He pulled a San Bernardino sheriff's radio he had clipped to his back pocket and set it on the window sill. I hadn't seen him with it before, and I too should've thought of the tactic to monitor the surveillance activity. He kept his eyes on the window and tossed a wave over his shoulder. He realized that if a threat came, it would come from the front: a biker rolling in, a patrol car responding to a call; he'd see it first from where he stood.

"Hey," I said.

He took his eyes off the crack in the curtain.

"I'm glad you're here."

He smiled. "Me too. Why don't you get in there in case your fat buddy goes psycho and kills one or both of those prospects! We don't need a murder rap during the course of a robbery."

I nodded and followed down the hall. Murder during the course of a felony made the suspect eligible for the death penalty. I had forgotten that Mack still thought differently than I did. I didn't want Drago to kill anyone, and would fight him to the death to keep it from happening, but I had already made my peace with the possible consequences. I had to, or I couldn't operate otherwise, at least not in a cogent, effective manner.

I found the two bikers in the large room that didn't match the living room area. This one contained a nice maple desk and an expensive Asian area rug. A Remington bronze of a cowboy riding a bronc sat on the desk. Overhead, a Tiffany lamp hung from the ceiling. The room had been professionally decorated with a generous budget, money obtained through tyranny, extortion, pain, and blood. Tongue-and-groove knotty pine panels covered the walls, where pictures hung depicting Clay Warfield with public figures at dinners, charity events, and political rallies. The face, the figurehead, the leader of the SS International organization.

We were kicking a sleeping giant.

CHAPTER FORTY-TWO

I have little or no knowledge about safes. This one took up one corner of the room. A real monster, olive green with a double door. Older looking, with twin dials. A beautiful mural on the front depicted a stagecoach with a team of black horses at a full run fleeing masked gunmen on wild-eyed steeds.

Drago set both bags down by the safe.

"Is it the same safe?" I asked. "Is it in the same position as you remember?"

He looked at me as if he had not thought of that, took a step back, and reexamined the safe. He scratched his dome. He walked back to the door where we entered, turned, raised his hands, spread them wide, looking through them gauging the space, the same as a director of a movie. He carefully paced off the distance back to the safe. "Shit. I can't tell for sure if it's in the same place or not, but it is for damn sure the same safe. I'm absolutely sure of that."

"You can't tell for sure if it's in the same location? You're kidding, right?"

"Well, you asked me. I'm here to tell ya, I'm not sure. And come on, man, it was a long time ago. It does seem to me that the safe's in the right place. But maybe...I don't know, maybe it should be another two or three feet farther that way. That wall seems closer for some reason. But man, that can't be right." He scratched his head. "Since I got out, I've been goin' a little crazy. I notice things from before, that in my head I remember different from this time around. I was in a small concrete cell for twenty-five years and everything to me feels bigger now, huge even. That concrete box really fucked with my perspective, man."

Drago came back and shoved the solid maple desk out of the way as if it were constructed of balsa wood. His mood changed back to all business. "You watch these two assholes close, I'm serious." He looked at the safe, appraising it, then down at the bags we'd brought in. "I'm not gonna need all these tools like I thought. This isn't the model I thought it was. They call this one the butter model, cuts like butter."

He opened the bag, took out a sledgehammer, raised it high and came down on the first dial. The dial broke off and skittered away.

Slim Jim said, "You're insane—that's Clay's safe. You just committed suicide assh—"

Drago spun around, the hammer of Thor raised high overhead, ready to strike.

I stepped in front of the two idiot prospects to keep their mouths from killing them.

Drago's eyes cooled. "Sit them down over there and tell 'em to keep their mouths shut, or I'll cave in their little pea brains." He did not bluster. I had no doubt he'd do it.

By the way Drago talked and acted, he didn't like bikers much. I hoped that's what was causing his overreaction to the situation, and not that he realized the safe might have been moved. Had the safe been moved even two or three feet, the doughnut, in all likelihood, would not have been used in the reinstallation, as it had not been needed in the first one to begin with.

Drago swung the big sledge in one fluid movement and knocked off the other dial. He went back into the duffel and came out with a unique device, an aluminum rack or frame attached to a huge drill. He looked back to check on me. "Hey, I'm tellin' ya, don't watch me, watch those two assholes. They'll go on you, you give 'em half a chance. They have to. Like I said, they get their asses kicked now by us, or by the gang when they catch up to them. It'll happen as soon as those two ass-wipes grow a pair of balls."

Of course, he was right. I understood the primitive and archaic mentality. I just had difficulty comprehending anyone still employing it. I sat on the edge of the desk, facing the two biker wannabes who sat on the floor with their backs to the wall. They kept their eyes on me as the drill's rpms whined and the bit cut into steel.

Their eyes filled with anger and, in some small way, smothered any hope I had for humanity.

Time did not play fair. It slowed to a pace akin to soldiers, exhausted, slogging along in two feet of sludge, mired in endless miles of mud.

The pitch of the drill changed as the bit broke through. The whine stopped. The lack of noise filled the room with an eerie silent echo. I fought the urge to watch what move Drago did next and asked, "How long?"

"I don't know."

My head jerked around all on its own. "What do you mean you don't know? Haven't you done this before?"

He smiled. "Hell, no, I'm a stickup guy, not some crotchety old yegg or cheesy little sneak thief who prowls the night afraid of his own shadow. I hate sneak thieves, hate 'em with a vengeance."

"Why didn't you tell me you never broke into a safe?"

"Cracking a safe. They call it cracking a safe, or peeling a safe, depending on which method you use."

"How do you—"

"Chill, man. I had twenty-five years to study up on it. Enough time to earn eight college degrees in the subject. I got this. You'd better pay attention to your shit."

I turned back just as Slim Jim and Roy Boy shot up from the floor in a unified attack. I buried my head in my arms and elbows. Their two cuffed hands grabbed my shoulders beside my neck. They'd been going for my throat and missed as I reacted. With their free hands, they pummeled me on both sides with rock-hard fists of youth. The blows rained down on my forehead and ears and neck with a burst of pain and bright lights. I expected a lion's roar as Drago counterattacked. Surely, any second, Drago would dispatch them with his hammer. Smash and crush their bodies. Fling them up against the wall like so much human garbage.

But the counterattack didn't come. The whine of drill started again. He'd warned me, and now I had to take care of my own error. Another biker mantra, "Take care of your own shit."

The blows continued to fall. I turned numb.

While on the street as a deputy working South Central Los Angeles, I had been jumped twice, once by four suspects and another by five. Four and five were better than two to fight any day. With more in the mix, they got in the way of themselves and even struck one another. Back then I had covered up and picked my shots, making them count, meting out all takedown shots. When two of their cohorts went down hard, the momentum of the gang broke and they had fled.

Now in Clay's office there were only two, who were younger and more motivated. I had to make a sacrifice. I opened up my right side in order to take a shot with my best stroke, a right uppercut. I made my move. Roy Boy came in with knuckles to my temple on the weak side that shook me to my heels and made the lights in the room flicker. My uppercut was already on the way, a short violent stroke that I put in everything I had left. My fist connected with the bottom of Slim Jim's jaw. His head snapped back. His broken jawbone radiated through my wrist and up my arm. He went down as though I'd switched off a light. His cuffed hand pulled Roy Boy off balance just enough. I came around with a left hook, the diversion, and followed it up with the heat, a right roundhouse that caught him flat on the nose. He went down on top of Slim Jim.

Mack heard the ruckus and burst into the room just as it ended. He came over and propped me up. My knees wouldn't cooperate, not entirely, and I had to sit on the edge of the desk. Mack asked Drago, "Hey, asshole, how come you didn't help out over here?"

The drill whine went on for another long minute, or maybe

it was two, as we both waited for his answer. A thudding pain bleated in my eyesight.

Drago shut off the drill and pulled down his goggles. "I warned him twice about these turds. I don't have the time to do both his job and mine."

My injuries settled down to a constant throb. My head rang with several bell tones, and I tasted a metallic wetness in my mouth. "He's right," I said, "this was all on me."

"Oh no, it's not," said Mack. "We're a team here."

Drago scowled, turned back, went into his bag, and came out with a small flashlight he put in his mouth and a long thin piece of metal. He leaned over the holes he'd drilled and probed with the thin shiv, first in one hole, then in the other. "This was much easier than I thought it would be."

Mack patted my back. "You okay?"

"Yeah, sure. I just had my bell rung, that's all. I'm too old for this shit."

"Yes," said Drago. He dropped his tools and took hold of the two handles. He hesitated and then turned them. The handles moved. A loud clack sounded as the doors swung open.

The large safe was empty. Absolutely and conspicuously empty.

"Shit, we've been had," Drago said.

"What are you talking about?" asked Mack.

"Son of a bitch, who's watching the front?" Drago ran for the office door as he yelled, "That safe should be filled with guns and ledgers and computer disks." He made it out the door into the hall with Mack and me close on his heels. Drago said over his shoulder, "They cleared it out for a reason. And there's only one reason it can be."

In the big open room, the front door burst open. Three Sons of Satan came right at us with M16 rifles leveled at our bellies. They yelled, "Get on the ground. Get on the ground now."

I eased to the ground amongst all the debris, trying to take it all in, trying to understand how we had screwed up, how we could possibly get out of this mess.

The fat bikers with guns jumped in close and kicked us. I was slammed down against the crusty rug. Pain radiated up and down my leg from a kick to my hip.

Out the front door, a van had backed up right to the house entrance. The double doors to the van stood open. Two more men stepped down out of the van and into the house. I recognized one from the photos I'd seen. Clay Warfield, the president of the Sons of Satan International. He'd aged and his shoulders had slumped slightly, but he was easy to recognize. He still possessed that crazed look in his eyes, a fire that wouldn't extinguish until someone cut off his head and buried it ten feet from his body.

CHAPTER FORTY-THREE

Drago held his fists up chest high, ready to take on the M16s with muscle, bare knuckles, and pure, insane stupidity. Two bikers covered Mack and me on the floor with their guns, as the third moved in closer. "Get on the floor, fat man, or I'll open you up like a tomato soup can."

"Come on, Drago, do what he says," I said. "They got us cold."

"Do it, fat man. Do it right now."

"Drago," I said, "come on, what good's it gonna to do if you get yourself shot." My words didn't penetrate his anger. I could see that at any second he'd pull his internal trigger and go on them, take his best and final shot.

"Hey, Meat, do what he says, get on the floor," said Clay Warfield. "We're just going to talk here."

"Let 'em shoot, the cops'll come runnin'," Drago said. "The cops are watchin' the clubhouse. You want the cops all up in your shit, Clay? I don't think so."

Clay broke into a smile. "Looks like we're in what you'd call a white trash stand-off." The smile intensified the crazy in his eyes. "What'd you do with Roy Boy and Slim Jim? You put 'em down?" He said it casually, as if their deaths had been expected and the prospects meant nothing to him.

Clay turned to a quiet biker dressed in chinos and a long-sleeve blue shirt. "Sandman, check it out."

The Sandman walked by us and down the hall to the office. He stuck his head in and came back. "They've been spanked but they're still breathin'. The safe's open. Dipshit here ruined it, just like you thought he would. I liked that safe. A damn fine antique, and he drilled two huge holes in it."

I got up and brushed off my hands. "You want to talk, let's talk." One biker jabbed the barrel of his rifle into my gut, a fool's move. I could've taken it from him. But then we all would have died. He yelled, "Get back down."

Clay held up his hand to stop him. Mack got up and peeled off a cheeseburger wrapper from Bakers stuck to his leg and let the trash drop back to the floor.

"Get their guns and pat them down," said Clay.

This time the biker played it smart and handed his rifle to a partner. He put us up against the wall, relieved us of our pistols, and patted us down. He took the sheriff's radio, looked it over, and tossed it into the debris on the floor.

Drago had not changed his posture. "We got nothin' to talk about. And you tell your man to keep his dick-beaters off me or we're gonna have a problem."

"Sure we do, Meat, we have a lot to talk about. Tell me true, do you have a gun on you?"

"Don't call me Meat." He lifted up his football jersey and did a slow turn. The maneuver had a dual purpose. Showed Clay's foot soldiers his tattoos, showed them exactly who they were messing with. Drago sneered at them. "You can kill us but you can't eat us."

Robby Wicks had said the same thing a few times when we had our asses in a crack.

Clay Warfield nodded to one of his men. "See to Slim Jim." One guy peeled off and hustled back to the office, the long chain from his belt, hooked to his wallet, rattled as he quick-stepped, the only noise in the silent room except our heavy breathing.

"The safe's empty," I said. "No one's here but two prospects, and you come in using a Trojan horse when you're supposed to be on a Toys for Tots run. We were set up. How did you know we were coming?" As soon as I said it, the answer popped up all on its own. What a complete dumbass I'd been. This whole thing never had been about the money.

"I can see by the look on your face you know who it is, so why don't *you* tell me his name?" said Clay.

"His name's Jonas Mabry."

"I don't know him. Who is he?"

"He's the guy who set me up."

Clay nodded. "I know that, asshole, but why? This Mabry called me, gave me most of the details, but wouldn't give me his name."

"He's someone who wants the worst kind of harm to come to me."

"He did a good job, because I'm going to oblige him. Break into my house, try to steal my shit. You're going to die in the worst possible way."

Mack spoke for the first time. "You can't shoot us. Like Drago said, it'll make too much noise." Mack took a step toward the front door. "We're leaving, and you're not going to stop us."

The other two bikers with guns threw down on him. Mack hesitated.

Clay said to Mack, "I would strongly advise you to rethink what you're about to do."

The other biker came out carrying Slim Jim like a mother would a child, and semi-dragging Roy Boy, his nose bloated and bloody. Did all of these assholes have superhuman strength?

"What did you do to them, and which one of you did it?" asked Clay.

"I did it," said Drago.

"No, I did it," I said. "They jumped me and I defended myself. I think I broke his jaw."

"What about Roy Boy?" asked Clay.

"I just knocked him silly. His nose might be broke. He'll come out of it okay."

Clay scoffed. "Broken jaw I can see, but just gettin' your dick knocked in the dirt isn't good enough. Neither of them made a decent enough show of themselves. We'll settle up on that later. Take those cuffs off."

The biker who'd dragged them out and set them on the floor pointed his M16 at the chain.

Clay yelled, "Hold it. Hold it you, dumbass. Haven't you been paying attention to what's going on here? Never mind. Jesus! I'm surrounded by idiots. Sandman, deal with that, would you please?"

Sandman went over, took a key from a key ring in his pocket, and undid the cuffs. Then he slapped Roy Boy until he came around, his face pink, his eyes going wide when he saw who had slapped him. Sandman jerked him to his feet.

Clay grabbed the rifle from the closest biker and shoved it into Roy Boy's hands. "Now, you do exactly as I say when I say it. Do you understand?"

Roy Boy nodded. Clay said, "These three who desecrated our revered clubhouse don't think I possess the brains or the balls to shoot them because the cops are right outside watching. Do you understand?"

Roy Boy again nodded as he held the gun, uncomfortable, as if it were an alien ray gun. Like Drago had said, he hadn't made his bones and hadn't been trained yet. Maybe he was about to get both accomplished at the same time.

"They're burglars, you understand?" said Clay. "If I say shoot them, you shoot them. We'll all leave in the plumbing van the same way we came in. You wait for the cops. You'll get three years for manslaughter and be out in eighteen months, you got it?"

Roy Boy nodded. The truly scary thing about it, Clay was right.

"When you get out in three, you'll have earned your patch," said Clay. Roy Boy stood straighter, pulling back his shoulders.

"Right," said Mack, "shoot us with an illegal machine gun, because that's what that gun is classified as, and you'll get life, guaranteed."

That quick, Roy Boy lost motivation. His shoulders slumped. He looked at Clay for confirmation.

"Son of a bitch," said Clay. He reached inside his denim jacket and pulled out a beautiful H&K P9 from a shoulder holster. He jerked the M16 from Roy Boy's hands and shoved the P9 into them. He spun on Mack. "Who the hell are you?"

"Like you said, I'm a burglar."

"Chickenshit, sneak thief burglars don't know the law. Not like that."

Mack shrugged.

Clay turned back to Drago. "Drago, you want outta this mess? I'll give you one chance. You tell me true, I'll reinstate you with full privileges."

Reinstate him? He'd said he was never an SS.

Drago sneered. "Not a chance in hell. You killed Willy. No, you assassinated Willy. Gunned him in cold blood. Walked right up and put the gun to the back of his head and pulled the trigger. And for no good reason other than you just didn't want to cut the money three ways. He was with us. He told us which armored car to hit. He was my friend. No, *Mr.* President, you're going to have to kill me first."

Willy. That name sounded only vaguely familiar until Drago said the part about the armored car job, then it locked in. Willy Frakes. Drago hadn't killed the guard after all—Clay had. Clay had been in on the armored car heist all those years ago. Now it all made sense. Drago lived by the code that you did not rat. He couldn't get even with Clay, not by ratting him out. But he could rub it in Clay's face by hiding the money from the job right under Clay's nose. The gold protected by the club to whom he'd sworn his oath and an allegiance. I realized my jaw had dropped open.

"What's the matter with *you*?" Clay asked me.

I turned to Drago. "You didn't shoot that guard."

Drago didn't acknowledge that I had said anything at all.

"You went to prison for twenty-five to life for something you didn't do."

"Don't get your panties in a wad, Bruno," Mack said. "He's not some darling angel. He was in violation of the felony murder rule. Someone died during the course of a felony, whether he pulled the trigger or not. That's twenty-five to life, too."

"Very good," said Clay. "You're not some kind of sneak thief. Now I know that for sure. You're a cop. Who do you work for?"

"Los Angeles County Sheriff's Department. They know I'm here. You shoot me and you know what will happen? All hell's going to break loose. It'll drop right down on top of you like a hot pile of dog shit."

"Not if you just quietly disappear." Clay turned to Drago. "You had time to think about my offer? Full reinstatement. You went to prison without saying a word. For your loyalty, I'll give you half the money from the armored car job."

Drago's eyes bulged and spittle flew from his mouth. "Half? That's big of you, asshole, considering you don't even know where I hid it. Cause it's all mine. And guess what? I'm not afraid of you. I know you for the greedy bastard you are. You're not going to kill me. Not till you find your precious money."

Clay remained calm and collected. "This is true, I don't know exactly where. My mystery caller," he looked at me, "according to you, this Jonas Mabry didn't give me all the necessary details. He just said there was a million point two in gold. That's why we didn't roll right in. We gave you some time, but as you can see, that didn't work out. I have to hand it to you, Drago, my man, hiding it here was truly a piece of advanced thinking."

"Fuck you and the plumbing truck you rode in on."

Clay looked to Roy Boy. "Before we rolled up, did you hear anything about what they were doing, where the gold's hidden?"

Rob Roy shook his head. "They came right in, went right to the safe, and started working on it."

"What good are you?" Clay turned to Sandman. "That doesn't make sense. How could he hide that much gold in a safe without expecting me to see it?"

Sandman shrugged.

Clay said, "What good *are you*? We'll take them somewhere else and have a little chat until we find out. Zip-tie their hands."

"The fuck you will!" yelled Drago. He took a giant step toward the already scared Roy Boy, who jumped back, his eyes wild with fear and indecision, the gun jittering in his hand. Drago did it on purpose to solicit a gunshot. Did he hate Clay enough to sacrifice his life to bring the cops down on him? In the short time we'd been together, I'd gotten to know Drago a little better.

"Hold it," Clay yelled. "Looks like this whole damn thing's going to get screwed up if I don't take a personal hand in it." He said this looking up at the ceiling, as if talking to himself, a sure sign of mental instability. "Watch them for one minute. Can you assholes do that much? Huh?" He hurried down the hall and disappeared into the office. Something scraped on the floor. The desk. And then another scraping noise. He returned with a second H&K P9 while screwing on a silencer. He finished tightening it. From three feet away he shot Drago in the foot. Drago went down without a sound. "Now zip-tie them like I said, and do it quickly before I lose my cool and decide I need new prospects." Prospects always did the dirty work, the menial labor, no matter what their physical condition, until they made their bones and earned their patch.

The prospects put the plastic zip-ties on our hands behind our backs. They had to use three on Drago, one on each hand, and then one to link the two hands together.

Clay's phone rang. He answered it and listened. "Okay, hold on." He put his phone on speaker. "Go ahead. Deputy Bruno Johnson can hear you now."

Jonas Mabry said, "Hello, Deputy Johnson."

CHAPTER FORTY-FOUR

"Bruno, what did you do to this guy?" asked Mack.

"I guess I made the mistake of saving his life," I replied angrily.

"Now that sounds like a story I gotta hear," said Clay.

Jonas, on the phone, yelled, "Hey, pay attention, or I'm going to hang up."

Drago lay on his back, writhing silently in pain. He tried to reach his foot bending backward, his hands cuffed together, but he wasn't flexible enough. He'd been shot in the foot on the same leg where I'd shot him in the thigh. I moved over to help him. No one stopped me. I sat down, slid my hands down past my feet and around to the front.

"Jonas Mabry, where is this gold you told me about?" asked Clay.

"They didn't find it?" asked Mabry. "Sounds like you moved in a little premature. I warned you about that. But you have ways to deal with that problem after you fulfill your end of the bargain. I need to talk with Deputy Johnson."

I took my shirt off over my head, slipped it past my tied hands, and ripped it open to get it past the flex cuffs. I knelt down and untied Drago's boot.

Clay addressed Mabry. "You're not doing shit until I tell you to, you understand?"

Jonas Mabry chuckled and hung up.

Clay yelled, "Hello? Hello? The little shit hung up on me. You believe that?"

With my hands still zip-tied together, I slipped Drago's boot off as gingerly as I could. I tied my shirt around the bloody mess the 9mm round had made. The round went right through the top of the boot and imbedded in the sole of his boot. The entry wound on top had already swelled to a mound of red and purple, and oozed blood.

"Thanks, man," Drago said. "That does feel a little better."

Now Drago had two bullet holes in him, one of which I had put there. One I now regretted. I didn't know him or what he was about when I'd shot him.

"Do you believe the balls of this guy, hanging up on me?" asked Clay.

Sandman came over and grabbed my now-naked arm. "Look at this." He pointed to the BMF tattoo. "This guy's a Brutal Mother Fucker. He's one of those LA cops who took down Joe Dick."

Clay's cell phone rang. He answered it as he walked over to me. He said into the phone, "Hold on a minute." I stood from my crouch.

Clay and Sandman came right up close. "That right? You the one who took down our friend Joe?"

"I have one of those tattoos," Mack said. "Here, look. What's the big deal?"

Clay smiled. "You're too young, and we heard a nigger took out Joe. Looks like we're in for a bigger party than I thought. Grapple these guys up and take them to the warehouse. Call in the rest of the club, they're going to want to watch this." Clay tapped his phone. "Okay, go ahead, you're back on speakerphone."

Jonas said, "Are you talking about my friend Deputy Johnson? I know you must be. How absolutely perfect." His voice pulled away from the phone. "You hear that, Mom? The biker assholes know Deputy Johnson. They've promised to make his last minutes on this earth memorable ones. What? Yes, I wish we could be there, too."

Sandman did not move away. Pure hatred emitted from his eyes into me as though in waves. He pulled back and slugged me in the stomach. I bent over. His knee came up. I saw it coming and turned my head, took it on the side. I went down and feigned unconsciousness.

"Wait," Jonas said, "Before you go too far, I need to tell him something."

"Where's the gold?" Clay asked Jonas.

"I told you, he didn't tell me. That fat slob Drago, he knows for sure. No doubt, you can get it out of him. Now let me talk to Deputy Johnson. A deal's a deal. If I hadn't called you, you wouldn't have known about this, and then where would you be? Out on your toy run while your clubhouse was taken down."

Clay brought the phone down closer to me. "Okay, go ahead, he's listening."

Clay didn't care if I was conscious or not. I kept my eyes closed, my body lax.

Rustling on the other end of the phone, then. "Mom, you do the honors. You've waited a long time for this." Another voice came on, a woman. I didn't recognize Bella, I had never heard her speak. She said, "You ruined everything. You are a cold and insensitive man."

Clay asked, "Is this going to take long? Do I need to get a beer?"

Bella continued. "You shouldn't have kicked in our door that day. You had no business doing that. You should've left us alone. Now you'll pay a price for it, a dear price." Her voice came over strong, not weak like someone who had only two weeks to live. She coughed, and the one cough set off a string in rapid fire.

Jonas took the phone. The coughing continued in the background. Jonas said, "We really wanted Deputy Johnson to be with us when he found this out. And we would have if he'd gone along with our first plan. We would have grabbed him when he made the payoff. We would've had him and the money. But it's not about the money, never has been. That would only have been the bonus."

"Get on with it," said Clay. "I'm growing old here."

Sandman kicked me in the side.

I hadn't been ready for it and curled up.

Sandman laughed. "He was faking it." He kicked me again.

"Do it again and I'll rip your head off," said Mack.

"Right, all tied up like that," Sandman said.

"Enough," said Clay. "I want to hear what this little shitass has to say. Go ahead."

"No, it's fine if you want to go ahead and hit him some more."

"Talk or I'm hanging up. I don't have time for this."

"As I was saying," said Jonas, "we had originally intended on grabbing you and clipping off each one of your fingers and toes, one at time. But then I didn't know how resourceful you were, how you'd come across a pot of gold. When we met out at Whitewater, I had a chance to meet your lovely wife, Marie. Would you like to talk to her?"

My world slid over the edge. I went into free-fall.

CHAPTER FORTY-FIVE

"No!" Mack yelled, and tried to wiggle his feet free.

Roy Boy and Slim Jim jumped over and put the boots to him, kicking relentlessly.

Sandman laughed and grunted as he tried his best to kick the life out of me. I covered up, squirmed, and dodged the best I could. I saw Mack take one to the head. He went limp.

Clay threw his head back and laughed. "You have his wife? Really? That's perfect, absolutely perfect."

With the kicking, my anger rose. Nothing mattered now except Marie. I curled tighter. The blows became distant thuds. I yelled, "Jonas, you gave me until eight o'clock tonight. I will bring you the money tonight at eight. Are you a man of your word? Are you?"

The beating stopped.

Clay looked surprised. "Where are you comin' from here, boy? You aren't goin' anywhere. We're taking you to the warehouse. We're gonna have some real fun and games. And then—and then you gonna have an urgent appointment with a hole in the ground."

I ignored him. "Jonas, what do you say?"

Clay clicked off the phone. His spittle flew. "Get them in the van."

Drago didn't move. I couldn't tell if he was breathing. He'd probably lost too much blood. Three men half-carried, half-dragged me out to the paneled utility truck backed up to the front door. I didn't resist, I needed to reserve my strength. If Jonas had Marie, that meant he also had Eddie. I had to get away. I had to take these guys down and find Marie.

The answer came to me as to what had happened. That the night before out in Whitewater, Jonas hadn't given up Eddie because he was injured or because Eddie wouldn't talk. Jonas had used Eddie as bait. Jonas must have put a small GPS in Eddie's shoe. Who would have thought to look? I should have. Jonas had lain back and taken Marie and Eddie at his leisure. Now getting free was the only thing that mattered.

They left me in the truck and went back for Mack. My hands were still in front of me. I floundered around looking for anything to get the flex-ties off. Then I remembered training from long ago. Friction. Heat. I fumbled with swollen hands, undid my shoelace, and tied one end to the inside support to the truck's metal shell. I threaded the lace through the flex cuff binding my hands. I tied the lace to another bulkhead brace below the first one, making a bow. I pulled the lace taut and worked the lace back and forth in a rapid manner like the pioneers did to make fire.

Less than ten feet away, back at the entry to the house, Roy Boy said, "Look at all that blood. I didn't think one body could have that much blood." He was talking about Drago.

I seesawed away at a furious rate. The friction sliced through the flex cuff. I was free just as the group returned dragging Mack. I laid down where they had left me and didn't move. I looked up. I'd left the lace. They wouldn't know what it was for. I fought down my anger and the urge to jump them, right then. Beat them all to a bloody pulp for what they did, and for keeping me from my Marie.

They tossed Mack in next to me. He grunted and groaned and went silent. His face was unrecognizable. His eyes were welded together with purple and red. His nose bled and his lips were split. Blood trickled out of his mouth and down to his neck. I hoped like hell he didn't have internal injuries. I'd worked the street too long, seen too many beatings. I knew. My gut ached at the pain I had caused him.

Roy Boy and Slim Jim had stayed at the open back end of the truck. Roy Boy said, "How we going to get fatass all the way over here and into the truck?"

In the distance, Clay yelled, "Don't be a bunch of pussies. All five of you get on that pig and get him in the truck. Quit dickin' around and get it done."

"Hey buddy, you okay?" I asked Mack.

No reply. I nudged him. He didn't even groan. He needed immediate medical attention. I looked back. The three bikers and the two prospects, with great effort, were hauling Drago along the trash-laden floor of the club. I leaned up far enough to check the ignition. The keys were gone.

The truck was a one-ton with lots of floor space. The bikers grunted and cussed, lifting Drago to the back edge. They paused, huffing.

"You two assholes get up there in the truck and pull," said Clay. "You three stay down here and push."

With great effort, they hauled Drago over the edge and into the truck. Roy Boy stumbled over me and stepped on my hand. Bones crunched. I yelled.

Roy Boy said, "Hey, this asshole's cut his flex cuffs off."

Shit.

Everyone stopped. A welcome diversion to rest.

Clay stood at the end of the truck. "Dumbass, what do you think you should do about it?"

Roy Boy kicked me.

"No, dipshit," Clay said. "Cuff him up again." He tossed in more flex cuffs.

My only chance was gone. Without my hands free, what could I do? I fought the urge to make a play before they recuffed me. A stupid move that wouldn't work anyway. But if they succeeded in getting us to that warehouse, all was lost.

Roy Boy put the flex cuffs on too tight. My blood flow was cut off. If I didn't get the cuffs off soon, I'd lose my hands for sure.

They pulled Drago in the rest of the way. His dead weight

leaned in on Mack. I fought to keep Drago from flopping over. In Mack's condition, he'd be smothered.

Clay closed one back door. "You think you two dipshits can haul this load of garbage to the warehouse?"

Roy Boy answered. "Yeah, sure boss, no problem." Clay closed the other door.

I fought to keep from leaning on Mack. I couldn't feel my hands already. I couldn't reach the derringer if I wanted to. Short of a miracle, I had no idea how we could escape.

CHAPTER FORTY-SIX

Drago groaned.

"Are you okay?" I asked. "How are you doing?"

"Not too good. If it were raining pussies, I'd get hit in the head with a dick. I've been shot twice, kicked, and drug across a sea of trash like a slab of meat. And to top it off, I'm tossed in the back of a truck with a cop and a—"

He hesitated, waiting for me to tell him not to say it. I didn't have the energy.

"A darkie."

An improvement, however minor.

"Thanks for that, I think."

He chuckled. "Man, you're all right."

"For a darkie."

"Yeah, that's what I said." He laughed some more.

"How can you laugh when these white trash, cracker ass-holes are going to torture and kill us and bury us out in the desert, where no one will ever know what happened to us?"

"I got no one who cares, so that last part is no big whoop."

"I care."

Drago laughed again. "Yeah, thanks for that."

"Mack's in a bad way."

Drago stopped laughing. "He's a friend of yours?"

"Yeah, a good friend, a great friend."

"I guess we'll just have to get him to a doctor."

He said this so casually, with so much confidence, I chuckled at the irony.

His big paw came up and rested on my shoulder. I took a full second to realize the implication. He had freed himself with the knife.

Roy Boy and Slim Jim jumped in the truck and started it up. The engine roared up in the cab. We were off to the warehouse.

I chuckled.

"What's funny?" whispered Drago.

"You."

"That right?"

"Yeah, because you're touching a darkie."

We both laughed out loud. He jerked his hand back out of sight.

"What's going on back there?" asked Roy Boy. Then to Slim Jim, he said, "You better check 'em. We screw this up and we're gonna be the ones takin' a cold dirt nap."

Slim Jim couldn't talk with his broken jaw. He had to be in enormous pain and hating me for it. He leaned over as Roy Boy steered the truck down the driveway ramp and bounced into the street. Drago's weight pressed into me, as I craned my neck to see into the driver's compartment, all while trying to keep us off Mack. I caught Slim Jim's eyes. After a long hateful look, he turned back and nodded to Roy Boy. He hadn't seen Drago's free hands.

Sunlight came in through the windshield. I figured the time to be about noon. Eight hours to get away and find Marie and Eddie. Who was I kidding? Nothing would keep them alive until eight o'clock.

Drago's hand found mine behind my back. He cut the flex cuffs and the feeling rushed back in my hands. He'd used the dirk that the biker had failed to find on him when they searched us. The same biker who was too homophobic to check my crotch when he searched me. I had depended on that. The derringer was safe.

"You got a plan?" whispered Drago.

"I'm working on it."

"You don't have much time."

"Do you know where this warehouse is?"

"Twenty minutes or so, up in Cajon Pass, at the dead end of a dirt road called Whitehall."

Out the window, buildings and treetops flashed by. Roy Boy drove us up to Baseline, then went west. He took us in and out of side streets, avoiding the freeway and on up into the Cajon Pass. I couldn't wait much longer to make a move. If we made it to the warehouse all would be lost. I'd waited too long already for Mack. He needed a hospital now.

The derringer had only two shots, against two prospects with large guns. That wasn't the problem. The problem was that I couldn't, in cold blood, just shoot them both in the back. I couldn't do it. And if I threw down on them, I would only give them a chance to overpower me. I'd get one shot off, and if the other held his mud, he'd have time to shoot me.

My only option was to shoot Roy Boy without warning. Shoot him right in the back of the head instead of his back. He'd crash the van. If we survived, I would have one shot to hit Slim Jim. I had to do it. Too many lives depended on it.

I wiggled around until I had my hand down the front of my pants. Drago whispered in my ear, "Hey, buddy, now's not the time or the place."

He must have been giddy from blood loss.

"You ready?" he asked. "We're gonna have to jump them in the next couple of minutes or it'll be too late, we'll already be there. And to tell you the truth, I don't feel so hot right now."

"We're not going to jump them. I have a gun. Just gimme a minute, would ya?"

"We don't have that kinda time. Gimme the gun, I'll do it."

"No, I got this—"

Drago reached around and, before I could react, he smothered my hand with his big mitts and snatched away the gun. He didn't hesitate like I would have. He rolled to one side, extended the derringer, and fired right through Roy Boy's backseat.

CHAPTER FORTY-SEVEN

The explosion in the confined space sounded like we were in a church bell tower. Slim Jim whipped his head around too fast, banging his broken jaw on the seat's back headrest. His eyes rolled up and he fell back out of view into the footwell.

The van didn't waver; we kept on a steady path. Roy Boy didn't seem affected at all. He hadn't even acknowledged the gunshot. Maybe the bullet had not penetrated the seat. Robby Wicks and I had been in a shooting where that had happened. The seats, to cut back on the weight, weren't solid, and had a mesh frame for support made out of cheap steel.

Drago struggled up on his knees. I did the same. He extended his arm, cocked the hammer back a second time, and aimed at the back of Roy Boy's head. I put my hand on the gun. He lowered it.

Roy Boy looked up in the rearview mirror at us without expression. "You gone and killed me for sure." A bit of blood trickled out of the corner of his mouth. He fell forward and his head hit the steering wheel. The truck veered out of control. I wiggled between the seats.

Too late. The truck went over the curb, peeling off some speed with the minor impact. We crossed two front yards, disrupting shrubs, flowerbeds, and a hedge that all spit out the back behind the truck. We plowed broadside into a lime green Volkswagen Jetta in someone's driveway and shoved the heap perpendicular.

The crash threw me forward, and then I tumbled backwards and was shoved up against the back doors.

I scrambled like a spider. "Mack? Mack, are you okay?" A light trickle of blood ran out of the corner of his mouth. I checked his pulse, thready, barely there. I crawled to the back doors and opened them to bright sunlight.

A large woman in a muu-muu with frizzy red hair came out the front door at a fast waddle. "What the hell? You crashed into my car. Are you kidding me? My car was parked in *my driveway*. You totaled my car. My God, you totaled my baby."

Bold as a biker prospect, she came up and took hold of my arm. I shrugged her away and stumbled to the front driver's door, opened it, and dragged out Roy Boy. He plopped onto the driveway. I dragged him farther into the yard, out of the path I'd need to extricate the truck from the yard.

The muu-muu woman screamed, "What are you doing? Get him out of my yard. You can't leave some dead biker in my yard. I'm calling the police." She put a cordless phone to her ear.

Drago hadn't killed Roy Boy, like Roy Boy had thought. His chest rose and fell uninhibited. He was far better off than my friend Mack.

The smart move would be to walk away. Muu-muu would have the cops and paramedics here in no time. "In no time" could take too long. I couldn't risk it. Mack meant too much to me. I had to see this through. By the time the police arrived and then they called paramedics, I could already have him in the hospital being treated.

I got back into the truck, shoved the gearshift into reverse, and gunned the accelerator. The back wheels dug in, spinning up sod and azaleas. Muu-muu woman screamed into the phone. "Now he's leaving. It's a hit and run. Hurry. No, wait, okay, I got it. The license plate is—"

I shoved the truck into drive and bounced over the curb into the street. "Drago, are you still with me?"

"I'm here, but I got nothing left, partner. I think I broke my leg."

"Which way to the closest hospital?"

His voice faded. "I'm not sure exactly where we are—"

"Drago, what's the name of the hospital?"

"St. Bernadine's." His voice was barely a whisper. "Man...you can't take me to a hospital. They'll call the police, they'll violate my parole. I'll go back in on...on a violation. I gotta get that gold, I gotta get—"

He went silent.

He'd slipped into shock from the multiple gunshot wounds, the beating, all the blood loss, and now the crash where he broke his leg. Even men like Drago had a vulnerability threshold.

I headed south and typed in the hospital's name on the dashboard GPS. The route popped up and the woman with a calm voice told me what turns to make, told me we had a seven-minute ETA. I planned to cut that in half.

I'd pull into the hospital's emergency entrance, get a nurse or orderly to come out, and I'd be gone. I'd take off right then. I wanted to stay with Mack, but hospitals attracted cops, and I needed to find Marie. There was too little time.

I fought with the speed. My foot pushed harder on the accelerator, my hand tapped on the steering wheel. I had to continually correct by slowly easing off my foot. Slim Jim groaned and struggled to climb out of the foot well. I stopped for a red signal. I wanted to move. I impatiently tapped faster on the steering wheel.

Slim Jim managed to almost crawl back up in the seat. I leaned over and slugged him right in his broken jaw. He wilted back to whence he had come. The light changed. I hit the gas.

I turned into St. Bernadine's and followed the signs around to the emergency entrance and stopped.

A black-and-white San Bernardino police patrol unit sat in the slot next to an ambulance. Another unoccupied police unit was parked farther down. No time to consider possible consequences; everyone in the truck needed emergency medical care. I pulled around and backed into the only slot open, 'Ambulance Only.' I got out and came around the back. Two cops stood at the back door talking. I said, "Please help me. I have an officer down." Words that never failed to send chills through any cop who heard it. They ran over. One said, "What happened, who is it?" while the other climbed in.

I took a step back, a little farther away from the truck. "Please hurry," I said. "The guy on the left is Detective John Mack with Los Angeles County Sheriff's Department. The guy in the front seat is one of the Sons of Satan who beat him."

"This detective is in a bad way—get some help!" the officer inside said.

I took another tentative step backward.

The cop outside reached up to his lapel mic. "Two-Paul-Three, we have an 1199 at the back of St. Bee's, officer down. We are code four." He ran into the hospital to get a doctor.

Distant sirens came from all over the city. When an "officer down" went out, everyone dropped what they were doing, no matter what it was, and responded. Nurses and doctors rushed out with gurneys. More cops.

I backed up more and kept going. I'd almost made it to the front end of the truck where I intended to turn and casually walk away, when one of the cops who'd been inside came out said, "Hey, it's Leon Johnson."

He was one of the cops who'd stopped me outside the Quick Stop store my first night here. I turned and ran.

CHAPTER FORTY-EIGHT

The two cops behind me took chase. Their feet slapped pavement. One yelled into his radio, "Four-Paul-Five, foot pursuit behind St. Bee's, a 187 suspect."

I ran with everything I had left. My body ached all over from the beating and didn't want to cooperate. I pushed hard and couldn't kick it into gear. The air felt too thick to run in.

Dispatch said, "Any officer to assist in Four-Paul-Five's foot pursuit behind St. Bee."

The radio behind me came back jammed with cops responding. They had to believe I was the suspect in the officer-down call. The asshole responsible. I had awakened the brotherhood of cops. Every cop in a twenty-five mile radius would be coming: adjoining cities, California Highway Patrol, University Police, and the Sheriff's Department. They would coordinate and seal off the entire area. I didn't have one chance in hell.

I rounded the first corner to a long driveway leading down the side of the hospital that dumped out into the street. Halfway down the block was a park. If I could make it to the park, I'd have a chance to get lost in all the trees and bushes. I put on a burst of speed. The two cops behind came around the corner with their cop noise, running boots, creaking leather, jangling equipment.

Up ahead a cop car bounced into the driveway from the street, red lights and siren blaring, cutting off my escape route. In a last-ditch effort, I turned, hit the eight foot chain-link fence, and started up, fingers clawing for purchase.

A hand grabbed my ankle. "Got you, asshole."

They pulled me down and jumped on top. The cop car stopped with the bumper right at my head. They kicked and slugged and hit me with batons. They cuffed me and shoved me into the back of the car.

Tears of frustration filled my eyes. No way would I get out of this. Mack would not be there this time to rescue me. I didn't care about me. Now Marie didn't have a chance. Who would look for her?

The driver headed onto the San Bernardino Freeway. They'd transport me to the jail to book me in on the murder charge. A tick-tock pounded in my head. Time was against me. An evil, un-stoppable enemy who sped along unabated.

Outside, eucalyptus trees whipped by in an endless proces-sion. If only I could somehow escape and get into those trees. I put my face up close to the cold black screen that separated me from the cops and tried to see the MDT, the Mobile Dispatch Terminal, searching for any information that might help me get out of the car. There wasn't much time. Once inside the jail, all would be lost. Tick-tock. Yards sped by and turned into miles.

We exited at Etiwanda Avenue. A quarter mile later, we turned into the driveway of The West Valley Detention Center. The tall sally port opened to let us pass into the jail yard. I pivoted in the seat to watch out the back window as the gate rolled be-hind us and clanged shut with a finality I would never forget.

The two uniforms got out and stowed their weapons in the trunk of the unit before they both came around, opened the door, and pulled me out. Each held firmly to an arm even though I could go nowhere but through the solid steel door into the jail. I was their prize catch. A murder suspect, a shooter of cops, and they were the captors.

The one with sandy hair leaned up close to my ear as he stut-ter-stepped to keep up. "Say good-night, asshole. You're goin' away forever."

I stopped dead and stared at him. Sandy hair smiled and yanked on my arms. We continued.

They sat me on the concrete bench and filled out the booking slip and the health screen. I gave them the answers to all their questions by rote. My mind was spinning out scenarios of escape, any kind of plan. I needed to calm down and focus, or I'd be nothing better than a trapped animal banging around in a cage.

The intake deputy on the other side of the reinforced glass window asked, "You want to make a phone call?"

A phone call. I could call someone, anyone who might help. But who? The moment, however brief, lingered. There was no one. "No. No phone call, thanks." Thanks? Why'd I say that?

I sat on the bench with five other malcontents, all lacking teeth here and there, dirty hair, and reeking of body odor. All waiting to be classified. Street people who'd be better off with a warm place to sleep, a roof over their heads, and three meals a day. Except one, whose clothes, a rumpled disheveled suit that hung off him. His hair was mussed, his eyes watery, the classic drunk driver. He looked right at me from two crooks over and leaned in. "Hey, man, I know you? Sure, I know you. You're some kinda celebrity, right?" His breath was sweet with bourbon and cherries. A soured ignorance wafted my way.

"You've mistaken me for someone else."

"No, no, I never forget a face. I've seen you someplace." He sat back on the bench with a look of consternation as he tried to pull up the memory of my face the thousand times it had been shown on television nine months ago, a featured program on *Most Wanted*.

I looked at my wristband. Damn. They'd figured out my real name. They had booked me under the alias Leon Byron Johnson I'd given them, but they must have later found my real name through a CALID fingerprint check. Since they had my real name, the warrant must have popped. I was caught. Booked on a warrant for the murder of my friend Chantal, back from before when we fled the States for Costa Rica. I didn't do it. My old friend Robby had set me up to take the fall. I was boxed in tight. Robby was the only witness, and he was dead.

No, don't think that way. Every problem has an answer. There have to be options.

I put my head back and closed my eyes. The drunk down the way leaned over. His odor spoke before he did. "*Survivor*, right? You were on that one in Bali, or some shit. The guy who ate that lizard and got sick, right? Kicked off the island because you ate that lizard. Hey, man, that chick on there, the one with the short red hair, was hot. Did you have a chance to do her? Did you get a crack at that?"

I couldn't think with his yammering. I opened my eyes wide and leaned over. "The name's Bruno Johnson."

The smile in his eyes faded first, followed by the one on his mouth, as his alcohol-soaked brain cells kicked in and he put the name to the face. He turned face front and shut his yap.

Gradually, my mind eased and drifted back to where all this had started. How simple life had been working a cabana bar on the beach. Going home every night to see Marie's smile, the glow in her eyes, the joy of having the children, the tone in their perfect little laughs and giggles. Then the memories sped up. Images of the last two days came faster and faster in a kaleidoscope of color and pain, emotional and physical. I sat forward. A possibility, a small, ever-so-minute answer, burst to the surface. Sure, sure, that might just work. It had to work, there wasn't anything else.

I jumped up. "Hey, I want that phone call now."

The custody deputy took me out of the classification holding and into the hall to use the phone. I dialed Barbara Wicks. On the other end her phone rang once. She didn't pick up. Her phone readout would tell her the jail was calling. She'd have to know the caller was Bruno-the-dumbshit-Johnson on the line. Her phone rang a second time. She didn't pick up. If she didn't answer, the weak plan forming in the back of my brain wouldn't see the light of day.

Her phone rang again. She picked up, but said nothing. I said, "Hello." My tone was far too desperate.

She said nothing.

"Barbara?"

She said nothing. Her breathing came over the phone. *She'd asked me not to take Mack along. She'd begged me.*

"Barbara, please?"

More breathing. In the background a PA system paged a doctor. She was at St. Bernadine's with Mack.

I said, "I know it's not fair for me to ask a favor, but I desperately need one."

Her voice came over terse and angry. "You've got a lot of nerve, Bruno Johnson, calling me after what you've done."

My face flushed hot. "I have the nerve? Who's the one who came down to Costa Rica to ask *me* for a favor? Who had the most to lose?"

"How dare you throw that back at me," she yelled. "John's in surgery right now." Her voice broke with emotion. "His odds aren't good. He has internal injuries. He's bleeding internally."

"I'm sorry. You know I didn't mean that to happen."

"Didn't mean that to happen? What *exactly* did you think was going to happen when you took Karl Drago, a degenerate murderer, into the Sons of Satan clubhouse to commit a robbery?"

"It was a risk I had to take." My voice trailed off. She was right. How imbecilic raiding the SS clubhouse for a pot of gold. No, for a golden doughnut.

"I asked you not to take John with you," she said in a quieter tone.

"Wait, Barbara."

Her voice again caught with emotion. "He's in custody, Bruno. He comes out of this alive, he's going to do time for what happened. He'll never be a cop again. Being a cop defined him. It's all he's ever wanted to do."

I gripped the phone, put my head against the wall, and closed my eyes. I knew exactly how that felt. "I've really screwed this up, I know, and I have no right to ask you for a favor."

"Damn straight, you don't."

"Wait, wait, don't hang up."

Her breath came hard into the phone, but she didn't hang up.

"Barbara, Jonas has Marie and Eddie."

Her breath caught. "Oh my God. You're sure?"

"Yes."

"Do you have any idea where he's holding them?"

"No. Are you going to help me?"

"You're in jail on a murder warrant. I told you. You get picked up, there would be nothing I can do for you."

"I just need you to make one phone call."

CHAPTER FORTY-NINE

I sat alone in the holding cell watching the clock. I had told Barbara to tell the US attorney one hour or the deal was off. I didn't know if what I had to deal was enough, but it was all I had. And I needed them moving fast. One hour ticked by, then another fifteen minutes. I had calculated in the extra time this part would take. The assistant US attorney would want me hungry for the deal; they'd want the extra power driven home with the emphasis that they were the ones in control. They didn't know what I had in mind, what I wanted to negotiate with, they just wanted a cop-out, a confession to make their jobs easier.

At one hour and twenty minutes, the deputy came for me and escorted me to a large, comfortable interview room, not one often used for regular crooks. I sat in a hard plastic chair at a hard plastic table, hands cuffed in front of me.

I didn't have one minute to spare. I looked up to the ceiling where there had to be a pinhole camera and said, "No more bullshit games. Get in here right now or the deal's off."

I watched the clock on the wall. The red second hand swept around the dial once. The door opened. Three men and one woman came in, all wearing suits. They didn't sit down. The men folded their arms and leaned against the wall. The woman said, "Just to be fair, we don't think you have anything worth trading, not enough to let you go on a murder charge. We are here at the express request of Montclair Chief Wicks."

"First off," I said, "I know you've had the time to check out the case that this murder warrant is based on. I didn't kill Chantal. She was my friend and, if it goes to trial, there is every likelihood that I will walk."

I didn't want to tell her that Robby Wicks, my old supervisor, my friend and husband to Barbara Wicks, had killed Chantal. Any defense put forward would have to put Robby out front, and I didn't know if I could do that. Even after all that Robby had done.

One of the men, shorter, stout through the shoulders, wearing a blue suit with gray pinstripes, said, "And there's the other matter of the kids."

Was he now referring to the kids I had taken down to Costa Rica? I had left no evidence behind. They knew about Wally, but not the others, not for sure they didn't. They only had rumors, supposition, circumstantial evidence. When Robby was alive, Robby had been hunting the children. He and I had played a little game of fox and hounds. I was sure he had told no one. Now that Wally had been reunited with his father, the pressure had come off. What they had was conjecture, speculation, and, most of all, embarrassment for being outsmarted.

I played dumb. "What kids?" When I said it, I remembered they had me on video putting Jonas in the trunk at the mall. They thought I had the two children, the little girls Jonas had taken, Elena Cortez and Sandy Williams.

Blue suit said, "Chief Wicks told us you didn't take those kids. But you did grab Jonas Mabry, and you will have to answer to that if and when we capture him."

He had tipped his hand, the first to give up something. I might grow to like him. I looked at him. "FBI or AUSA?"

He shrugged.

"Tell us what you have," said the woman.

I looked her in the eyes for a long moment, then shifted back to blue suit, where I was getting a little slack. "I know the FBI set up Karl Drago to be killed by the Sons of Satan in order to get a RICO on Clay Warfield."

His eyes twitched. He wasn't ready for such a large serving of truth and reacted with his expression. I had him.

The woman's mouth dropped open. She hadn't known. She wasn't a Fed. She recovered and said, "Speculation and conjecture. Not enough to trade for a murder charge."

I looked back at her. "You're County, aren't you? You're with San Bernardino County District Attorney's office?"

She smiled. "Wrong. Los Angeles. Your murder occurred in LA county. And because of all your past crimes, I've been instructed not to negotiate with you."

"I told you, it's not my murder. You drove all the way out here *not* to negotiate with me?"

She dropped the smile. I looked back at blue suit. "I have enough circumstantial evidence to go to the press with you using Karl Drago as a staked goat."

He held eye contact and shrugged. "Do what you have to do."

They turned in unison to leave.

"I can give you Clay Warfield and most, if not all, the SSs in Southern California. I can do it with one predicate crime."

They froze and slowly turned back. Blue suit asked, "How?"

I'd said the magic words. "Ill-gotten gain, proceeds obtained through a criminal enterprise that will also establish tax evasion." The same thing that took down Capone. I wasn't handing him a murder and mayhem predicate, but RICO carried a lot of years, and the blue suit would understand that you put enough defendants under that kind of pressure and they will start to roll. The whole SS organization would fall.

"Where is it?"

"I need a signed, court-authorized agreement that all charges will be dropped on me and John Mack and Karl Drago."

"No, not all charges," the woman said. "Reduced time only. You are not in any position to negotiate."

"And you said you were told not to negotiate at all. You just gave up reduced time."

Blue suit pulled a chair out and sat down. He offered his hand. "Special Agent Dan Chulack."

I took it and smiled. He'd been the man Barbara called and told that we had recovered Eddie. Chulack was the special agent in charge—the boss. He had not broadcast his authority when he walked in. I liked him that much more.

"What do you have?" asked Chulack.

I let go of his hand. "I need a signed agreement first."

"You were a deputy, a street cop, and, from what I under-stand, a very...ah, effective one," he said. "You know how this works. We don't jump through a bunch of hoops with a load of legal red tape until we have a proffer that can be validated."

"You're right. I do have a great deal of experience. So here's the deal, Dan. If I tell you here and now, I give up my leverage. You'll simply walk out, and I'll never see you again. So I guess you're going to have to trust me."

"You have evidence?"

"Yes."

"Where?"

"There again—"

"This is absolute bullshit," the woman said. "We are not go-ing to go along with something this thin. Especially not without an offer of good faith."

"I know I don't have the best reputation but, I promise you, I can deliver to you the SS organization on a silver platter."

A gold doughnut platter, anyway.

Dan looked from her, back to me. "We'll bring you the agree-ment and it will be signed, but I won't hand it over until you give us the information, and then only when that information is deemed satisfactory."

"It has to be completed within two hours. I have to be walk-ing out the door in two hours."

Dan was getting up and stopped. "That's impossible. Why two hours?"

"Jonas Mabry has Eddie Crane, Elena Cortez, and Sandy Williams."

He nodded.

"Jonas also has my wife, Marie. Chief Wicks didn't tell you?"

"No, she didn't. I'm sorry. But what can you do if you get out? This doesn't make sense. Do you know where she's being held?"

"No, and *when* I get out, I'm going to track Jonas down."

I held his eyes a long time.

Finally he broke, turned, and said to the others, "Let me have a minute."

They didn't argue, but went out and closed the door.

"You don't know me, but I am going to ask you to trust me," he said.

I hesitated for a second, worried about the room camera. But he wasn't. I shook my head "no."

"Barbara told me what she did, how she flew down to Costa Rica to find you."

I sat down. "Is she in trouble?"

"No, this isn't going any further than me. This conversation goes no further. I believe everything you've told me, and now you're going to have to trust me. *You* know how long this kind of thing takes. The contract has to be drawn up, it has to be reviewed by both sides, supervisors then managers have to approve it, and then we have to get a judge to sign off on it. We'll be lucky to have this deal cut in two days, let alone two hours."

He was right. "So what are you asking?"

"I'm asking you to trust me."

"The FBI?"

"That's right."

He didn't look away for a long drawn-out moment. "My way is the only way you'll have a fighting chance at finding your wife."

I nodded. "How do you want to do it?"

"Where is this evidence?"

"It's in the clubhouse. There's proof there that will support a RICO indictment on Clay Warfield and, by extension, all his henchmen."

He shook his head. "We hit that place with a warrant two weeks ago and tore it up. We didn't find anything, and I mean nothing at all. These people are organized. They have attorneys on retainer, they even have a public relations firm looking out for their reputation. They are being repackaged and rebranded as good guys, community leaders."

"The evidence is there. You just didn't know what to look for. It's there. Get your old warrant and have a judge standing by to sign an addendum. And get me out of here. We go to the clubhouse, hit it, and if I'm right, you let me walk right then and there."

"The LA district attorney's not going to be happy."

"You ask me to trust you, now you'll have to trust me. You let me go, then after I track down Jonas Mabry, I'll surrender myself to you, and we can complete the paperwork on this little deal while I sit in custody. You have my word on it."

"Barbara said you are one of the most honest men she has ever met." He offered me his hand.

I took it. A lump rose up in my throat as I recalled that I had promised her I would not take Mack with me, and I had let her down. This was my chance to redeem Mack too.

CHAPTER FIFTY

The concealed FBI radio speaker under the dash spoke continuously, the voices eager and anxious, setting up the raid I had orchestrated. I sat in the rear of a sleek black Cadillac Escalade with the windows blacked out in reflective limo tint, in a rundown neighborhood with tired houses and weed-filled front yards. Kids rode bikes and skateboards back and forth, waiting for something to happen, trying to peer in. The air conditioner ran on high.

The clock tick-tocked in my head. I didn't want to look at the digital time on the dash, the little red numbers that never stopped marching on and on. I couldn't take my eyes off them. Six-oh-five. I had less than two hours to find Marie. How could I do it in two hours? I couldn't think of any past scenario when I had worked on the Violent Crimes Team that fit into what had to happen and allowed a resolution in less than two hours. I wished Robby Wicks sat next to me to lend some of his arrogant confidence. He'd have a plan, no matter how cockeyed crazy or over the line into the gray. But he'd have a plan and be able to sell it to me. "A cake walk," he'd say. "We'll take these bastards down and be drinking a beer in one hour and twenty-five minutes." No way could he back up his outrageous claims, not with credible reason. Even so, I'd find myself saying, "Yeah, I'm with you, let's do it."

I tried to peel my eyes off the clock and force my brain to think. I didn't even know if the golden doughnut would still be there. We had the safe open, but we had fled before taking that extra step to check. The golden doughnut could possibly link the SS organization to the armored car robbery. Planned and executed by them. Robbery was a predicate crime. The statute of limitations was up on the robbery. But the guard had been killed, and there wasn't any statute limit for murder. The worst part about the plan, I had to throw Drago under the bus. He would have to testify. He wouldn't, of course. He had that misplaced loyal gangster code coursing through his veins. I only hoped Dan Chulack would let me go pending trial. If nothing else, the recovery of a million two had to be worth something, a big feather for the FBI.

The FBI agent assigned to watch me sat in the front seat, his jaw set tight from anger at having to babysit. I said, for the fifteenth time, "Where's Dan Chulack? The deal was for two hours, it's been almost four." The inactivity and the inability to control the situation made me want to smash the window, climb out, and run down the street, moving somewhere, anywhere, at least doing something.

Finally the FBI SWAT team arrived in a long caravan. They got out already suited up, dressed all in black. Their long guns hung from team slings across their chests. The ballistic helmets and goggles made them look like aliens from a foreign world.

Okay, here we go. From another car, Dan got out and walked up to the SWAT team leader. They spoke a few words. Dan shook the man's hand, wishing him luck. Dan walked up to the Escalade, all too slowly. Couldn't they all move a little faster? Just a little? Didn't they know what was at stake? A woman's life and three small, helpless children?

Dan got in.

"What the hell? You said two hours."

He held up his hand. "I know, I'm sorry, I had a lot to coordinate. I just got the warrant addendum signed. We had to do this right. We want it to hold up in court later."

"What, at the risk of the lives of a woman and three children?"

"I said I'm sorry. After we do this, I'll personally put every possible resource at your disposal. Is there something I can do right now, something we can get started on?"

I couldn't think of a thing and it gave me a headache.

"How's my friend John Mack doing?"

"I'm sorry, I should've told you, but as I said—"

"Just tell me."

"He's out of surgery and his prognosis is great."

I sighed and sat back. I took a breath, "What about Drago?"

"Banged up. He's got a broken leg. He's shot in the foot, that one's recent, and he's got a gunshot wound to the leg." Dan smiled, "You know anything about the gunshot wounds?"

I didn't answer and said, "That's great about Drago. What about Roy Boy?"

Dan shook his head, "He's alive, but they think he might be paralyzed from the chest down."

Dan paused, then said, "Well?"

He wanted the information about the evidence for the predicate crime needed for the RICO indictment.

"Can you call Chief Wicks and have her meet me at the clubhouse—"

"Here she is now."

Barbara pulled up in a maroon Crown Victoria. She got out and came up to the Escalade as the SWAT team mounted the step-sides of the SWAT vehicle and held on to the exterior rail at the top. We were finally rolling. Barbara got in the back next to me, cool, not catching my eye. I didn't blame her. The Escalade started up. We moved in behind the SWAT vehicle. We were two miles away from the clubhouse. I didn't know what to say to her.

"Mack's going to be okay?" I asked.

"Define okay. He's going to prison, and he won't ever be a cop again."

"I made a deal."

Her head whipped around. "You what?"

"That's what this is all about. I made a deal that Mack walks if we find enough evidence to put away the SS."

Hope in her expression faded as I said the second part about evidence and the SS. "Evidence?" She said, "Did you actually see anything at all while you were in there?"

I looked away.

"That's what I thought. This is a fishing expedition."

"It damn well better not be," Chulack said.

We rode in silence for a few seconds. Every increment of time went by far too slow. Tick-tock.

"Do you have the file on Jonas, the one that was in the back of his T-Bird?" I was grasping at the least little bit of intel that would help bust through the mental road block.

She still didn't look at me. "No."

My mind scavenged around for something, anything at all to keep her talking. I had the need to hear her voice. Maybe we would happen on something of mutual interest, and that would once again bring us close together as friends. And, as friends, we could figure this thing out. I had an itch, a niggling in the back of my brain, that I had missed something. Something vital and I just needed it to float to the surface. Talking with her could trigger that effect if we could put aside this emotional wound between us.

We rounded the last turn and headed for the clubhouse one block away.

"What happened with the car?" I asked.

"What car?"

"The Rent-a-Wreck Jonas rented two years ago?"

"That was a dead-end. It comes back to a vacant house on Roswell Avenue in Montclair. No one's lived there for years. He used it as a dead drop, an address only, for the rental forms, social security, and a fake driver's license."

"Roswell?"

Ahead of us, the SWAT vehicle smashed through the wrought-iron gate to the clubhouse and sped right up to the front door. The team jumped off and ran. The lead man threw the ram through the door as men lined up and entered, long guns at the ready, all of them yelling, "Get down. Get down."

We pulled into the parking lot and stopped, waiting for the "all clear." This time the parking area was loaded with Harleys of every style and model. Most had the ape-hanger handlebars. Toys, stuffed animals, and games were strapped to various parts of the bikes with bungee cords, highly visible on purpose, the rebranding, their attempt to shift the public's perception. I could only hope the public did not easily fall prey to such elementary school tactics.

Six fifteen. An hour and forty-five minutes left.

Within seconds, the SWAT leader came out and gave Dan the thumbs up. Dan and Barbara got out. I opened the door and put a foot on the ground. Dan blocked my exit.

"The location is secure. I fulfilled my end of the deal, now tell me where inside? What are we looking for?" He wore anxiety like a wild, unwanted monkey on his back, an emotion that didn't suit him. He liked to be in control, and now everything depended on me. He'd gone way out on a limb, and I still held the saw.

Barbara came up behind him. I lowered my voice, said to him, "No, your end, the difficult end, is when you have to let me walk."

He nodded and didn't say anything else. He didn't want to risk my anger, or to hear me suddenly burst out in laughter, that this had all been an elaborate gag just to ruin his career and make the FBI out to be a bunch of buffoons.

I pushed past them, my hands cuffed in front. "Follow me," I said.

CHAPTER FIFTY-ONE

For the second time in the last seven hours I walked into the Sons of Satan clubhouse. This time at least sixteen bikers sat on couches in the front room, hands zip-tied behind them. Another eight lay face down on the floor amongst their biker detritus. Most had shaved heads, all had ugly antisocial tattoos that blared out to the world that they would not cross the street to help a person and that they'd rob you while you were down. Some wore bandanas around their heads or hanging from pockets. All wore their denim 'cuts' with the SS rocker and death head accented with their evil, angry scowls. By not wanting to look like everyone else, they'd ironically created their own conformity. What a bunch of lost sheep.

Clay Warfield sat amidst the people he lorded over, pretending to be just one of the guys. "Come back for some more, Deputy Johnson?" he asked.

I didn't answer. Clay saw my handcuffs. "That's right, *now* you have the right man. You don't have a thing on us."

"Have you read the warrant to him?" I asked Dan.

Unlike in the movies, which take short cuts for dramatic effect, the warrant had to be read to the person in control of the premises before any search could be completed. Dan nodded to an agent in a blue windbreaker. The agent took out a folded piece of paper and a micro recorder. He read from the paper.

Clay smiled, unconcerned. He knew there wasn't anything in his clubhouse, so why should he worry? He smirked. "When you assholes get done with your little game of cops and robbers, I want to press charges against Deputy Johnson for burglary and grand theft auto. He stole our plumbing truck. Roy Boy will also press charges for kidnap and attempted murder. What do you think about that, Deputy Johnson?"

I looked at Dan. "The gold's in Clay's office."

Clay lost his smile. "There isn't any gold in my office." He tried to struggle up off the couch. His zip-tied hands, and the other bikers packed hip-to-hip, made the move impossible. "You're not going to plant any evidence, not on me you won't. I'm going along. I'm going to watch."

Dan nodded to the agent who'd read the warrant. The agent helped Clay up off the couch. We all walked down the hall through the trash, most of which by now had been flattened against the crusty carpet.

We entered the once-immaculate office still tossed from our last visit.

"Okay," Dan said, "What gold, and how does it work as a predicate crime?"

I had taken a big chance believing Drago.

Clay yelled, "There isn't any gold in here. If there was, I'd know about it. Don't you think I would know about it?" His eyes blazed a hole right through me.

Dan asked again, "What gold? Where?"

"It's in the safe," I said.

Clay's anger shifted away and he smiled. "Go ahead and look, there isn't any gold in the safe."

"We don't need your permission to look," said Dan.

Someone had closed the safe doors. The dials were still knocked off and the holes Drago had drilled still in the door. Dan moved quickly over to the safe and swung open the heavy doors. His head whipped around. "It's empty."

Clay threw his head back and laughed. "Just like I told you. Is this the best you got?" He snapped back to anger. "Now untie my hands and get the hell out of my clubhouse. You'll be hearing from our attorneys. We're going to own the federal government."

"Johnson?" asked Dan.

"It's underneath the safe," I said.

Clay's eyes went wild. He didn't know what was under his own safe and didn't want to find out. "Hold it, stop what you're doing. I want my attorney here before you do anything else."

Dan smiled, sensing victory. "You don't have that right. In fact, you don't even have the right to be in this room right now. You're here out of courtesy."

While he spoke, I moved over to the safe. I had to see the four bolts Drago had described.

On the safe floor, inside, I counted four holes through the thick steel. *No bolts.* All the air left my body. I staggered back a couple of steps until my butt came up against the desk's edge.

Barbara Wicks took hold of my arm. I'd forgotten she was there. "What's the matter?"

Dan, too excited to notice with his longtime goal now in sight, yelled to his men, "A couple of you move that safe, slide it to the side."

Two agents tried, but couldn't budge it.

"Get two more agents," Dan said. "Find a fulcrum." An agent ran from the room.

Clay calmed. "There's nothing under the safe. Deputy Johnson has been a bad boy. He's been yankin' you all's dick."

Two big SWAT guys came in with the ram they'd used on the door and a pry bar they must have retrieved from their assault vehicle.

Barbara whispered to me, "What's the matter, Bruno?"

"I think I'm in deep shit."

She socked me in the arm, just like Marie would have. The move brought Marie foremost in my thoughts and, with it, a terrible ache in the pit of my stomach.

The two SWAT guys put the ram down on the floor at the farthest end where the safe sat closest to the wall. They got on the pry bar intent on flipping the safe onto its side.

Clay laughed, not a nervous one but one with confidence. "The Feds are going to have to rename the Lincoln fucking

Memorial, call it The Clay Warfield Memorial, after I get done suing your asses."

The weight of the safe thwarted the agents' best efforts. Not that it mattered; I already knew the outcome.

"You two," said Dan, "get over there and put your backs into it." Two agents with blue windbreakers moved over to help. One of the agents started to wiggle between the safe and the perpendicular wall on the side.

Clay jumped forward. "You assholes are in enough trouble. You damage or break something, and I'll have your jobs. You hear me?"

The two SWAT guys and the two windbreakers got on the lever, as the guy in between the safe and the wall pushed at the top of the safe. The safe slowly started to rise. The agent in between the wall and the safe, his face turning red and bloated with exertion, pushed harder. The drywall behind him caved in with a loud crack. The safe's top started to yield and lean. Dan yelled, "That's it. That's it. Push. You got it."

The safe fell over. The agents jumped clear. The dead weight thudded to the concrete floor. The entire clubhouse gave a little shudder.

Underneath, where the safe had sat, revealed nothing but smooth concrete. No bolts rose out of the concrete floor. No gold doughnut painted gray and inset as a gasket. Drago had been so believable. How had I fallen for his lie? But why had he lied? There could only be one reason. Drago was batshit crazy to make up a juvenile tale of a pirate's gold with safes and SS. His lack of sanity did not bode well for my family's future.

CHAPTER FIFTY-TWO

Dan rushed over to me, his face right up in mine. "Is this how you return my trust?" He pointed to the overturned safe. "This was a big joke all along, wasn't it?"

I couldn't speak, and shook my head "no."

Dan put a finger up by my eyes. "Now, you are going to rue the day you crossed me. I am going to file every possible charge. You'll never get out of prison."

Clay laughed loud and hard, most of it forced to help rub it in.

Dan pointed at me, "Get him out of here."

The two agents wearing the blue windbreakers moved in. One came away from the corner, away from the damaged drywall, that was now visible. Right above the smooth concrete where the doughnut should have been.

My mind locked on to the obvious solution, I physically struggled. "Wait."

The agents on each of my arms kept dragging me along.

"Chulack, wait. Wait."

The two agents hesitated and looked to him for direction.

Dan pointed his finger to the door. "I said, get him out of here."

The two agents resumed their tug-of-war in earnest. I violently swung my shoulders one way, then the other, and broke free. I ran to the overturned safe, the agents close behind, and picked up the ram on the floor. They were all over me.

Dan was almost to the door and turned toward the disturbance.

Clay's eyes went wild. "Get that asshole away from there."

"Wait, look," I said. "Look at Warfield. He knows I've figured out his game."

Clay yelled, "I'll sue you assholes, I swear to God, I'll sue you until you don't have a penny left to your name."

Dan took a couple of steps back from the doorway. "Bruno?"

"You asked me to trust you. Now *you* need to trust me on this."

Dan nodded. The two agents let me go. I took a deep breath, pivoted my hips, and slammed the ram into the wall. Clay yelled and leaped at me.

"Restrain him," said Dan.

The two agents jumped Clay with relish and took him to the ground harder than he needed. Dan came over and looked me in the eyes.

In a low tone, I said, "They moved the wall."

Clay continued to yell.

"Shut him up."

The two agents sat on him. Clay grunted. Now he could only focus on breathing.

Dan nodded, took hold of the ram with me, and we swung it, throwing our backs into it. We hit a two-by-four stringer supporting the drywall and caved it inward. We swung again and again until we were out of breath and we had a large enough hole. We dropped the ram. Drywall dust hung in the air and stuck to the sweat on our faces. Dan took a small, powerful flashlight from his belt. He carefully stuck in his arm with the flashlight. He looked back at me one last time and then stuck his head in the hole.

He moved his feet and tried to force more of himself inside. I held my breath. From inside came a muffled "Holy shit."

In the short time I'd known Special Agent Dan Chulack, he'd never used unprofessional language.

He pulled out completely, with a huge smile. "Call for backup. I want every one of those swinging dicks in there booked on RICO, conspiracy to commit murder, robbery, and kidnap." He pointed to the two SWAT guys. "You two. Take this ram, and I want you to take down this wall right here, but don't go any farther than right here." He indicated another place on the wall.

Before the SWAT guys moved, I stepped in close and held out my cuffed hands. Dan smiled and handed me his flashlight. I stuck my arms in the hole and then my head. I couldn't get in nearly as far with my hands cuffed, but far enough.

Clay had needed a place to run his organization. He knew there would be search warrant after search warrant served on the clubhouse, and he had to have a way to keep evidence out of the hands of law enforcement. He built another wall in his office to partition off a four-foot-wide room. There had to be a secret lever that accessed a hidden door. We didn't need the lever or the door; we had the ram.

An odor of gun oil and sweat came at me hard. The flashlight lit up the narrow space.

Inside, on one wall hung all the tools of the trade, sawed-off shotguns, machine guns, pistols—including the two H&K P9s with silencers—one of which Clay had used to shoot Drago in the foot. That's what he'd done when he left us in the living room with Roy Boy, Slim Jim, Sandman, and the other cronies. He'd gone into his office, activated the lever, entered the room, and gotten to the H&Ks. I thought that I had heard the desk being moved when it had been the secret door.

I marveled at all the guns and weapons as the light panned down the length of the wall. At the end, on the floor sat a smaller safe, shorter, the one that would contain the books, the records tracking all the ill-gotten gain for the SS International. I moved the flashlight above the safe. My breath caught. I whispered to no one, "What a damn fool." On the narrow four-foot-wide wall at the end and above the safe, Clay had thwarted so many search warrants in the past that he'd grown arrogant and invincible, enough to pin up old Polaroid photos and trophies from his past. Dead enemies of the SS. Witnesses, bikers from opposing gangs, and all those who failed to fall into line under their tyranny.

I started to pull back and remembered Drago. I pointed the flashlight straight down. On the floor just on the other side of the new wall, Clay had done a poor job with instant concrete mix. He'd tried to cover the hole where the safe used to sit. The shadow outline of the golden doughnut, still painted lead-gray, rose a quarter inch from the concrete, hardly visible at all unless you knew what to look for, a true Bluebeard's treasure. The doughnut would not draw any attention from the FBI forensic people coming to document and seize the evidence.

I pulled back out, stunned. Barbara stood close. I handed her the flashlight. She went up on tiptoes to look in the hole.

Dan moved in close and immediately put the key into my handcuffs. "What do you need? You name it. You can have all the manpower you want. I'll even pull in all the officers from the Joint Terrorist Task Force."

"I don't have any time left for that. I find my wife and the kids in the next hour or it's not going to matter." I walked out, down the hall, and out to the front yard. The sun colored everything orange and yellow as it went down ending the day. I leaned against the closest Harley and closed my eyes. Now that I had freedom, the pressure of not going to prison, clearing Mack and Drago, I could think straight.

I was barely aware that Barbara stood close by. In my mind, I deliberately went over everything that had happened since Barbara Wicks came back into my life, step-by-step, scene-by-scene, from the time she walked up from the beach. I replayed the dialogue from each conversation.

The common denominator was the city of Montclair. Montclair continued to come up in all the information. Jonas rented a car and used the Montclair address. He used an underground doctor at a Montclair address. He used a Montclair address as a dead drop, a vacant house—

I opened my eyes.

"What?" asked Barbara.

I looked at her. "We have to go. We have to go right now."

Her expression turned professional. One of the many FBI agents came out of the house, escorting a biker. She said, "I need your car keys, give them to me."

He shook his head. "Not a chance in hell."

Dan came out right behind him. Dan took hold of the biker the agent was escorting and said, "Go with them, do exactly what that man, Bruno Johnson, tells you to do. Do you understand?"

The agent nodded.

We ran for his car.

CHAPTER FIFTY-THREE

I had to slow down to let the agent guide us to the right car. He bee-lined to one of the many navy-blue Chevy Suburbans parked on the street just outside the wrought-iron gate. I went to the front with him and said, "Give me the keys, I'm driving."

"You're not an agent. You can't drive."

Barbara, with her hand already on the back door handle, said, "Didn't you hear what your ASAC just told you?"

The agent looked at me, his eyes falling to the BMF tat-too on my arm as he weighed the options. I couldn't wait. I grabbed the keys from his hand and hit the fob to open the doors. I said to the agent, "You get in back. Barbara up front with me."

This time he did as instructed. Barbara ran around and got in. I started up, put it in drive, and hit the gas. "Gimme me direc-tions to Kadota off of Mission."

She didn't answer.

I had to concentrate on negotiating the huge vehicle in and out of traffic at high speed, and couldn't look at her to see her ex-pression as to *why* she'd didn't answer.

"Bruno, that's in Montclair," she said.

"That's right." Then I caught on. If I was correct, the location would be in her city. "Snap out of it. We're talking about Marie and the kids here. We can worry about public relations later."

"Of course, you're right. Go down to the San Bernardino Freeway and take it west, get off at Central and go south."

"Right, now I remember."

"Why do you think it's back in Montclair?"

"Everything links back to Montclair, specifically, Mission and Kadota."

I checked the rearview and caught the FBI agent dialing his phone. He was going to alert his fellow agents to this hot new lead.

"Barbara, take his phone." She didn't hesitate, whipped around, leaned in between the seats, and snatched his phone.

I checked my driving path and then looked back in the mirror. "What's your name?"

"Price."

"Your first name?"

"Zack."

"Give him his phone back," I said to Barbara. "Zack, I'm sorry, there's a lot at stake right now, and I need you on my side. We can't have a lot of cops swarming the area until I know for sure which house we're going to. There are lives at stake. You understand?"

"Yes. If you want, I can call and have them stage out of the area."

"Not yet."

He nodded. Barbara handed back his phone.

"I had a detective and forensics check out the place on Kadota," Barbara said. "It was vacant."

"Forensics?"

"Yes. There were signs someone had been there, but the place had been wiped clean. I told you that house is a dead end."

"What about the house the car came back registered to?"

"What car?"

"The Rent-a-Wreck with Micah's body?"

"That house was neg—"

"What street was the car registered to?"

"Roswell."

I looked at her as she deciphered the new information. "How close together are Roswell and Kadota?" I asked.

"Kadota's the next block over. Oh my God, why didn't I see that?"

"There isn't any reason why you should have. It could just be a coincidence, but the coincidence is all we have right now."

I hit the freeway and opened up the Suburban to 120. The sun was completely down and dusk settled in.

"So what are you thinking?" she asked.

"He's used this same area twice. There has to be a reason why."

"Maybe it's because he's familiar with it?" Zack said.

"Good. Can you have your people do a record check on Jonas? See if he has any friends who live in the area? Maybe Jonas listed someone on his booking form the times he was arrested, the 'in case of emergency' contacts." I checked the mirror. Zack had already dialed, and the phone was up to his ear.

I came up on Central Avenue too fast and had to push the brakes so hard the seatbelt bit into my shoulder. I hit the off ramp, checked the intersection, and ran the red signal to southbound Central.

Zack closed his phone. "No luck."

I said, "Call back and have them check…" I looked at Barbara and said, "Have them check what?" I was running out of ideas. If we didn't come up with something, we were going have to go door to door, three blocks' worth of houses. It was seven fifteen.

"It's a long shot he's even in the area," she said.

I hit Mission and took a long sweeping right. "Point out Kadota."

"Right there."

I took a hard left, pulled over, and parked. "Let's go on foot from here."

We got out and met on the sidewalk. "Bruno, we checked this out. I'm telling you, there's nothing here."

"Jonas has been bold," I said. "He let the FBI tail him. He hid in plain sight because he knew we couldn't do anything to him. He knew our only way to get the kids was to follow him. He has to be right around here, and I'm betting it's going to be right here in plain sight."

"He didn't know we were tailing him," Zack said.

"Yes, he did. He wanted me to find him, to personally rub my face in it. He's been three steps ahead of us the whole time."

We came to the house with the Mercury Marquis parked in the front yard behind a chain-link fence. I went through the gate without hesitating. We were running into a dead end. What next? What else could we do?

I took several quick breaths to force down the panic and continued up the walkway in the dimming light.

"What's that?" asked Barbara.

"Residue, blood from Jonas' gunshot foot. When I dropped him off." The foot I'd shot and later regretted. I didn't regret shooting him now.

The door was open. Inside, the house was unearthly quiet and smelled of musty carpet and dust, with a faint hint of antiseptic. The blood trail did not transect the threshold. So we didn't have solid evidence he entered this house.

I checked the entire house, two bedrooms and one bath. Nothing. None of the small stuffy rooms had furniture or anything sitting on the threadbare carpeted floor. Wallpaper with an old floral design peeled away in long tongues, exposing the lath and plaster. Dust-laden weeping curtains let in the fading sunlight.

"You're right," I said, "If they did actually use this place, they did a good job of taking everything with them."

Zack got down on his hands and knees and put his face close, parallel to the carpet, looking for micro evidence or unique disturbances. I respected the man for trying.

In the kitchen, I tugged on the back door. It wouldn't budge an inch. I examined it closely. The door had been nailed to the frame, the window in the door covered over with plywood. "Hey?"

Barbara and Zack came in. "What?"

"Did your detective say anything about checking the backyard?"

She shook her head. "No, they didn't find anything inside so...son of a bitch." She turned and went out the front at a fast walk. I took one side of the house, and Zack followed Barbara around on the other. Darkness took the opportunity to hinder us further. I dodged overturned trash cans, pieces of wood, a stained sink, and a pile of used red brick. A detached garage sat back away from the house in the long lot. All the furniture from in the house had been tossed into a tall pile in the dirt and weed backyard.

Barbara pulled up on the one-car garage door. It came up a few inches.

"Hold it," said Zack. He pulled his service weapon, backed up the drive, and got down on one knee, aiming his gun and his little flashlight under the door. "Go ahead."

I didn't think anything would be in the garage, but it did make me realize I didn't have a gun. I took one side and helped Barbara lift the door open. Discarded trash bags went almost to the rafters. The sour reek backed us off. Nothing. I pulled the garage door back down.

"I guess we have to go check the Roswell street address." The back gate caught my eye, and I looked down at the concrete walk leading to it. Nothing remarkable. "Come on, let's check the alley."

They didn't argue or complain and followed along. Through the unlocked gate the alley contained degraded asphalt with weeds pushing up in untended cracks. Both sides of the alley had abandoned cars and trash cans but still left room, if need be, for one car to drive through. In the eerie darkness the cars looked like dead animals.

"You guys go that way," I said. "I'll check this way."

Zack headed off.

Barbara stayed with me. Good thing, since I didn't have a flashlight. "This is a dead end," she said. "I know you don't want to believe it, but it is. Let's move on to something else."

I stopped. "What? What else is there?"

She shrugged. "We could check—"

"Over here," called Zack.

We turned and ran to him.

CHAPTER FIFTY-FOUR

Zack pointed to a small bloody splotch, almost indiscernible on the broken asphalt with scattered tiny rocks.

"What do you make of it?" I didn't want to hope too much.

Zack said, "If your assumption is correct and he did receive medical attention in that house back there, then he might have walked away with a freshly bandaged foot."

Barbara finished it for him as she walked farther down the alley. "And if he walked away, it took until right there where that splotch is for him to bleed through the bandage."

We walked faster down the alley. The dried blood spore grew in size and frequency as Jonas had walked faster. I looked up periodically, watching our forward progress, not wanting to walk fat, dumb, and happy, right into Jonas. He had been three steps ahead of us at every turn. Did he know we would eventually get this far and wait in ambush for us?

We came to the cross street, the first east-west street south of Mission, Howard Avenue. The blood trail stopped at the edge of the road. This time I didn't have to ask Zack what he thought.

"Looks like he had a car waiting," he said.

I sat down on the curb, put my head in my hands, and closed my eyes. I'd been so sure this would do it, but I couldn't give up. Screw it. Zack and Barbara stood close by. Eyes still closed, I said, "There has to be a reason why he chose this area. Why Montclair of all places? What could possibly have drawn him to—"

I stood. Next to me, Barbara was nothing more than a dim shadow. "What do you have?" she asked.

"Do you have access to the county assessor's office?"

"Yeah, why?"

"Get them on the phone."

She pulled out her phone. "And ask them what?"

"Ask them if Bella Mabry or Micah had a house in Montclair."

Barbara shook her head as she dialed and muttered, "Son of a bitch."

"No, wait." I pointed to Zack. "Call your people and have them check marriage records and get Bella's maiden name. Then you," I pointed to Barbara, but she was with me now and waved her hand.

Zack dialed. When the other end picked up, he said, "Priority flag, ASAC Chulack cleared. I need an immediate record check for a marriage license in the name of Micah Mabry." He paused. "I don't know, check Los Angeles County and San Bernardino." He looked at me for confirmation. I nodded.

Barbara said into her phone, "This is Montclair Chief of Police. Stand by, I'm going to need an immediate record check on a residence in my city."

"Dobbs, Bella Dobbs," Zack said.

"Bella Dobbs," Barbara said. "I need you to check the tax records for a Bella Dobbs."

"Keep him on the line," I said to Zack.

Zack nodded. "Hold on one."

We waited, standing on the sidewalk, looking at each other. Barbara shook her head "no."

I said to Zack, "On the marriage license, get the first name of Bella's father."

"Now the first name of Bella's father," he repeated into the phone.

"Jack," Zack repeated to me.

Barbara paused a moment, confusion in her expression, and said, "Check Jack Dobbs."

A long moment passed. She closed her phone and took off running. We caught up. She said, "One street over on Pipeline. I'm calling in for backup."

"No, wait. There are three of us. Let's scout it first. We don't want—"

She hit speed dial. "This is Chief Wicks. I want three patrol units to stage at Mission and Central. I want them there now but without lights and siren. Call out the SWAT team and have them stage in the same place. No one moves without my go-ahead." The last came out gasping as she ran and talked at the same time.

We turned left and ran up Pipeline. "It should be about halfway up," she said. "It's an even number, so it's going to be on the left."

The houses on Pipeline were different than the tract homes on Kadota. These were unique, custom built, but years ago, decades ago, with wide, deep lots. I looked halfway up the long block. Right in the middle stood a house wider, taller than the rest. Barbara saw the house at the same time. She stopped running. Her breath came hard. "Let's go easy. Move in slow."

I didn't want to stop, I wanted to get there. My Marie was in that house, I knew it.

Barbara stopped two houses down, pulled her gun, and stood behind a tree with a wide trunk. "I know this house. Every cop in Montclair knows this house. When I heard the name, I wasn't sure. Now I am."

I didn't want to ask. "Why?"

"I've never met Bella, and I didn't put it together until right now when I heard Jack Dobbs' name. It happened long before I came on the department."

"What did?" I spoke but couldn't take my eyes off the dark house. No light at all escaped, which didn't bode well. Zack stood close with his gun drawn.

Barbara's breathing returned to normal. "The house's been vacant for forty, fifty years. All the rookies are driven by it and told that it's haunted. You know, a rookie hazing kind of thing. I pulled the old report back when I was running the detective bureau. Forty years ago April, it was in the spring, Millie Dobbs walked into the police station and said her husband was molesting their daughter."

All the air went out of me. I whispered, "Bella."

Barbara nodded. "A detective and a uniform went out to contact Jack. He barricaded, held his daughter—"

"Bella," I said again.

"He held Bella hostage. They negotiated for two hours while Jack held a gun to his daughter's head. They didn't have SWAT teams or trained negotiators back then."

I finished the rest of the scenario because I had seen it before. "The cops shot Jack while he was still holding Bella. Her father, the one molesting her, died with his blood all over her."

Barbara nodded. "Hit him with a shotgun close range."

I looked away. Poor Bella.

I didn't have time to commiserate over this. I had to shift my thoughts to tactical.

Two conical towers rose on one side of the Victorian with windows around all sides, a perfect place to observe. I pointed to the tower. "Look, Jonas picked the house on Roswell because he could watch it from up there. He knows we're here. The lights are off to give them the advantage. We have to move."

CHAPTER FIFTY-FIVE

"I'll take the front, you two go to the back."

Zack said, "Not to put too sharp a point on this, but you don't have a gun."

Zack had brown hair and eager blue eyes, and looked young to be a special agent with the FBI, maybe twenty-six.

I held out my hand. "Gimme your backup."

He hesitated, his eyes not leaving mine as he thought it over.

Barbara said, "Do it. Give it to him."

He reached down to his ankle and pulled a Smith & Wesson five-shot snub nose. He didn't hand it over right away. "You can have this, but I go through the door first."

"No deal, it's my wife in there." I made a grab for the gun.

He pulled it away. "I'm wearing body armor." He opened his blue windbreaker to display a new Second Chance vest, a threat level four, the best there was with the added trauma plate inserted over his chest.

"Take that off, let me have it," I said.

"That's a no-go."

"Your boss said to do exactly as I say."

"I'm with Zack on this one," said Barbara. "When's the last time you went through a door?"

I tried to think back. It'd been many years. But it was like riding a bike. You held your breath, kicked the door. You button-hooked right or left, as long as you got out of the kill zone, the instant you went through the doorway—the window of death.

"I'll say it one more time. I have operational command of this situation. Give me the vest." He wasn't going through any door and getting shot when I was the one that should be doing it.

He held my eyes for a long moment, handed me the gun, reached up, and pulled on the Velcro straps to the vest. "Okay, but I'm not taking the back. I'll go in right behind you. I'll be covering you."

I took the vest and put it on over my head and strapped on the Kevlar to my chest. The vest was still warm. "Fine by me. That gives you the back, Barbara."

"No one's going to run out the back. I'm going in right behind you two macho assholes. We're wasting time." She opened her phone and hit speed dial. "This is Chief Wicks. We're hitting 12736 Pipeline. Have one patrol unit come down the alley to the west, the rest go to the front. I have two detectives with me in plainclothes. Advise patrol to watch their friendly fire." She closed the phone. We took off running.

An untended hedge surrounded the front yard. Without water the bushes had died in spots and looked like the brown rotted-out teeth of a meth freak. I took the lead up the flagstone walk to the front door. The porch had been sturdy long ago, but time and lack of care let dry rot take over.

The question snuck in unbidden: *Had this been the position the detective took forty years ago when he shot Jack Dobbs dead as he held the ten-year-old Bella?*

I forced out the distracting thought and pointed to one side of the door. Zack took it. Barbara took the other. I held up three fingers, dropped one. Dropped two. I rose up and kicked the door with everything I had.

The door flew open, banged hard against the wall, and bounced back only a little. Before I could rebound, before a fraction of a second passed, my eyes caught the image of an emaciated, semi-bald woman sitting in a wheelchair in the entryway right in front of me. Too late. The shotgun blast took me in the chest. The force of the nine, .32 caliber pellets striking me in unison lifted me off my feet and threw me backward. I flew in slow motion.

Marie screamed, "Bruno!"

Zack rushed into the door opening, following his 9mm, firing, firing, firing. The shell casings flipped over his shoulder, slowly making their way to the ground, flying the same as me. The empty brass clinked on the flagstone.

Sirens.

Zack, move. Get out of the doorway. Get out of the window of death.

His 9mm rounds continued to pelt Bella. Her body jerked. She dropped the shotgun. With each impact and thud, a fine bloody mist rose in the air.

I landed on my back.

From down beyond my feet, off to the side of Zack, on the other side of the doorway, a shirtless Jonas fired a pistol.

Time sped up again.

Zack spun and went down. I caught a flash of his expression—shock, confusion, and something else. His youthful eagerness had disappeared, stolen from him.

Jonas followed, still shooting, advancing. Coming out to finish us off. Barbara, her eyes alive with anger, stepped around from the side of the door, her gun pointed. She fired as she moved in. Not stopping, not afraid of this deadly threat. Her rounds struck Jonas, the first one in the throat, the next three in the chest over the heart.

Maybe three seconds had passed.

Shock shielded me at first. The injury caught up, sucked breath from my lungs. I should've been thinking survival, but instead, I saw only the tattoo over Jonas' heart, the heart tattoo brutally penetrated by Barbara's bullets. Bullets doing the job Bella's bullet should have done all those years ago.

Inside the house, down the entry hall, a side door crashed open with Marie holding a desk chair she'd used to ram the door down, loose rope hung from her wrists.

Then Marie, my Marie, was all over me, crying, trying to hold me down. "Bruno. Bruno, are you okay? Say something. Breathe." Her hand moved all over my chest until she found the Velcro strips to the Second Chance and pulled them. She took the panels off just as air entered my lungs in one large gasp. I grabbed her and pulled down, buried my face in her neck, and took her in, her scent, her feel. For one long moment.

I pulled away. "Help Zack, help him."

Cop cars out front skidded up, their red and blue lights a kaleidoscope on the houses and trees.

Barbara ran out and yelled at the patrolman exiting his patrol car. "Roll paramedics, we have an officer down. Get an airship for immediate evac."

Barbara went down on her knees by Special Agent Zack Price and put both hands over his bloody wound on his abdomen, applying pressure.

Marie wouldn't leave me. "How are the children?" I asked.

"They're all fine. Jonas and his mom never intended to hurt us. They just wanted to die together at the hands of the man who'd robbed them of the chance before. That's what this whole messed-up thing was about. Psychotics, the both of them."

"I'm okay, Marie. Help Barbara. Help Zack."

"You sure?"

"I'm good. Go."

Marie moved over to Zack to help out. I rolled over and fought to get on hands and knees. My body didn't want to comply.

Marie said to Barbara, "The abdomen wound is serious, but if we don't stop the bleeder on this leg it's not going to matter. Give me your belt."

With bloody hands, Barbara pulled off her belt. Marie wrapped it around Zack's leg and tightened it.

I made it to all fours and struggled to my feet, fighting dizziness and a light head. Cops flooded in from the street.

Barbara stood. "Hold it. Hold it. The scene's secure. Tape it off. You and you find a spot for the helicopter and keep it clear. You, check on the ETA of the paramedics. You, tape off the street two houses each way. No one comes in, no one, you got it?"

I staggered past them. Zack lay on his back with blood soaking his white t-shirt, a small black hole in his lower right abdomen. His eyes were closed, relaxed. If he had been wearing his own body armor—no time to think about it.

I looked down my knuckles, blanched white from gripping the revolver. I let the gun drop to the ground with a clatter. No one noticed. I grabbed the doorframe for support and stepped across the threshold. Bella couldn't have weighed more than eighty pounds, her hair wispy and thin, her body ravaged with bullet wounds put there by Zack. Her head lay cocked to one side, her eyes and mouth open in death. On the floor, not two feet away, lay Jonas Mabry, the child I had scooped up twenty-five years ago and raced to the hospital. His open eyes stared at the ceiling. His mouth a dark vacant hole. I had somehow intervened in fate, and now fate had returned to make the correction.

The sound of whimpering brought me out of my funk. I followed it down the hall.

CHAPTER FIFTY-SIX

All three children huddled together in the kitchen, half-scared to death from their ordeal, and now all the gunfire. They didn't move when I approached them. They'd slipped beyond scared and teetered on the razor's edge of shock. If they went over that edge, they would need immediate medical care. I cooed to them and stroked their hair until they calmed down. There wasn't much time. I got down on one knee close to Eddie. "How are you doing, partner?"

He said nothing.

"We're through the worst of it, I promise, really we are. But we have to get somewhere safe, you understand?"

His eyes wide, his mouth in a straight line, he nodded.

"I'm going to need some help. Are you up to it?" He shook his head. I didn't blame him, not after all that had happened, those scars on his back from the electrical cord.

"I'm not going to leave you, I promise. But I need you guys to hold hands and walk with me, okay? Can you guys do that? We have to go now. We have to hurry."

Sandy Williams all of a sudden came alive. "Well then, let's get with it, let's go."

I tried not to react. She'd spoken. I didn't want to make a big deal out of it and said, "Good, good."

I picked up Eddie. He resisted for just a second. "It's okay, partner, no one's going to hurt you. No one's ever going to hurt you ever again. I give you my word on that. Shake on it."

I held out my free hand. He hesitated, took it, and shook.

"All right, little man, let's get out of here. Sandy, you take Elena's hand." She did. With trauma and shock, these eight-year-old kids acted more like four- or five-year-olds. Kids are resilient, and with a little bit of love and attention, they bounce right back. The courts and social services had already failed them twice, put them back into abusive homes. I couldn't, I wouldn't, let that happen again.

"Come on, kids, what do you say let's make like sheep and get the flock out of here?" Eddie giggled a little. He was already bouncing back.

We went out the back kitchen door and into the overgrown yard. I left the door open. We picked our way in the dark until we came to a cedar plank fence fallen over in long sections. We carefully negotiated past it and into the alley. The cop car Barbara had sent to cover the back must've been recalled and gone around to the front to help out and to get into all the action.

Eddie wiggled. I stopped in the dark. "What's the matter, partner, you want down?" He didn't want to be carried when the girls were walking. "Okay, say it. Say, 'Bruno, please put me down.'" His eyes, shadowed in the dark, kept me from seeing how he reacted. "Okay, partner, I understand. If you want down, pat me on the shoulder." He did.

I set him down. He immediately took hold of my hand. My heart swelled and a lump rose in my throat. How could a kid who'd been through so much go back to trusting that quickly? No time to ponder.

I turned us south into the alley. We had to hurry. We'd made it to the cross street Howard Avenue when Marie caught up. She didn't say a scolding word or ask me where the hell I was going with the kids. She just fell in step and took hold of Elena's other hand. We continued over to Roswell and to the FBI Suburban. We got in, buckled everyone up, and I steered us south.

With the threat gone, the kids leaned into each other and

immediately fell asleep, a natural reaction. We hit the Mexican border in an hour and a half. Rosarito Beach in another thirty minutes. We abandoned the FBI vehicle and took a cab the rest of the way to Ensenada.

The next day, Marie went shopping and bought suitcases and the basics we'd need for the freighter trip to Costa Rica. In the hotel room, I watched CNN news as they covered the Sons of Satan clubhouse story and the shoot-out in Montclair. FBI agent Zack Price was hospitalized and expected to make a full recovery. Barbara stood behind her podium in full dress uniform, a hero in her city for taking down the kidnappers, for personally braving the gun battle. The investigation still continued for the missing children, and she said she would not rest until there was closure in the case. She looked up from the podium, and I thought for a brief second her professional demeanor cracked. She smiled, a small one at the corner of her mouth.

I watched Elena and Eddie and Sandy eat a huge room service breakfast. I told them they could order whatever they wanted. They didn't believe me when I handed Sandy the phone. She looked at me funny. I took the phone back. "Okay, if you don't want to order." I started to order one of everything. She hadn't said much to me since we'd been together. She smiled and I handed her the phone. All three huddled around the menu and ordered big. Eddie still had not said a word and could not be coaxed into it. He pointed to what he wanted. When the food came, they fell upon the cart like a starving horde.

I carried the phone into the bathroom and called St. Bernadine's Hospital, told the nurse my name was Scott Drago and that I wanted to talk to my brother Karl.

"Hello, Franc? Is this Franc?" He pronounced it like the French dollar.

I didn't know if Karl had a brother. I'd made up the name Scott. "No, Drago, it's me, Bruno Johnson."

Silence. Then faintly, "Bruno Johnson? Oh, yeah, yeah, the darkie. How the hell are ya, buddy? I've been watching the news and you really put the meat to the SS. I owe ya for that. Clay's picture's been all over the news. That son of a bitch finally got his. Damn good job. They'll kill him in the joint, you know. Dumbshit kept all those pictures. What an asshole."

"How you holding up, Drago?"

"Good. I'll be out of here in a couple of days. They came by and took the restraints off, said I was free to go, said you took care of all the problems. I owe you big for that."

"Who's that? Who came by?"

"Guy in a suit. Chuck-a-luck or some shit name like that. Was real anxious to know if I knew where you were."

"Did they drop the charges on my friend John Mack, the Los Angeles County detective?"

"Yeah, yeah, fact we're in the same room together because we were both on lockdown and under guard, and now we're not. He sleeps a lot. He's asleep right now. You want to talk to him?"

"No, that's okay." Guilt kept me from speaking to him. The charges were dropped, but he'd still lose his job.

Drago laughed. "Saw you took out that Jonas asshole. But the news didn't say nothin' about those kids. Johnson, you got those kids?"

"Drago, listen, about the gold."

"Yeah, man, I know, I saw it. The safe was moved. Son of a bitch nothin' was there. Someone found the gold. Probably a long time ago."

"How do you know the safe was moved?"

"I asked that Chuck-a-luck dude. He told me, thought I might know more than I did about the SS. They had to move the safe to get into the false room. But I already knew the safe had been moved. When I opened the safe, there were only the bolt holes on the floor of the safe, and no bolts."

"You didn't tell him about the gold, did you?"

"Are you crazy? Cop out to possession of stolen property?

No way. Too bad. I wanted that money. You have no idea how bad
I wanted that money. Dreamt about it for twenty-five years. Now
that it's gone, it feels like someone cut a chunk outta my gut, you
know what I mean?"

"It's still there, I saw it."

He yelled, "It's what?"

"Yeah, it's still there. I saw it. Clay moved the safe, put the
wall up, and just poured concrete over the top of your golden
doughnut. You can barely see it, but it's there."

"No, shit. Hey, when I get out, I'm goin' back for it. You
wanna come along? I like the way you work."

"I'd like to, but I can't."

"I owe you some of that money, and I always pay what I owe."

"Thanks, but no. You keep it. I'm glad you're feeling better. It
was nice meeting you."

"Hey, you're gonna still come around, right? When I get out
of this hospital, right?"

"Good-bye, Drago."

I had one more phone call to make, one I dreaded and had
not told Marie about. I called the FBI office in Los Angeles and
told the agent who picked up that I was Barbara Walters' personal secretary and asked for ASAC Dan Chulack. He came on the
line. "Special Agent Chulack."

"It's me."

"I figured you would call." He went silent.

"I have a big problem," I said.

"Yes, you do."

"I gave you my word I would come back and face the murder
charge. I wrapped everything up here and I'm ready to come in."

"You're no longer wanted for the kidnapping of Jonas
Mabry," he said. "He can no longer be a viable victim."

"Our deal was for the murder charge."

"Yes, our deal was for the murder in Los Angeles. I adopted
that case from LAPD, took it federal. I put five agents on it. Seems
you're no longer a person of interest. That warrant's been recalled."

I put my head against the bathroom wall, closed my eyes, and whispered, "Thank you."

"Don't thank me yet. You're still a person of interest in the abduction of a number of children and—"

"Been nice talking with you, Dan."

"Bruno? Don't come back."

"I won't. Thanks again." I hung up.

***

While I waited for the counterfeit passports, Marie flew down to Costa Rica to help Dad with the other children and his medical treatments. Chulack knew I had Eddie, Elena and Sandy. I was now a person of interest for kidnapping and interstate flight. But based on the phone call with Chulack, they weren't going to look too hard. It was easy to assume that if we stayed low and under the radar, the Feds would not chase us. Chulack knew the kids were in a better place.

Wally Kim was with his father and Mr. Kim would never press charges, he understood the motivation for taking Wally from his toxic environment. Without a witness or victim, the Feds didn't have a chance at a successful prosecution. And as for the other seven—my grandson Alonzo, the Bixlers, Toby and Ricky, Melvin Kelso, Tommy Bascombe, Randy Lugo, and Sonny Taylor—the Feds didn't know about them, that we had them safely in Costa Rica. At least, I didn't think they did. Officially those children were still listed as missing under suspicious circumstances, foul play suspected, meaning kidnapped. And they were going to stay that way.

In two weeks, as soon as the counterfeit passports came through, I planned to meet Marie along with Eddie, Elena, and Sandy in Costa Rica. Three plus seven equals ten.

AUTHOR'S NOTE

The first two years

I had not been long out of high school, not long living away from home, and nothing more than a kid myself, when I responded to a real case that inspired *The Replacements*, which I first entitled *The House That Bled*. I experienced incidents—much worse—in those first few years. To this day, I don't know if my emotional reactions and responses back then were *normal*. I had nothing for comparison. I do know that back in those early days, I pushed those terrible images into the far recesses of my mind, shoved them into a room, and locked them away. I never intended to take them out, turn them over, examine them. I never shared these particular stories with friends.

I cannot tell you exactly when the shift occurred because time compresses and changes memories, but as I've grown older, I've found I can no longer hide these images behind that locked door. They roll back on me, unbidden.

In those first years, I learned death did not play favorites. Brutal lessons came hard and were difficult to accept. I have five brothers and sisters; two were very young when I started my career. I saw in comparison how tender and vulnerable, and how fragile life could be when dealing with children.

In those first few years, while alone wearing a uniform—me, nothing more than a kid given a gun as a tool and tasked with protecting the innocent—I chased an evil man on foot. This man grabbed up a five-year-old child, put a gun to his head. He said that if I did not stop chasing him, he would shoot the uninvolved child. I wasn't given a choice that night. I was forced to shoot that man.

Bruno Johnson is a fictional character who champions the rights of the innocent. While he is drawn from real-life experiences, in the Bruno Johnson novels, I have tried to instill the emotions, the sights and smells, the images that continue to haunt me.

David Putnam